Her Nanny's Secret

Her Nanny's Secret

Jan Baynham

Stories that inspire emotions!
www.rubyfiction.com

Published 2022 by Ruby Fiction
Penrose House, Crawley Drive, Camberley, Surrey GU15 2AB, UK
www.rubyfiction.com

A CIP catalogue record for this book is available from the British Library

ISBN: 978-1-91255-060-9

Printed and bound in Great Britain
by Clays Ltd, Elcograf S.p.A.

For Alan and our lovely family.

Acknowledgements

I'd like to thank my husband, Alan, for his unstinting support as always. Thank you, as well, to all family members who are forever spreading news about my books, far and wide! You are all superstars in my eyes!

Thanks are due to so many people in the writing community for their encouragement and generous support, especially those in my writing group, The Cowbridge Cursors, members of the *Cariad* Chapter and many, many more writers online.

Special thanks are due to Alan, daughter Jo, Helen Beckett and Sandra Mackness for reading early drafts of *Her Nanny's Secret* and giving useful feedback. Thanks, too, to writing buddy, Sue McDonagh, for the many messages, Facetimes and Zoom meetings talking about writing, to Carole Fearn for chats about horses and stables and to Jo McGill and Gil Crocker for conversations about wills and inheritance.

I am indebted to Ruby Fiction for its faith in the novel and to the designer for another striking book cover. I was delighted to be working with my lovely editor again, and huge thanks are due to her. The team at Ruby Fiction includes a panel of readers who passed the manuscript and made publication possible. A special mention to: Isabelle D, Rosie Farrell, Jenny Mitchell, Carol Botting, Carol Fletcher, Dimita Evangelou, Alma Hough, Gill Leivers, Lynda Adcock, Honor Gilbert, Helen Maddison, Sharon Walsh.

Thank you all!

Prologue

At the end of the lane, the stone farmhouse appeared even greyer under the slate-coloured sky. The trees were laden with rain that had now stopped, and everywhere looked as bleak as Odile Lefèvre felt. It had been an exasperating morning. She'd collected the brochures as she'd been directed, but there'd been Germans everywhere. Men in grey uniforms on every corner of Ville de Roi, huddled together smoking their strong cigarettes, laughing and joking whilst her country men were starving and being murdered. When she'd caught the scent of the smoke from the *Gauloises* cigarettes, she'd shuddered in horror, remembering one particular German officer. Gustav. His name was imprinted in her innermost thoughts.

She'd crossed over to the other side of the street, carefully hiding her bundle of propaganda leaflets under her swagger coat with its hidden pockets, and heard the crude comments she'd come to understand in their mother tongue. How she wished this war would end! People in the surrounding villages in this part of northern France were suffering hardship like other parts of the country, and Odile was determined to do her bit. The *résistance* movement was strong in her town, and the rural community she was a part of was a proud one. They would never give in or surrender. She told herself that every small gesture and undercover deed she could do for the cause was worth it. But no one knew how involved she was. There was one part of her *résistance* life she kept concealed, even from the movement's members. Only Lucien, the leader of the local group, knew how she obtained the German soldiers' secrets she reported to him …

Odile wheeled her bicycle into the large, covered barn at the side of the farmhouse. It was gloomy and shadowy at that time of the afternoon, and Odile didn't want to stay there any longer than she had to. She made her way to the wooden double doors to secure them for the night when she heard the rafters in the upstairs loft creaking. The hairs on the back of her neck stood on end and her heart thumped. Several Nazis had been found hiding in neighbours' barns. They'd been trying to find out who were resisting the occupation and were listening for evidence. She froze to the spot, hardly daring to breathe. Another creak. She wasn't imagining it. What should she do? If she crept away, maybe she could warn her parents and they could get away … but where would they go? Horrific stories of what happened when local farmers had resisted the Germans had circulated around the villages from Sainte Marie-Hélène to Mont St Michel. Another sound in the floorboards above. Maybe it was just a rat. Odile was used to hearing and seeing vermin of all sizes living on the farm. *Yes, that was it.* She picked up a broom and crept up the stairs into the hayloft.

She felt her heart quicken as she neared the top step. A skittering across the planked floor convinced her she was right and she relaxed, loosening her grip on the handle of the broom. She smiled to herself at the ridiculous notion she'd had of a German soldier hiding in the hayloft. She stood up to full height as she reached the top of the stairs. It was then that she saw what – or rather who – had been the reason for the floorboards creaking. She gasped.

'*Mon dieu.*'

Relieved to see that the young man cowering in the

shadows was not dressed in Nazi grey with a swastika emblazoned on his jacket sleeve, she was still wary. She held the broom up in front of her.

His clothes were dirty and torn. A jagged hole on one trouser leg revealed a cut where blood had dried and crusted. Judging by the amount of stubble on his cheeks and the grime on his face and neck, it was a good while since he'd been able to wash. A nasty gash ran down from the corner of one eye to his jaw line, but it was a deep wound on his head that looked the most serious. Blood had matted into his hair. Although lank and greasy and clinging in strands to his scalp, his hair was obviously very fair and, even in the poor light, she could see that his eyes were an unusual shade of lavender-grey. So different to the swarthy, handsome Antoine; her first love. Odile's heart skipped a beat, and she berated herself for admiring the looks of this poor wounded man who was obviously in a state of distress.

'*Vous parlez français?*' she asked.

'*Oui, un petit peu.*' He held up his hands, seemingly in defence.

He did indeed speak some French, but from his accent it was clear he was British.

'*Qui êtes-vous?* Who are you? Why are you here?'

She was surprised when he answered her in her own language, hesitant at first.

'My fighter plane was hit and I parachuted out. I landed a few fields away and found your barn unlocked. I'm ...' He rubbed his face with his hand and visibly blanched. 'I don't know my name. I can remember every detail of bailing out, but my name ... it's gone.'

Chapter One

February 1941, rural mid-Wales

Annie glanced around the empty cottage. It was just her and her father now. Her youngest brother had left that morning after signing up, and she had been the only one up to see him leave. The row between her father and Reggie still resounded in her ears. She could hear the panic in her father's voice disguised as bellowing, as he played the heavy-handed head of the household. But she knew the fear was there, fear that another of his sons was going off to war, never to return. He'd been the same before, when seventeen-year-old Alf had forged his sign-up papers to accompany his older brother, Jimmy, and had gone and got himself killed in the first battle. Jimmy was somewhere in France, but no one knew where. After her mam's passing five years previously, the Beynon family had never been the same. She'd died giving birth to another brother who also hadn't survived. The sparkle had long gone, and Reggie leaving was only the latest blow.

She began to cook the bacon in the enormous frying pan on the range, the three rashers looking strangely lost as they sizzled; her mam had once cooked enough for six. She didn't feel hungry, and her heart weighed heavy in her chest.

'You up already, *bach?* You're a good 'un, aren't you, staying with your old da like this?' Ted Beynon appeared and sat down at the table laid for one.

Annie smiled at her father. She cracked two eggs into the sizzling bacon fat.

'You knew I was getting up to see Reggie off.' Her father's mouth formed a thin straight line and he remained silent. She continued, 'He's just as scared as we all are, but he wants to do his bit. I think we should be proud of him.'

'There was no need for him to go. He's a farm worker, and they already do their bit working on the land. Isn't it enough that he's got one brother dead and another God knows where?'

Annie placed the cooked breakfast in front of her father and poured strong tea into his large enamel mug.

'What are you having?'

'I'm not hungry. In any case, I'm off up to the Court to find out if Reggie's job in the stables is still going. See if I can catch Sir Charles.'

Her father's knife and fork clattered on to the plate in front of him. He placed his hands on the table and sat up straight. 'That's no job for a young slip of a thing like you, Mary-Ann. Your place is here, doing all the jobs your mam did, God rest her soul. I forbid it.'

Annie stood and faced her father. 'I'm sorry, Dada. My mind's made up. It's only you and me now, so it won't take me all my days to cook and clean for the two of us. There aren't many young boys around to become stable lads, in any case. He may be glad to let me carry on where Reggie left off. I used to spend enough of my time down in the paddocks with him anyway. The horses all know me. You can forbid it all you want, but I'm going there now.'

Her father's mouth dropped open. Annie had never stood up to him like that before. Always one for keeping the peace, she was. She knew her own mind though and would wait for the right moment to persuade him. It was always Reggie who went spoiling for an argument. But he was gone now, wasn't he? 'Please, Dada.' Her eyes filled with tears.

Her father sighed, stood and held out his arms. 'Don't let's fight, Annie. You're all I've got now. I don't like it, mind. You're your mam's girl all right, *bach*. If her mind was made up, there was nothing I could do or say to change it.' He kissed the top of her head. 'A chip off the old block, I'd say. At least Cefn Court is just up the road.'

The sun trickled through the sparse trees and cast dappled shadows on the narrow road. It would soon be spring, Annie's favourite time of year, when everything was bursting into life with luminescent shades of green. As she cycled nearer to the imposing manor house, she had a good feeling. Perhaps she would be taken on as the first stable girl at the Court.

Before going up to the house to speak to Sir Charles, she called in at the stables situated to the side of the main house. She had visited every day on her way home from school when Reggie worked there. Each of the horses had a character of its own. Some were quiet and thoughtful, gentle to stroke, nuzzling into her arm as if for affection, whereas others were frisky and temperamental, liable to kick out or rear at the slightest noise. Her favourite was a beautiful chestnut mare, just under fifteen hands high, called Kenna. She belonged to Edmund, the son of Sir Charles and Lady Delia. Reggie was Edmund's groom and despite the differences between them, one master and one servant, they had become firm friends. It was Reggie who had trained Kenna and calmed her fiery temper, encouraging her to become the elegant, well-mannered mare she was now. She had been born in one of the stables there at Cefn Court on an evening with one of the most magnificent red sunsets Radnor had ever known, according to Reggie, so it was right that they had given her a name meaning "born of fire". Annie remembered how her brother had become animated and alive whenever he talked about his beloved horses. A lump formed in her throat as she thought of Reggie and what he would be facing now he'd signed up.

Kenna trotted over to the wooden fence which edged the paddock. Annie took a carrot from her coat pocket and held it out for the beautiful mare.

'Here you are, my lovely girl. Are you missing Reggie?'

The horse snuffled the carrot and lowered her head so that Annie could stroke her silky chestnut coat that gleamed in the late winter sunshine. Then Kenna raised one front leg and pawed the lower strut of the fence with her hoof.

'I know, I'm missing him, too, girl. Let's hope this awful war will soon be over and we can go back to how things were.'

Kenna whinnied and moved along the fence.

'You've got company, I see, my beauty.'

Annie would have recognised that cultured, mellow voice anywhere. Her heart skipped a beat, and she turned to see a tall, handsome young man grinning at her. Edmund Pryce was dressed in a smart riding jacket and jodhpurs, his leather boots clinging to his calves so that he seemed taller than the last time they had spoken. A flush crept along her neck and her cheeks felt hot. Every time she saw him, he had the same effect on her.

'Oh, hello, Mr Edmund. I didn't hear you. I hope it's all right for me to come to see Kenna now that Reggie's gone.'

'Just Edmund, please. Of course it is, Mary-Ann. It still doesn't seem right that Reggie had to enlist and go off like that. I'm sure my father could have got him off to help the war effort here on the estate. A damned shame. I apologise for my language, but I don't know how I shall manage without him.'

Annie hesitated. That was what she had come up to the

Court for after all, so why not come straight out with it? That way she would be working with her beloved horses *and* helping Edmund out by taking her brother's place. So, what was stopping her? Before she could broach the subject, Edmund had entered the paddock and was leading Kenna into one of the stables.

'Like this, for instance,' he called. 'Reggie would have her all saddled up and ready for me to start my ride.'

Before long, Edmund reappeared on Kenna's back. He and the horse cantered away from the paddock into the adjoining field, with Edmund leaning forward as the speed increased. Annie waited until they became an indistinct dot in the distance. She imagined the thrill of riding Kenna, encouraging the mare to go faster and faster, just as she'd seen Edmund do. She closed her eyes and imagined feeling the wind stinging her cheeks with her long auburn ringlets flowing out behind her. But that would never happen. Her dada worked all hours God sent as a hedger on the land for Sir Charles. Even then, there was barely enough money to buy food for the two of them. Owning a thoroughbred horse like the ones in Cefn Court stables was out of the question and always would be. No, the only way she could be with horses was to do what her brother had done and become a groom.

She turned to continue her walk down to the Court.

The front door to the main house was huge. Wide oak panels were carved with intricate patterns of foliage, and the bolts and hinges were made of heavy black cast-iron. Her hand shook as she pressed her finger on the bell and she swallowed, trying to moisten her dry mouth.

She heard dogs barking and footsteps approaching. The door was opened by a young servant girl wearing a black dress and a starched white apron, her dark brown hair dragged back behind a matching white hat.

'Yes?' she said.

'I've come to see Sir Charles.'

'Have you got an appointment?'

The girl had obviously rehearsed what she had to say on such occasions. Annie's heart drummed in her chest. She should have guessed. He would not speak to a mere slip of a thing like her.

'Please tell him Nellie's girl is here to see about a job. Thank you.'

After telling her to wait there on the doorstep, the servant closed the door. Annie's mother had been well thought of by the family, and she hoped that the mention of her name would be enough for her to get a meeting with the master of the house. *Poor mam, if only you were still here. You'd put a good word in for me, wouldn't you?* The door creaked open.

'The master says I'm to take you to the drawing room.'

Chapter Two

Annie had not heard a word since she had wheedled her way in to Cefn Court to ask Sir Charles for a job. She did not expect to. On hearing her mother's name, he had assumed she was asking about a job in the kitchen. It was what her mother had done once she was no longer needed as a nanny for Mr Edmund.

'*You* working in the stables? That's no job for a young girl,' he'd said.

A flat refusal. He would not even discuss it.

Annie was ironing sheets and bolster cases when her father came in from work. Taking the iron off the stove, she spat on its flat surface to see if it was hot enough to get the creases out of the white cotton.

'Heard anything from Sir Charles? I was hoping you'd forgotten all those ideas of following Reggie into the stables. Mucking out and such like, you don't want to be doing that. Even Reggie used to hate that part of the job.' There was a break in his voice and it became barely audible. 'I wonder where he is now. Daft bugger. Should never have signed up. They said on the wireless it's only a matter of time before they ship more of the boys out to the action in the Middle East, and he'll be one of 'em. Just you watch.'

'You needn't worry. Sir Charles said the same as you. No job for a girl.'

Annie stood the iron on its end and took an enamel dish over to the blackened pot that was hanging over the fire. She ladled out the lamb *cawl* that was bubbling hot. 'Here, Da. Get some of this inside you. That scrag end you managed to get from Sid the Meat has done us for two days now.'

'There. I told you so. If old Charlie boy paid a bit more, you wouldn't have to look for work – but I'm not sorry he didn't give you a lad's job. At least he's got a bit a sense.'

Annie didn't comment or show him how disappointed she was. She just resumed the ironing, hanging each item as it was finished on to the wooden airing rack. Another job done. She raised the rope pulley and wound the cord in a figure of eight around the prongs. The heat from the fire would air the clothes properly and she would strip the beds in the morning.

She was putting the ironing board away in the scullery when there was a knock at the door. Who could be calling at Beech Cottage at that time of night?

'See who that is, *bach*.'

Annie walked through the narrow passageway to the front door and opened it a fraction, not wanting to let in the cold air.

'Good evening, Mary-Ann. May I speak with your father?'

A serious Edmund Pryce stood on the doorstep, fidgeting from one foot to the other.

Annie's pulse quickened. What could be so important that Edmund had come to their modest cottage? What could not wait until her father started work in the morning?

'It's not Reggie, is it?' Annie blurted out her fears and Edmund's face broke into a smile, his lavender-grey eyes twinkling.

'Gracious me, no. I've got something to ask your father. Something I need to discuss with him.'

'I'm sorry. Please come in. It's just after losing Alf and Jimmy, I'm terrified something is going to happen to Reggie too.'

Edmund patted her arm and tingles fizzled through Annie's whole body.

'I understand. It must be awfully hard for you and Mr Beynon. I shall miss your brother terribly. He's an exceptionally good friend to me. I want him back safe and sound too.'

Annie led Edmund into the parlour. She pulled across the heavy curtains that acted as a blackout before switching on the lights.

'Please take a seat, Mr Edmund.'

'I wish you'd call me Edmund. We were friends when we were little. There was no "mister" then, was there?'

Annie smiled, remembering the fun they'd had playing in the grounds of the Court when Edmund had come home from boarding school. Her mam had treated them all the same, boxing the master's son's ears as well as her own children's if they misbehaved.

The room was cooler than the rest of the house, so she turned on the one bar electric fire to take off the chill. A faint smell of burning filled the air but soon disappeared. Annie knew that not much dust could have settled on the filament. She dusted the room every day, just as her mam had done all those years before, despite it being kept for "high days and holidays". *You never know when someone important will come.* Her mother's words resounding in her ears, she went to fetch her father. Edmund Pryce *was* important.

'Da, it's Mr Edmund. He wants to see you. I've taken him into the parlour.'

'What the blazes does he want at this time of night?'

Her father stood, smoothed down his trousers and checked his collarless shirt was tucked in at the waist. He left Annie in the kitchen, and she could hear the unrecognisable tune he always whistled when he was apprehensive as he made his way to the parlour.

Annie would have loved to have known what they

were saying but resisted the temptation to eavesdrop. If it was not bad news about Reggie, could it be her dad's job? Weren't the Pryces happy with him? If he could no longer work, would they lose their home? It was one of the estate's tied cottages, after all. She knew her father was slowing up. He never complained, but it was obvious his back and knees were giving him a lot of pain. She had caught him rubbing liniment into his joints on many an occasion, the pungent smell filling the room. *Your da's the best hedger around these parts*, her mam had told her. But he was older now and being out in all weathers was taking its toll. She heard voices in the passageway.

'Just give it some thought, Mr Beynon. I wouldn't ask if I didn't think it would work out. I can't think of anyone better. And my father will pay the same rate.'

Her father shook Edmund Pryce's hand and saw him to the door.

'I will, Mr Edmund, but I'm not making any promises.'

Edmund saw her standing by the kitchen door and called, 'Goodbye, Mary-Ann.'

She rose her hand.

Her father closed the door and followed her back into the kitchen

'Seems you haven't told me everything, young lady.' Her father's glare unnerved her. 'I thought you said the master didn't like the idea of you working with them horses.'

'You knew I was going to see Sir Charles – and he *did* refuse me the job.'

Ted Beynon's voice rose and he banged his hand on the table. Annie's pulse raced. She rarely saw him angry. Ever since her mother had passed, he had been so gentle and caring towards her, his only daughter. What was so wrong about working with the animals she loved best in the world just because she was a girl? It was not heavy work. Lifting leather saddles, bales of hay, keeping the paddock fences and gates secure, that was all. It would be messy at times, mucking out and cleaning the stables, but being a chambermaid in the main house would not be any better. And there would be the bonus of brushing and grooming the horses. Reggie had been allowed to ride them too, especially when his master had been away. And there was one other attraction to the job that Annie had not even admitted to herself until that moment. She would see Edmund Pryce every time he came to ride or check on Kenna. She felt her cheeks burn.

'Please, Da. Anyway, as I told you, Sir Charles said the same thing as you. But I know I can do the job. And I'd be good at it. Reggie let me help him, so I've picked things up from him. Is that what Mr Edmund wanted to see you about?'

Her father sat back down on a chair. 'Yes. He said you'd be ideal for the job. His mare's missing Reggie and pining, so he says. He said he watched how you were with her. His father was dead against it, but he said he stood his ground. Sounds like someone else I know. In the end, Sir Charles said as long as I agreed, he would give you the job.'

The thumping in Annie's chest increased. She realised that if she handled the situation correctly in the next few minutes, perhaps her da would relent after all.

'What harm would it do, Da? I'd be earning a bit of money at last. Surely that would be a help? As soon as Reggie is back from the war, I'd give it up in an instant. I'll ask for a job in the kitchen then like you want. Think of me as guarding the job for him until he gets back. If they had to get someone else, they wouldn't give it back to Reggie, would they? When I write to him, I'll be able to tell him all about Kenna and how she's doing. Please, Da.'

Ted Beynon did not say a word. He put his elbows on

the table and held his hands together, spreading out his fingers. To Annie, the silence was deafening and seemed to go on for an age. Eventually he spoke.

'Put like that, I suppose it makes sense. For our Reggie, then. But if I hear them other stable lads are not treating you right or are swearing and cussing in front of you, there'll be 'ell to play, understand? You can tell the gaffer and his son with the fancy ways in the morning. I mean it, *bach*. Stable girl? I don't know what the world's coming to.'

Annie stood up and rushed over to her father, flinging her arms around him in a big *cwtch*. 'Thank you, Da. Thank you.'

Chapter Three

Annie took down the blackout card from her bedroom window. Dawn was breaking and pale pink sunlight filtered through the thin curtains into the room. It seemed to her that she had only been asleep for a short while after she had taken such a long time to drop off. She had tossed and turned, her mind full of sleek chestnut horses and the noise of hooves galloping over the fields behind her cottage. Racing to the front of the crowd was a rider clad in a stylish red riding jacket and tight jodhpurs. When she realised the date, her stomach tightened into knots and she jumped out of bed, determined not to be late on her first day.

Her father had already left for work and the pan was still on the stove for her to cook something. She wasn't hungry but, remembering her mother's voice telling her not to start the day on an empty stomach, she went into the pantry and cut a doorstep of bread, before spreading a thick layer of beef dripping on it. There was still tea in the pot so she poured herself a cup and gulped it down.

By the time she cycled along the lane from Beech Cottage, the sun was higher. The sky was streaked with coral-pinks and lemons, and Annie hoped that the weather would be fine for her first day. She parked her bike in one of the sheds by the stables and immediately spotted Edmund walking up from the Court.

'Good morning, Mary-Ann. Nice and early, just like your brother. I thought I'd meet you myself on your first day – introduce you to the others and show you the ropes.'

'Thank you, Mr Edmund – I mean ... Edmund.' Annie's heartbeat quickened as he flashed her one of his dazzling smiles. *There's no point in thinking of him like that, my girl. He's your boss and you're his servant.* But there was something in the way Edmund's gaze met hers that made her wonder …

He led her into the main area, where there were eight stalls in all. He explained that not all of them were currently being used.

'All the horses are named and the two other grooms are responsible for the other horses. You'll be in sole charge of Kenna.'

Annie walked to each of the bays and read the names. 'Are you sure it's all right to only have one horse to look after? Won't the others mind?'

It was then that two young lads arrived and joined her and Edmund. She knew them from school and remembered her father telling her that the previous grooms who had been there for years with Reggie had also enlisted.

'Ah, here they are now. Harry, Fred, I want you to meet the new groom who'll be working with you. This is Mary-Ann Beynon.'

The boys looked at each other in what Annie soon realised was disbelief, and then looked her up and down.

'A girl. What use is she going to be?' muttered Harry, the tall, gangly one.

'More work for us, then,' grumbled Fred.

Edmund ignored their comments and turned to Annie.

'Harry and Fred have been here a few weeks now, so they'll show you what to do. They look after the horses that drive the carriage and also after Sir Charles's horse, Ebony. Lads, Mary-Ann will be looking after Kenna for me. She knows her well from when her brother was my groom and will be exercising her as well as feeding her, along with general stable duties. I want you to make her welcome, show her what a typical day in the stable looks like. I'll call back in about an hour to see how you're getting on.'

Edmund strode away, and Annie felt the hairs on the back of her neck stand on end. It was obvious that she was not welcome with the two stable boys.

Harry spoke first. 'Ooh, Mary-Ann, eh? Rest of us 'ave to call you Annie Beynon. Only got the job because of that brother of yours, did you? If you know the place so well, you won't need our 'elp – will she, Fred?'

Fred was stocky and shorter than his friend. As he passed Annie, the bucket he was carrying swung to the side and tipped liquid over her boots before she could step back out of the way. The stench from its contents caught in the back of Annie's throat. 'Oops, sorry. Didn't see you there.' The two boys walked off to the back of the stables laughing. 'Ruddy cheek, thinking she can do the same job as us' she heard, in a loud exaggerated whisper.

Annie found a tap near the stable bays and ran clean water over her boot. It was obvious that she would have to find her own way around the work involved. She went into the tack shed where the saddles and harnesses were stored. She found some brushes and went to find Kenna. Her stall was empty and the wooden door was open. Annie heard whispering and noticed the two boys leaving through the open doors. She rushed to the paddock and saw them letting Kenna into the field with the others.

She caught up with them. 'I thought that was my job,' she said.

'Help you, 'e said. That's all what we was doing, wasn't we, Fred?' Harry raised his eyebrows. 'You need to get that pretty backside of yours into gear a bit sharpish if you're going to stay the blue-eyed girl with Eddie boy.'

Fred leaned against the wooden fence. 'Yeah, that's right.'

Annie stormed off in the direction of the horses. Kenna had no bridle on, so she had to stroke her and speak softly to persuade her to come back to her stall. The boys were nowhere to be seen, and Annie relaxed for the first time that morning. Had she made a huge mistake? She knew she would have to keep herself to herself and concentrate on Kenna; making sure the horse was happy and contented until Reggie returned from the war was all she had to do.

Brushing the mare's silky chestnut coat was very soothing, and once she had finished, she put on her bridle and led her out into the fresh air.

'I'll be back to ride you in a little while, my girl.'

As if she understood, Kenna seemed to nod her head and trotted into the open space of the field. Annie returned the brushes to the tack shed and cleared the stall floor before putting down fresh straw.

'Getting on with things, I see.' Edmund was back as promised. 'Have Harry and Fred been all right with you? Don't take any nonsense from them. It's just banter. If it gets anything more, you let me know.'

Annie looked down. 'Everything's fine.'

She was determined it would be and anyway, it was worth putting up with things just to hear the mellow tones in the voice of the man standing opposite her.

Chapter Four

Annie came to dread arriving at the stables each morning, wondering what Harry and Fred had planned for her. Morning would arrive all too soon after hours of tossing and turning. She'd drag herself out of bed, skip breakfast and leave the house. Her da had noticed how she'd changed in just a few weeks.

'You don't have to stick at it, *bach*, if it's too much for you. You've given it your best shot. Reggie will understand,' he'd said, only the night before.

But it wasn't the job. She was determined that two layabout lads from the village were not going to break her. She drew in a deep breath and set off for the stables. As she cycled along the lane, signs of spring were now visible everywhere. In the shade of the budding hedgerows, clumps of pale yellow primroses dotted the grass like jewels, and powdery catkins dangled in the breeze. It was always the skies that amazed Annie at that time of the morning on bright, clear days. That day was no exception – streaks of apricot merging into pale pink hung above the hills in the distance. Giant oak trees grew there as if guarding the village that had been named in their honour. By the time she arrived at the stables, her mood had lightened and the knots in her stomach had unravelled a little. Even better, there was no sign of Harry or Fred. She walked round to the stable block.

Kenna's stall was empty. There was muck tipped all over the clean straw she'd put on the floor for the horse the night before, and the rack where the grooming brushes were stored was empty. On it was pinned an envelope bearing an untidily scrawled message: *NO JOB FOR A GIRL.*

Annie rushed in and screwed up the message, throwing it to the floor. The stench in the stall made her gag and she returned to the yard, her eyes streaming with hot tears. She heard a noise in the barn and a muffled giggle.

'You think this is funny, do you?' she screamed, running in through the barn door. 'What have you done with Kenna? How could you!'

In the gloom, she saw the two stable boys hiding in a corner.

'Don't know what you're on about. We've been in here shifting hay like Eddie boy asked us to – doing a man's job, han't we, Fred? Ain't that girl of yours still in her stall?'

'Yeah, should get 'ere early like us. Eddie's not going to be 'appy.'

Annie knew she hadn't been late, but she would never win with these two. Kenna was her priority. She stormed out into the bright sunshine, her pulse pounding. Hot, angry tears blinded her momentarily, and she blinked. There was no way she wanted Edmund to see her like this.

Kenna was in the far field and seemed unaware of the drama that had occurred. Once the stable boys had led her out of her stall, she had obviously cantered away into the freedom of the meadow. Annie searched for the horse's bridle and saddle, eventually finding them tucked in an empty stall behind a bale of hay. *Damn them!*

As soon as Kenna saw Annie striding across the field, she trotted over and nuzzled into her. That feeling made it all worth it. Annie would stick it out. They'd have to get sick of the taunting and trick-playing sometime, wouldn't they?

The next day, Annie was sweeping out the stall and turned to see Edmund striding into the paddock. She was alone and relaxed now that Fred and Harry were in the far field exercising the lordship's horses. It was only her and Kenna here, just the way she liked it.

'Good morning, Mary-Ann'. Another of his beaming smiles made her heart beat faster.

'Oh, good morning, Edmund. Lovely day.'

'Yes, we're going to have a spell of this fine weather for the next week, I believe. Can you stop what you're doing and come into the office for a moment, please?'

Annie's pulse raced. He was happy with how she was caring for Kenna, wasn't he? She placed the large broom against the wall and followed him into the poky room that had been sectioned off from the stable yard.

'Sit down,' Edmund said, pointing to the stool alongside the table where papers were stacked untidily. 'Kenna has really taken to you, Mary-Ann. I'm so pleased with my choice for Reggie's replacement. As you know, I'm leaving for my training soon. I've told my father what a good job you're doing and that you're more than capable of carrying on the job without any further guidance from me.'

'Thank you.' Annie thought of two people who would disagree but dismissed them from her mind.

'Kenna will be in good hands while I'm away.' Edmund smiled.

Annie took a sideways glance at the handsome man standing by her. The way he became so passionate when talking about his beloved mare endeared him to her even more.

'That's all, really. If you have any problems when I'm gone, please take them up with my father.'

'Thank you. I'm sure everything will be fine,' she said, sounding more confident than she felt.

They walked back into the yard. Annie's heart sank as she watched the young man make his way back to the Court. Apart from looking after beautiful Kenna, seeing

Edmund Pryce was the only thing that made her job worthwhile. How would she cope with the unpleasantness and taunts of Harry and Fred once he left for his RAF training in only six weeks' time? She took in a deep breath.

Two riders appeared in the distance; her fellow groomsmen would be back making her life a misery before she knew it. She returned to Kenna, saddling her up and putting on her bridle. Edmund had said to take her on a long ride, so that's what she'd do to get as far from the stables as she could. She led the horse into the yard.

'Madam's only now getting going, it looks like, Fred,' said Harry. 'You and me have been out for hours.'

'Bet she's been sucking up to Eddie boy. Gets away with blue murder just 'cos she shakes that tight little arse of 'ers.'

Don't rise to it, don't rise to it. As Fred passed her, he struck Kenna on the hind leg with his riding crop. The mare reared up in pain and dragged Annie along the ground. She let go of the reins and the horse trotted into the paddock.

'Oops!' Fred laughed, and he and Harry continued on their way into the stables.

Annie's eyes burned with tears. She picked herself up and stormed after the boys

'You monster, Fred Rhys. You can do what you want to me, but don't you *ever* mistreat my horse. Call yourself a groom and you do that. You're a bully!'

She turned on her heel and strode away to find Kenna.

Chapter Five

'Everything all right with you down at them stables, *bach*?' Annie was serving a dish of *cawl* to her father. Her heart raced and she felt a warmth creep up her neck as she sat down at the table next to him.

'Yes. Why do you ask?' She tried to keep her voice light.

'Oh, it's just I overheard summat in the shop today. 'Cos if you're having any bother with them lads, you say. That Fred Rhys is a nasty piece of work. And Harry Lewis just follows him like a sheep, no sense between the ears that un.'

'They don't like it 'cos I'm a girl, that's all, but I can handle them, Da. Don't worry. *Cawl* all right for you?'

Glad to change the subject, she wondered what it was that Fred was saying about her. But her conscience was clear. Whatever the boys thought was going on between her and Edmund was all a figment of their imaginations. The fact that she dreamed about her boss every night was a secret that only she was privy to, and that was the way it was going to stay. The fact that she'd sensed that maybe Edmund was starting to think of her in the same romantic way was just wishful thinking on her part, she told herself.

It was a fine, dry day and the canter over the surrounding fields was exhilarating. Feeling as free as a bird, Annie dismounted outside the gate from the paddock into the yard. All was quiet, and she sighed in relief that she could concentrate on grooming Kenna. The mare's coat glistened with a fine layer of sweat from the effort of the long, fast ride and her breath made clouds in the crisp air.

24

Annie covered her in a woollen rug while she collected the brushes, combs and cloths.

She led the mare into her stall and gave her clean water and some hay to eat, and then proceeded to brush her coat until it shone.

'There you are, my beauty.' Edmund had arrived. 'I must say Kenna's looking fantastic. You're doing a terrific job. Even better than your brother, maybe?' He smiled. 'Have you heard from Reggie lately?'

'Just a letter to say the training is going well.' Annie's heart pounded. She dreaded to think what her brother would be facing after that. Only last week there was talk in the village of more casualties.

As Annie led Kenna back in, she heard whispering and giggling. Fred and Harry must have been watching and listening to the praise heaped upon her by Edmund. They scarpered when they knew they'd been seen, but for some reason a shiver of unease ran through her. She dismissed it and cleared away all the grooming tack before making sure Kenna's stall was securely locked.

Beech Cottage was empty when she arrived home. There was time to peel the potatoes before tackling her muddy riding boots. It wasn't long before she heard Ted Beynon outside the scullery door, scraping his boots on the metal guard.

'That you, Da?'

He joined her by the sink. 'You look tired, *bach*. Them Pryces don't know they're born with all o' us waiting on 'em hand and foot, especially her ladyship. Always asking your mam to stay on and do extra, she was.'

Annie thought of Lady Delia with her sad eyes and sighed. Her father was in one of those moods. 'Come on, Da. Where would we be if we didn't have these jobs, eh? Most of the folk round here owe their livelihood to Sir Charles and Lady Delia.'

'I suppose you're right. But I still worry about you ...'

Annie didn't say any more. What she didn't tell her father was that working at Cefn Court was the only way she could see the man who made her heart beat a little faster and whose face she dreamed about every night.

Annie followed her father into the kitchen where he sat down in his chair next to the range. A hand-crocheted blanket was folded to form a cushion down the length of the back. She remembered her mam unravelling old socks and pullovers to get enough wool to make it, and she was sure her da kept it there as a last link to his beloved Nell.

'No matter how hard you work down with them ol' horses, you still get a hearty meal on the table. You're a good girl. What's it tonight? It smells tasty, whatever it is.'

Annie knew her da missed her mam, but as long as she could get a hot meal on the table for him after he'd been out on the land in all weathers, she knew her mam would be proud of her.

'It's a pie. I managed to get a rabbit from Sid the Meat yesterday. Skinned it for me too. You know how I hate that bit. Urggh! I got it all ready before leaving this morning. The potatoes should be cooked through now as well.'

She served the meal and they both ate in silence. Her father cleared the table and took the plates down to the scullery. He always insisted on washing up.

'You've cooked it, *bach*. So, I clear away. You can make us a cup o' tea.'

Maybe it was because her mam had gone, but he'd always been good around the house and very different from most fathers, according to her friends. When he'd finished, Annie took the cups into the living room and her father turned on the wireless.

'Another British vessel was sunk today,' said the voice on the BBC Home Service. 'These are a number of casualties and reports of bodies floating in the water. A rescue service has begun.'

Ted Beynon stood up and immediately turned the radio off. His face was solemn.

'Reggie will be fine, Da.'

'Silly bugger. I'm off up the garden. I'll see you in a while.'

When her father was worried or upset, she always knew where to find him. It was as if tending to his vegetable plot in the garden gave him solace. At this time of year, he was getting the soil ready for later in the year and sowing seeds. None of his beautiful flowers now. All the beds had been turned over to growing veg on the instructions of Mr Churchill.

Dusk was painting brushstrokes of rose pink and apricot along the horizon again. The earlier feeling of unease returned and Annie felt compelled to check on Kenna. She cycled along the lane from the cottage towards the stables. As she got closer, she heard the unmistakeable snort of a horse in distress. *Please don't let it be Kenna.* She pedalled faster and found the stable door wide open.

'Who's there?' she shouted.

Kenna was rearing up in the confined space of her stall. There were white and brown feathers scattered on the floor, and as Annie ran to the mare, a startled chicken made its escape through the stall door. The other horses were restless, but it was Kenna who was the most agitated and upset. Annie cuddled her around her head, speaking softly and stroking her nose.

'There, there, *cariad*. I'm here now.'

The horse calmed and nuzzled into her neck. Annie

felt her heartbeat slow back to normal. She *knew* she'd padlocked the stable door before leaving; it was her responsibility. Someone was trying to sabotage her, and she had a pretty good idea who that someone was. On the stone floor, she found the padlock and key neatly placed on a piece of paper with the word *chicken* written on it. They'd deliberately put the chicken in there, knowing how spooked Kenna would be! She would not keep this to herself. Sir Charles should know that the grooms he'd appointed were prepared to mistreat a beautiful animal like Kenna just to get at her. She began to cry. Once she started, pent up angry tears from weeks of bullying and taunting came flooding out.

She didn't hear Edmund come into the stables.

'Mary-Ann,' he said. 'What on earth has happened?' He took her in his arms and she allowed herself to be comforted.

'The door was wide open. Somebody put a chicken in her stall,' she said, pointing to the feathers on the floor around them. 'It was done just to get at me. And to frighten Kenna. That's unforgiveable! She was terrified when I got here.'

'My poor love. Did you see anyone?' Seemingly realising what he'd said, Edmund released Annie from his arms. He started to pick up the feathers and spoke softly to his horse.

'There are only two people who would do this,' she said. 'Fred Rhys and Harry Lewis.'

Edmund's mouth dropped. 'But why? I thought you were all getting on now.'

Annie had kept quiet for long enough. She told Edmund about every incident and how she'd tried to deal with it herself. 'I think they overheard you earlier telling me how pleased you were with my work. And they're spreading rumours about us in the village too. My father heard something in the village shop. They hate me, Mr Edmund.'

The young man suddenly pulled Annie towards him and kissed her tenderly on the lips. Annie's stomach flipped and her skin tingled. He stood back immediately.

'I'm sorry, Mary-Ann. Uh, uh … that was very wrong of me. I should never have taken advantage of the moment like that.' His cheeks were flushed and he could no longer make eye contact with her. 'You get off home. I'll see to Kenna now.'

Still reeling from Edmund's kiss, Annie did as he suggested. Ted Beynon was dozing by the fire when she got in so she didn't have to tell her father where she'd been.

That night, in the pitch darkness of her bedroom, Annie relived Edmund's kiss; the memory of his soft lips on hers, and the knowledge it would always be her secret because he'd made it clear he'd crossed a forbidden line.

Chapter Six

It had been several days since Fred and Harry had been dismissed by Sir Charles. Annie had been starting work earlier and leaving later to help Edmund with the extra workload. At first the two grooms had denied any knowledge of the incident, but, in the end, Harry had admitted taking the key from its not-so-safe hiding place at the back of the stables while Fred had raided the chicken coop.

One evening Annie was cycling back from Brynderi after meeting Gwennie, an old school friend. She'd forgotten all about the trouble at the stables for a few hours. When she approached the main entrance to Cefn Court, the sky was streaked with fiery shades of scarlet. Annie imagined it looked similar to the night Kenna had been born. Beautiful, maybe, but something made her cycle down the lane to check on Edmund's mare. *You're getting paranoid, bach*, her father would say, but she had a feeling something wasn't right. Crows perched on the wooden fencing edging the paddock, their black silhouettes against the glow of the sky. Their raucous calls heightened the feeling of foreboding. The metal gate was open, and there was carnage when she entered the stables themselves. The stalls were empty. The floor was strewn with pails of stinking slurry. Saddles and reins were slashed and grooming tack scattered over the floor. Hay that was used to line the floors of the stalls was sodden with what smelled like Jeyes Fluid. Kenna's stall was the worst affected. The whitewashed back wall had been daubed with red paint to spell out a word. *SLUT*. Panic ran through her veins. She knew who'd done this. It was bad enough that they had it in for her, but how could people who had been employed to look after horses be so cruel? Annie went to the paddock and saw that Kenna and the carriage horses were roaming there. She called Kenna over and held onto her bridle. But what about Ebony, the beautiful black stallion belonging to Sir Charles? He was nowhere to be seen.

'Noooo!' screamed Annie. Frightened, Kenna reared and it was all Annie could do to hold on to her.

'What's going on?' Out of breath, Edmund arrived in the yard. He was quickly followed by Bert Pearson, the chauffeur, who had clearly been alerted by Annie's scream too.

Annie was sobbing uncontrollably, desperately trying not to let Kenna go. Edmund took the mare from her and spoke to his horse in soothing tones. 'There, there, girl. You're safe. Calm down, calm down.' Eventually the horse stopped pulling.

'Are you all right, miss?' asked Bert. 'What a bleedin' mess!' He looked slightly abashed despite the circumstances. 'Sorry for the language, Miss Beynon.'

Concerned, Edmund looked over at her. 'Yes, are you all right, Mary-Ann? I think I know who has enough of a grudge to do this, don't you? I never thought they would go this far, though.'

Bert looked puzzled.

'My father gave Fred Rhys and Harry Lewis notice. We've put up with their unreasonable attitude to Mary-Ann joining the team long enough. She hasn't told anyone how much of a misery they've made her job here. They obviously didn't take it well and are out for revenge by the look of it.'

'I'd heard the grumbles, but I didn't think it had got this bad,' said Bert, clearly in shock.

Edmund started to examine the damage. It was then that he noticed what had been written on the wall in Kenna's stall. He became scarlet in the face. 'That's preposterous!

Just wait until I get my hands on those two low-lives! I'm so sorry you had to read that.'

Bert came to his side to see what he was talking about. He gasped. 'That can't be referring to you, miss. To think, I've known 'em two all their lives. From good families, too, the Rhyses and the Lewises. They deserve a good whipping the two of 'em, and I'll be first in the queue to do it.'

Annie took in a deep breath. 'Mr Edmund … Ebony's gone.'

Edmund's face blanched. 'Are you sure he's not in the paddock? Surely even Rhys and Lewis wouldn't stoop that low …'

'I couldn't see him. Maybe we could check on the far side,' said Annie. 'All the stalls were empty when I came in. Look, his saddle is one of the ones slashed into strips.' She pointed to the damage.

'Bert, will you take Mary-Ann home in the car, please? It's not safe for her to cycle along the lanes at this time of night. I'll have to tell my father what's happened and inform the local constabulary. But the priority is finding Ebony.'

'What about Kenna? She can't stay here,' said Annie, tears trickling down her cheeks. She couldn't help thinking if she hadn't been so headstrong about taking on her brother's role, none of this would have happened. 'I'm so sorry. This is all my fault.'

Edmund put his arm around her shoulder. 'Mary-Ann, the only people responsible for this are the rotters who did the damage and neglected my father's horse. I'll take Kenna. I'll house her safely in the barn by the manor. Now, try not to worry and go and get some sleep. We'll take the carriage horses down there too.'

Ted Beynon was waiting for Annie when she arrived home.

The familiar smell of *cawl* she'd made the previous day greeted her and made her realise how hungry she was.

'I didn't expect you to be this late, *bach*. I was getting worried. I thought you were only going to see the Probert girl. An hour you said.'

'No, there was more trouble at the stables. Mr Edmund got Bert to bring me home in the car. I can collect my bike in the morning. The walk will do me good,' she said.

'Going up in the world now then?' Her father laughed.

Annie sat down at the table and burst into tears. Ted placed his gnarled hand on hers. 'Annie, *bach*? What on earth has happened?'

Once Annie started, everything came out. Everything Fred and Harry had done, how they'd made her life at work a misery. 'You and Sir Charles were right, Da. It's no job for a girl. I can do the job no problem. It's the resentment I can't get over.'

Ted Beynon stood and pulled his daughter up into his arms, holding her until the sobbing subsided. 'Let it all out, *bach*. It's all over the village that they've been sacked but I 'ad no idea it was this bad. Why don't you ask Lady Delia if there are any jobs going in the kitchen like your ma did? You'll still be able to visit that 'orse you love so much when you pass every day.'

Annie pulled back. 'You don't understand. Tonight they've ransacked the stables. Damaged the tack and soaked everywhere in water and Jeyes fluid. The stink was awful ... but the worst thing is that Sir Charles's horse is missing.'

Annie didn't tell her father what they'd written about her in red paint. It was best if the police dealt with the culprits; she didn't want Ted Beynon taking the law into his own hands.

After finishing her *cawl* and helping to tidy up, Annie

retired to her bedroom for an early night. But she couldn't sleep. She tossed and turned. One minute she was so angry at what Fred and Harry had done, and the next she was thinking of the one man who made her insides somersault whenever he was close to her. Why was life so complicated? Why couldn't Edmund Pryce belong to a family like hers? They could have met at Young Farmers' events and courted like lots of her friends. As it was, any hope of love blossoming would come to nothing.

She eventually fell into an uneasy sleep, but woke up bathed in perspiration with her heart drumming in her chest. She'd had dreams of a black stallion lined up among the cattle at the abattoir in Builth as a middle-aged man in a blood-stained apron led each animal in for slaughter. 'Noooo!' she yelled.

The next thing she knew, her father was bursting into the room. 'What is it, *bach*?'

'It's just a nightmare. Sorry, Dada. Go back to sleep. It's over now.'

Annie lay awake in the dark until dawn bathed her room in pale yellow sunlight. *A new day. What would it bring?*

Chapter Seven

By the time Annie reached the stables, Edmund and his father had cleared most of the mess. The floor had been cleared of the contaminated straw, the grooming tack was all neatly stacked back on the shelves in the shed and the undamaged bridles were hanging on hooks along the back wall. Sir Charles's slashed saddle was beyond repair and was placed by the door. The best news for Annie was that Kenna was settled back into her stall with fresh hay and the door secured with a new bolt.

'Good morning, Mary-Ann,' said Edmund, looking up from sweeping the flagstones. 'I trust you slept well.'

'Good morning. I did, thank you,' she lied. 'Is there any news about Ebony?' She hadn't been able to get the images of the slaughterhouse out of her head.

Sir Charles emerged from the stable office with an unsorted pile of papers in his hands. 'Good morning, Mary-Ann. I'm so sorry you were the first to come across that mess last night. Pure vandalism. Despicable.' He shook his head. His eyes looked sad, and grey, puffy shadows suggested he had not had much sleep either. 'In answer to your question. There is no sign of Ebony as yet, but the police have put a look out to all surrounding county forces. I told them about the white scar under his mane. It wouldn't be obvious to whoever stole him, but it would identify him. One of our shepherds, who knows the area well, has been here since first light and has agreed to travel to each of the farms around to look for him.' The older man inhaled deeply. 'We've just got to hope that he has not come to any harm. The good news is that Constable Thompson has arrested Rhys and Lewis, and they're currently in the cells in Pen-y-rhos. Denying everything, of course. He'll be up shortly to interview you. And, my dear, please don't hold back. Please tell him everything about what you've had to put up with from those two hooligans.'

'I will, Sir. What can I do to help?'

Constable Thompson arrived at the Court not long afterwards and made detailed notes of everything Annie told him. He wanted to know why she hadn't reported them until Edmund had found her upset after the first incident. She almost felt that it was as if he was siding with Fred and Harry. Perhaps he didn't agree with girls working as grooms either. But criminal damage, cruelty to animals? Surely nobody could think that the way they had chosen to behave after their dismissal was her fault?

The florid-faced policeman hesitated and flicked back through his notebook as if checking what he'd written. 'I have one more question before I finish, Miss Beynon,' he said. 'Have you noticed anyone hanging around the stables apart from the Pryce family and the two grooms we've arrested? Any vehicles you haven't seen before? Any horses and carriages not belonging to Sir Charles and Lady Pryce?'

Annie shook her head. 'No one. Why do you ask?'

'It's just that when we notified the Credenford police this morning, they'd had a similar incident a few weeks ago. Stables trashed. Expensive saddles slashed. A pedigree horse going missing and then turning up at a horse sale outside Bromyard.'

Annie's pulse raced. What if they'd all jumped to the wrong conclusions? She plucked up courage to speak again. 'Do you think it was a stranger, then? Not Fred and Harry?' she said.

'I didn't say that, Miss Beynon. The lads are denying everything and we're in the process of checking alibis. We have to look at all possible scenarios, that's all.'

Annie bit her lip and thought of the letters daubed in red paint. She hadn't told him everything. She took a deep breath before speaking again. 'I haven't told you about the thing that upset me most of all, Constable.'

'What do you mean?' He got his notebook out again.

'On the back wall of the stall where Mr Edmund's mare is housed was a word written in huge letters in red paint.' She blushed.

'What word, Miss Beynon?'

'I can't say it. But it was about me.'

The constable sighed. 'I need to know. It's evidence.'

'Slut,' Annie whispered.

'Ah,' said the policeman. 'I can see why that would upset you.'

'I'm responsible for Kenna, Mr Edmund's horse. How would they know a girl worked in the stables? And how would a stranger know I was responsible for that horse? It *has* to be Fred and Harry. They think I get special treatment from Mr Edmund.'

The policeman sighed before raising one eyebrow. 'And do you?'

'No, certainly not!'

'No one mentioned that when I attended the scene this morning. I understood everything was as it was when you found it.' He closed the notebook. 'If you do think of anything else, please let me know at the police station in Pen-y-rhos. That will be all for now, Miss Beynon. Thank you.'

After the constable had gone, Sir Charles escorted her back up to the stables. It was unrecognisable from the devastation she's witnessed less that twenty-four hours before. Men from the estate had repaired the stable stalls and the gate into the paddock had been given stronger struts of wood. The best sight was Kenna cantering freely around the meadow. All that was missing was Ebony.

'We're about done here now, Mary-Ann. Why don't you take yourself home and enjoy some rest? This is such an ordeal for you. I'll see you here at eight o'clock sharp in the morning. Let's hope we get some news about Ebony and we can put this awful business behind us. Father and I are already interviewing someone for replacement groom this afternoon. You'll be the first to know.'

Cycling along the lanes into Brynderi gave Annie time to think. Although she loved her job, her stubborn insistence that she could do the work as well as any stable lad had brought her nothing but unhappiness and trouble. She enjoyed looking after Kenna and working in the fresh air, but wasn't her main reason for wanting the position down to a certain handsome young man she knew she'd see every day? Edmund Pryce was all she thought, and her heart still beat faster when she remembered his kiss. But a memory was all it could be. It would only ever be a professional relationship between them now. She thought about how happy her upbringing had been with her parents. Neither of them came from money, and times had often been so hard that they'd sometimes gone without in order to feed her and her brothers when they were little. The Pryces had never known that sort of hardship. She and Edmund were from different worlds …

No, she'd admit she'd made a huge mistake. She'd wait for Sir Charles to get a replacement groom for Fred and Harry, and then she'd tell them her decision. There'd be plenty of strong local lads who'd jump at the chance of employment with the Pryces. Suddenly the spring foliage seemed a little brighter and she relaxed, letting the fresh breeze cool her cheeks. *Sorry, Reggie. I tried to keep your position open for you. Our da will be happy, at least.*

The cottage was empty when Annie arrived home. Her da was still out in the fields, the place was as neat as a new pin and she suddenly had the urge to do some baking. On checking the pantry, the rations of flour and butter were almost gone; not nearly enough for the Welsh cakes that were her father's favourites.

Taking her ration book with her, Annie left the cottage and walked down the hill into Brynderi. The village store was on the corner. Two middle-aged woman she knew from church were talking to Mrs Morgan the Shop when she entered. They looked around when the bell signalled her arrival, and immediately stopped talking. The way they looked at one another told Annie that she'd been the subject of their gossiping, and they stood aside as she walked up to the counter.

'Miss Beynon, what can I get you? We don't often see you at this time of day. I thought you'd be at work.'

One of the customers raised an eyebrow. 'There's bin a bit of bother up at the Court, I hear.'

Annie felt a warm flush travel across her neck. She took out her ration book and placed it on the counter.

'I've been given the afternoon off,' she said. 'Could I have my rations of butter, sugar and flour, please? I'm going to get on with some baking.'

The shopkeeper proceeded to weigh out the flour and sugar from the large storage jars behind the counter. She then brought out two packs of butter wrapped in grease-proof paper.

'These are already cut up into two-ounce pats, *bach*. Anything else? Your da keeping well?'

'He's fine, thanks. Very busy now the hedges are springing into life. Lots to do on the estate,' said Annie.

'More than you can say for Harry Lewis's mam,' whispered one of the women. 'Absolutely distraught, Florrie is. There'll be no money coming in there, what with her Dai passing on last year.'

Annie clenched her fists, determined not to rise to the bait. 'That'll be all. Thank you, Mrs Morgan.'

Once outside, Annie's eyes welled with tears. It wasn't her fault that Harry had lost his job. He'd been the one to vandalise the stables. Even if he hadn't been the instigator, he'd have gone along with Fred Rhys as he always did. She turned on her heel and hurried back home.

Once back in the kitchen, Annie relaxed and followed her mam's recipe. Soon the smell of Welsh cakes cooking on the ancient bakestone filled the air.

'Something smells good.' Her father's voice echoed in the scullery.

'Hello, Da. I got the afternoon off so I thought I'd surprise you.'

Her father walked in, his braces hanging down from the waist band of his breeches over his long-sleeved vest. He'd removed his dirty outer clothes and his muddy work boots would be stacked outside the back door.

'Just like old times, *bach*.'

Annie smiled, knowing her father was thinking of her mam, with her reputation of being the best baker of Welsh cakes in these parts. She always won first prize in the annual village show. Annie swallowed down the lump that had formed in her throat. It was left to her now to try to perfect the skill.

'It won't take long to clear up, Da. I've been boiling up some water for you and the kettle's almost done again. If you want to go and get the bath in, I'll disappear upstairs so you can have the kitchen to yourself.'

'Ah, you're a good 'un, *bach*. No more bother from them two ruffians today?'

'No. Sir Charles is already interviewing somebody to replace them,' Annie said.

For some reason, she didn't tell her father what she'd decided.

Chapter Eight

Annie never did give in her notice to Sir Charles and Edmund. One morning, a few days after the incident, she arrived at the stables and was met by a smart young man who looked to be in his twenties. Edmund came out of his office to join them.

'Mary-Ann, I'd like you to meet Frank Baker. He's joining us at Cefn Court to be groom for my father. There will be just two of you now, and I'm sure you'll get on.'

Frank Baker offered his hand to Annie and she took it. 'I'm very pleased to meet you, Mr Baker.'

'Frank, please. I've been hearing wonderful things about you and your skills as a groom. I'm looking forward to learning from you.'

Annie's mouth gaped open. She wasn't used to praise like that from a fellow employee. 'I'm sure you won't need any help from me. If you love horses, that's all there is to it. We can explain the routines, can't we, Mr Edmund?'

Edmund flashed her one of his smiles and her insides quivered. *Maybe now wasn't the time to leave her work here at Cefn Court.* She wondered what Frank Baker's previous experience was. As if reading her thoughts, Edmund said, 'My father has known Frank's family for years. Mr Baker Senior was head gamekeeper until he retired through ill health a few years ago. When this position became available, my father contacted him and Frank.'

'I've recently returned to Wales from working on an estate in Cornwall,' explained Frank. 'My father is not at all well now. As long as I'm doing my bit working on the land, I don't have to enlist and I'll be able to look after Dad at the same time.'

'I'm sorry to hear about your father. I'm sure we'll work well together,' Annie smiled at him before turning to Edmund. 'Is there any news on Ebony?' The stallion's stall was still empty, and there'd been no sightings in or around the village according to her father.

Edmund sighed. 'Nothing, I'm afraid. According to Constable Thompson, it's looking more and more like theft. Rhys and Lewis are adamant they had nothing to do with smashing up the stables or stealing my father's horse. The police seem to think the lads will be free to go soon. They have nothing on them. They admit the first incident and to the taunting and bad behaviour towards you, though.'

Annie's pulse raced. She'd been convinced it had been them and found herself guiltily imagining Florrie Lewis scrimping and scraping to feed her children because of her.

'They won't be coming back here, will they?' Panic sounded in her voice.

'No, it's just you and Frank now.'

Working at the stables with Frank Baker ended up being a far more relaxed affair than it had been before. Annie was still solely responsible for Kenna, but until Ebony was found, Frank's work was reduced to looking after the carriage horses. He was often taken away to do other work around the estate and Annie was left on her own. Every morning she prepared the mare for Edmund to ride, and although she scolded herself for feeling the way she did, she always looked forward to seeing him.

One afternoon, after enjoying Edmund's company earlier, Annie noticed a cream-coloured Bentley being driven slowly down the drive to the house. She walked to the furthest fence from the stables to watch. The chauffeur got out and opened the passenger door on the opposite side. A beautiful young woman with blonde curls and wearing a plum-coloured dress got out, followed by an elderly man with receding grey hair. The front door of Cefn Court opened, and Sir Charles, Lady Delia and Edmund emerged to welcome them. It was obvious that the Pryces and the older gentleman knew each other but introductions were made between the young woman and Edmund. Annie felt sick. It seemed a suitable match had been selected for the man she loved and had been invited to Cefn Court to let them get to know each other. *Not that they'll have much time for that before he leaves for his RAF training, will they?*

Annie turned, not able to watch any more. He hadn't mentioned a word of it that morning! How dare he be so lovely when all the time he had known about a visitor? But then it was nothing to do with her, his employee. She stormed back to the stable, saddled up Kenna and trotted into the paddock.

'Come on girl, let's have a good gallop.'

Her head down, she loosened the reins and they were soon riding away from the stables into the open field. Kenna galloped as fast as she'd ever done. The exhilaration of ride did the trick. When she dismounted back at the stables, all resentment to Edmund and the blonde woman had gone.

'Blimey, you were going some.' A smiling Frank Baker came out to greet her. He made a striking figure standing there. If he'd had the same effect on her as the son of the lord of the manor, it would be so simple. Even after only knowing him for a short while, she knew Frank was kind, good company – and he hadn't mentioned a wife. There was also the fact that he was an employee like her, just like others in the surrounding farms. But her insides didn't flip, her pulse didn't race for him.

'I just thought Kenna could do with a really good work

out,' she said, bending over to get her breath back. 'It was fun.'

'Here,' Frank said. 'Let me take her.'

He took Kenna from her, undoing the girth strap and removing the saddle. He placed a rug over the mare and led her to the stall. 'I've just had some good news, actually,' he called from inside. 'Did you see the visitors arrive in the Bentley?'

'Yes, why?'

Frank returned to the stable yard. 'Well, they own a large stable over near Cheltenham, and a couple of weeks ago they were offered a black stallion for sale. They said no, but the Pryces are now wondering if their horse is over in that area.'

Annie's eyes widened. 'Is it Ebony?' Annie grabbed Frank's arm. 'Please say it is.'

'All I know is what Mr Edmund told me. The police are involved and an investigation is underway. Let's hope the black beauty will be back here before we know it. He asked me to tell you. Oh, and did you see the daughter? Her name's Arabella, apparently. All the talk over at the manor is that the two families are trying to push her and Edmund together before he goes off to war.'

Annie felt sick.

Shortly afterwards, Frank returned to the manor house grounds. Before coming to see Annie with the news, he'd been helping with the early lambing in the top field and said he had plenty of work to do there. Annie spent the rest of the afternoon brushing Kenna until her coat gleamed. She then washed all the tack and the flag-stoned yard. Her next job was to check all the feeds and make sure the order and invoice book was up to date. She had her back to the office door when Edmund entered. She turned to face him.

'Mr Ed—'

Before she could finish her greeting, Edmund took her in his arms and kissed her on the lips.

She pushed against him. 'I don't understand. You apologised the first time you kissed me. You said it wasn't right.' It took all her reserve to push again. 'No! I'm your employee. You cannot play around with my feelings like this.'

Edmund drew his arms by his side. 'I know, Mary-Ann. I know I'm being unfair.' He hesitated. 'But I've fallen in love with you.'

Annie's heart raced. *How could this be happening?*

'Until this year, I thought of you as my friend. Reggie's little sister. But it's something far more than that. What I feel for you is love. Real love. I can't stop thinking about you, Mary-Ann. Yours is the first face I see when I wake in the morning and the last when I close my eyes to sleep.' He took Annie's hand, locked the office door and led her up the stairs to the loft space over the stable. 'We won't be disturbed up here. I want to talk to you and tell you how I feel.'

Annie didn't say a word, but she still couldn't believe that the thing she wanted most in the world was actually happening. Edmund Pryce loved her and she loved him.

Holding hands, they sat down under the eaves on a bed of hay that was covered in a woollen travel rug.

'Mary-Ann, we may be from different backgrounds but if we love each other, surely that's all that matters, isn't it? I think you love me too. I've seen the look in your eyes. Every time I've wanted to sweep you off your feet and tell you I feel the same, but I didn't think it was fair.'

Had it been that obvious? When Fred and Harry had been spreading rumours about her and Edmund, perhaps they had seen it too.

'Yes, I do love you, Edmund. Very much, but why today? Why did you choose today to tell me?'

Edmund was quiet for a moment. 'Today I had a visitor.

Lady Arabella Warrington-Smythe, accompanied by her father. Very beautiful, very accomplished … it was obvious that my family thought they'd found a match for me. Even marriage was mentioned.'

Annie shifted in her seat and looked away.

'No talk of love, no getting to know each other! They just expected us to become betrothed before I leave for my RAF training. I'm afraid I saw red. I apologised to Lady Arabella, of course. It wasn't her fault. I'm sure she'll find a suitable husband with no trouble. But it's not going to be me.' He stood up and began pacing the floor. 'She was awful, Mary-Ann. Nothing to say, just sat there looking bored out of her mind and answered only when prompted to by her father. I had to get out of the manor. I wanted to tell you how frightful it was, but then I realised that it wasn't the only reason I needed to see you. What if I go off to war … lose my life … and I'd never told you of my true feelings? There, I've said it.'

Annie reached for Edmund's hand and pulled him back onto the makeshift bed where they fell back in each other's arms kissing with passion. Through the tiny window in the gable end of the loft, she saw that the sky was overcast.

Edmund sat up and held Annie's hand. 'Let's keep this our very special secret. I don't think either your father or my parents will approve, so why spoil the time we have left? We'll deal with that when the war is over. You will wait for me, won't you?'

Annie grinned. 'Of, course I will. I shall worry about you every day you're away, and I'll write lots and lots of letters.'

When Annie cycled home that evening, she felt different. She was not imagining things. The man she loved with all her heart loved her too. And she'd keep that secret for as long as she needed to.

Chapter Nine

Annie and Edmund snatched every moment they could to be together. If Frank Baker suspected anything, he didn't let on. The stables were run efficiently, and Annie and Frank complemented each other in both temperament and the tasks they were given by Sir Charles and Edmund. Frank took great pride in making sure the carriage horses were ready at a moment's notice if Sir Charles needed to be taken anywhere. It didn't happen that often as Bert took him everywhere in the Daimler these days.

Any hope of getting Ebony back seemed to be fading fast, and his empty stall was a permanent reminder of the vandalism and theft. One morning, Edmund called Annie and Frank into the office.

'It's been a long time now since Ebony was stolen, and my father is missing having his daily ride. He has decided to purchase another horse. He's heard of a pedigree stallion up for sale at a stable in Gloucestershire, and he'd like both of you to accompany him to the sale and look the horse over with him.' Edmund stood at the office desk and shuffled a pile of papers. 'I shan't be coming as I have plenty to do before I leave and, of course, both of you as the grooms need to know the horse that is going to be joining Kenna and the carriage horses.' Edmund didn't make eye contact with Annie. She knew he would find the next six days as hard as she would. 'We'll never give up hope about Ebony but we have to face facts. He may be gone forever.'

The next morning, as the Daimler drove away from Cefn Court, Annie noticed Edmund at an upstairs window.

They'd spent the previous evening together in the stable loft, and Annie relived what it felt like to be in his arms. She felt her cheeks redden. He was the perfect gentleman, stopping them getting carried away completely even though their kissing had become more passionate and urgent.

'You're all I think about now I know that you feel the same way about me. But with me leaving soon, we can't let ourselves do something we'd regret, no matter how tempting it is.'

She'd agreed reluctantly, even though every inch of her body was tingling with desire. 'You're right. I want our first time to be the right time. Special, like our love.'

He'd kissed her again and gently caressed her neck. She wanted it to go on forever and make the days stop. *Only a few more days and he'd be gone.*

As Bert drove away, Annie discreetly rose her hand and waved. She then settled back into the seat and listened to the conversation between Sir Charles and Frank.

The gates into the farm where the stables were housed were tall and hung on solid metal posts, ribbed like stone columns. At the centre of the wrought iron spindles on each gate was a family crest. There was a dragon on each blue-and-yellow painted shield, under an image of a head in full armour and the name "Phillips".

'Very impressive,' said Sir Charles when the gates miraculously opened as they drove up to them.

At the end of the gravelled drive, a magnificent country residence with four towers and mullioned glass sash windows glowed in the spring sunshine. Annie thought of the two-up, two-down cottage where she and her da lived. It would fit comfortably under one of those windows.

'Major Phillips said to drive around to the left side and park in front of the stable blocks.'

'Right you are, sir,' said Bert.

There, a very tall middle-aged man emerged from the stable door to greet them.

'Good morning, Major,' said Sir Charles walking around the car to shake his hand.

'No trouble finding us, I hope?' He directed his question at Sir Charles.

'No, sir. Your directions were tip-top, weren't they, Pearson?'

Arthur Phillips ignored Annie and Frank. She took an instant disliking to the man.

'Now, let's get on with the purpose of our visit. I believe you have a pedigree stallion, sixteen two hands high, that may be what we're looking for.' Sir Charles walked into the stables behind the Major. Neither Annie or Frank were invited to follow the two men.

'He's a magnificent beast,' they heard Arthur Phillips say in a booming voice that carried across the empty barn. 'Even though I say it myself. He was bred here at these very stables. Here's his *mater*. He was sired by another pedigree horse on a neighbouring estate.'

Bert had gone back to the car.

'They're obviously not going to involve us,' said Frank. 'Let's have a look around.'

Annie agreed and the two of them wandered across the yard and entered a barn where the large double doors were wide open. Inside were more stalls, and all but one was empty. Annie gasped, grabbing Frank's arm.

'It's him. I'm sure of it.'

'Who?' Frank walked over to the stall, and the huge horse occupying it came up to him and nuzzled into his neck.

'*Ebony*! It's the master's horse. I'd know him anywhere.'

Frank looked sceptical. 'All black stallions look the same, surely.'

Annie stepped forward and reached up on tiptoe. She lifted the stallion's mane. About half-way down was the white scar. 'There,' she said. 'I remember Reggie got upset when Ebony got caught in some barbed wire in the fence when he was a pony. The vet was called and patched him up.'

'We'd better get back outside,' said Frank.

'But what are we going to do? We have to let Sir Charles know,' cried Annie.

Chapter Ten

Annie and Frank returned to the yard to find Sir Charles and the Major waiting by the car. Arthur Phillips glowered when they approached.

'I wondered where you'd both got to,' said Sir Charles. 'Pearson said you'd just disappeared.'

'We heard a horse's whinny in there.' Annie stared at Arthur Phillips for a reaction. 'You know us, Sir Charles. We love to see other people's horses.'

'Especially black stallions,' muttered Frank under his breath.

Arthur Phillips broke eye contact with Annie and appeared unsettled. 'Charles, I thought you wanted your grooms to see your new purchase.'

'Of course. I think you're going to love her.' He led Annie and Frank in the directions of the stables. Arthur Phillips hung back. Annie turned to see him talking to a young stable lad who'd appeared from nowhere. The boy suddenly dashed into the barn, leaving the Major to join them in the stables.

'What do you think?' asked Sir Charles, beaming. 'Meet Silver Shadow.'

In front of them was a magnificent grey mare, about fifteen hands high. Her coat gleamed in the sunshine and resembled polished silver. The horse's black mane and tail were glossy black. Annie hadn't seen Sir Charles so animated since Ebony had gone missing. Could she be wrong? What if it wasn't Ebony in the barn? Maybe the scar was a coincidence? That was her only proof. But if the horse had been stolen, perhaps Silver Shadow had too. *Oh, Edmund. I wish you were here to help me work out what to do.*

'She's beautiful, Sir Charles. Are you going to ride her? At the stables where I worked before, clients always did that. Or I could if you like?' cut in Frank.

Edmund had told Annie that his father valued Frank Baker's experience, and she hoped that he would agree to give them more time. Perhaps she could get Sir Charles on his own and broach the subject of Ebony?

'Frank has a good point. You don't mind, do you, Arthur?'

Arthur Phillips watched with his mouth pulled into a straight line and glared at Frank. The more she observed the Major, the more she was convinced he had something to hide. But if he did have Ebony, surely he knew that the man who had made enquiries about the mare he had for sale was the stolen horse's owner? Why hadn't he declined the visit?

'I suppose that's all right. But remember we already shook hands on the deal,' he said. 'I'll get someone to saddle her up for you.'

Sir Charles and Annie walked back into the sunshine and found a place by the dry stone wall edging the meadow to watch Frank canter away on Silver Shadow. Annie took a deep breath. 'Sir Charles. I have something I think you should know ... but I don't know how to tell you.'

'Goodness me, Mary-Ann. Whatever is it?'

'Frank and I wandered into the barn there,' she said, pointing. 'Well, there's a black stallion in there ... and I think it's Ebony.'

The older man's mouth gaped open and he steadied himself against the wall. 'Are you saying what I think you're saying? It can't be! I've known Arthur Phillips for years. Good farming stock and very well thought of in the military.'

Annie's pulse raced as she saw the Major walking towards them. 'I had to say something, sir.'

'Your groom's a good horseman, Charles. The mare has

taken to him. Here.' Arthur Phillips handed him a pair of binoculars.

Sir Charles brought them to his eyes and Annie noticed his hands were shaking. 'Arthur, you know why I'm here, don't you?'

'To buy the mare I have for sale?'

'And the only reason for that is that my horse has been stolen and the stables trashed. You haven't been offered anything in recent weeks, have you? The local police have notified other forces, so I'm surprised they haven't called on you, given your business,' said Sir Charles. He lifted the binoculars to his eyes again. 'She moves beautifully. Frank has already got her galloping at full speed, giving it its head. There's another rider out with him now. They seem to be having a race.'

Arthur Phillips went to take the binoculars off him.

'Hang on,' Sir Charles said. 'Is that the black horse you saw, Mary-Ann? I know you can't see from here, but I'd recognise that movement anywhere.'

Arthur Phillips went white. 'I don't know what you're suggesting, but as soon as your groom returns, I think you'd better go. How dare you? Black horses are two a penny. It's not much wonder yours was stolen. You obviously don't have the right security at your place.'

'Get in the car, Mary-Ann. As soon as Frank returns, we'll be off,' instructed Sir Charles.

Annie got into the back seat and Bert started the car. It spluttered until the engine purred. She watched as Frank rode closer to the yard and dismounted Silver Shadow. Clouds of the horse's breath resembled morning mist, and Frank bent over to get his own breath back.

'What a horse!' she heard him say.

Sir Charles took the reins and handed them to a fuming Arthur Phillips.

'We're going, Frank. I'll explain in the car.' Then he turned to shout at the Major, 'This isn't the last you've heard of this, Phillips. I'll be back to claim my stallion.' With that, he marched to the front of the car and slammed the door. 'Thank you, Pearson. I'd like you to drive me to the police station in Cheltenham.'

It was another fine morning when Annie arrived at the stables a few days later. The first thing she noticed was that Kenna was already out in the paddock, all saddled and bridled. Next to her, no worse for wear, was the magnificent Ebony. She broke into a wide smile as she parked her bicycle against the wall of the office.

'Here she is, Frank,' said Sir Charles. 'The heroine of the hour!'

Annie felt her cheeks burning. 'Anyone would have done the same. But I don't know what possessed me to lead Frank into that barn. We were trespassing, really.'

'Well, I'm very pleased you did, my dear. That scoundrel is now being charged with the theft of my black beauty. I can't believe you remembered about his accident with the barbed wire fence. That scar was the identifying mark that convinced them I was telling the truth. The gall of that man! It turns out that Rhys and Lewis had already broken into the stables that night and written what they did on the wall behind Kenna, leaving the doors unlocked when they left. Made it easy for his thieves when they arrived to steal the stallion. A convenience, really! They thought they'd got away with it when they heard two of our local lads had been charged. The police there had had a spate of horse thefts, and the man was stupid enough to sell his spoils from his own stables. I was completely taken in by him! Even that beautiful Silver Shadow had been stolen from some stables in Somerset.'

He left them then so they could get on with the jobs they had to do. Annie was suddenly struck again by how little time she had left with Edmund. He'd told her he wanted to spend as much time with Kenna as he could in those last few days. Annie knew what that really meant was spending precious time with her during her working day as well as every evening.

Edmund was true to his word. He arrived dead on two o'clock. Seeing him kitted out in his riding gear made Annie's heart flip as it always did.

'All alone?' he said, looking around him.

'We are,' Annie said, grinning. 'Frank's ridden Ebony over to the Manor for Sir Charles.'

Edmund took her hand and led her into the office where they wouldn't be seen. 'Well in that case ...' He pulled her into his arms and kissed her firmly on the lips. 'That's for what you did to get my father's horse back.' He kissed her again. 'And that's from me. A little clue as to what awaits you tonight.' His hands slid under her work shirt and caressed her skin, making her tingle with pleasure.

'I can't wait,' said Annie, beaming.

Suddenly there was commotion in the paddock, and they both rushed outside to see what had happened. They emerged to see Fred Rhys revving up his motorbike.

'What do you want, Rhys? You're scaring the horses.'

He revved again and Kenna reared up. Annie let herself into the paddock and managed to calm her down.

'Just come to collect what I'm owed. Your old man kicked me out without a penny, and now it seems the stallion was stolen and it was nothing to do with me or 'arry.'

Edmund's face looked as if it would explode, and Annie worried that he would retaliate against the boy's taunts.

'You will get nothing from us,' he said. 'You were sacked before the horse was even gone. Now get off my land or I'll call the police again.'

'Still got your serving wench, I see. Good between the sheets, is she?'

Before Edmund could get to him, Fred accelerated away, leaving Annie open-mouthed.

'Ignore him, Mary-Ann. My father has insisted you have the day off tomorrow to thank you for finding Ebony. I thought we could spend my last day together. Maybe take a picnic somewhere? I know just the place. Have I told you about the boathouse my grandfather had built? Hidden away, miles from anywhere.'

Annie's heart thumped in her chest. She would love nothing more than to spend time with him in the open air, but what if they were seen? Fred Rhys had just put paid to any idea they could spend time away from work in public.

'Edmund, it sounds wonderful ... but what if we're spotted? What would your parents say?'

He took her hand, and Annie glanced around to check there was no one to see. 'I don't know what the future holds, Mary-Ann. I don't know if there is a future once I get to France. My parents can't begrudge me time spent with a very dear friend. They needn't know that this certain dear friend is someone I love very much ... and I want to make her my wife if there is a future.' He kissed her on her cheek and fireworks sparked along her veins.

Chapter Eleven

Annie couldn't sleep. She listened for the chimes every hour, and when she removed the blackout card from the window, cool light filtered into her room. She stepped out onto the lino and drew back the curtains. It had rained heavily during the night, and the scene in front of her glowed in luminescent shades of green. The sun was creeping up from the horizon, painting brushstrokes of gold against the silver-grey sky.

What do I wear for the picnic? The only ones she'd been on had been with the Sunday School when she was a little girl. Today she was being picked up by Edmund in a horse and carriage. She decided on her best dress, smocked and tucked over the bodice in a bottle-green fine cord that suited her so well with her auburn curls. *The colour matches your eyes, bach*, her da had said. In case of a chill wind, she picked out a finely crocheted shawl to wear on top. Her best leather boots were polished until they gleamed. She brushed her hair until it shone and pinned it back over her ears with two tortoiseshell combs. Breakfast was a hurried affair, and her stomach felt queasy as she waited for Edmund to arrive. He'd told her just to bring herself and he'd see to the rest. 'A hamper of Cook's finest fare,' he'd said. 'I think madam will approve.'

Annie paced the passageway and watched the hands on the clock slowly creep to ten o'clock. She was glad her father wasn't there. He'd left at eight o'clock, and all she'd told him was that she was being treated to a day off by Mr Edmund and Sir Charles.

Dead on the hour, a horn sounded outside the cottage. Annie wrapped her shawl over her shoulders and took one last look at herself in the mirror. She gave her cheeks a gentle squeeze to bring some colour there and moistened her lips. Locking Beech Cottage behind her, she saw that Edmund was already at the passenger side to help her up into the seat.

He made a mock bow. 'Your carriage awaits, madam.' Taking her hand, he helped her up onto the side running board.

Annie beamed, and for the first time since he'd told her of his plans, she relaxed and allowed herself to become excited. Once seated, he spread a woollen travel rug over their knees.

'There, that will keep us warm. You look beautiful,' he said. 'I don't think I've seen you in anything but your riding wear and jodhpurs recently. A dress suits you.'

Annie smiled. 'Thank you, kind sir.'

He reached across and patted her hand, before taking up the reins and clicking for the horses to start on their way. They were soon leaving the village of Brynderi behind. As they rose up into the hills, it got cooler and Annie pulled her shawl more tightly around her. The view was magnificent and below them she could see the village and Cefn Court. Her da would be out in the fields doing his backbreaking job, and here she was being taken on a luxury picnic by the lord of the manor's son.

'Penny for them?' Edmund's voice broke her reverie.

'Oh, I was just thinking how different our lives are. But it doesn't matter … You haven't told me where you're taking me.'

The horse gathered speed now that they had reached the top of the hill, and Annie noticed a large oval lake in front of them.

'See that waterfall to the left,' said Edmund. 'Just to the side of that, the family has a boathouse. I thought we could have our picnic there. Afterwards, we'll visit the waterfall and walk off Cook's famous pork and ale pie.'

Annie couldn't stop beaming. 'It all sounds absolutely wonderful.' She leaned across and kissed him on the cheek.

'Giddy, up, gal!' He called to the mare trotting in front of the carriage.'

Annie squealed in delight. *This already has to be the best day ever*, she thought.

She searched the view in front of her as they descended the lanes down to the lake. As they neared the boathouse, Annie saw how pretty the building was, nestled in thick foliage of late spring colour. It was a wooden structure, painted in a pale blue with white window frames; a bit like the continental houses she'd seen in books. A wooden balustrade surrounded a veranda and steps led down to the water's edge.

'It's beautiful,' Annie whispered as the carriage came to a halt.

Edmund guided the horses to a space at the side of the boathouse. 'It is rather, isn't it? And the best bit for our family is that it's hidden away here and every one of us can escape if we need to. My grandfather travelled extensively before the war, and he had this built to resemble some of the summer houses he'd seen. It was left to my mother with the surrounding land when he passed away. I can vaguely remember coming here to stay as a little boy too … when my baby sister died.' He abruptly stopped talking and looked thoughtful.

Annie gasped and touched his hand. 'I thought you were an only child. I'm sorry.'

'It's a long time ago, now. I was about three. Marjorie was seven months old. She died of scarlet fever, and my mother has never got over it.' His voice cracked as he spoke. He helped Annie from the carriage and opened the door to the boathouse. 'Mother has always given me everything I could have wished for apart from one thing. Unconditional love. Oh, she'd deny it, but I'm not the daughter she craves and never can be. When Marjorie died that day, I think part of her did too. My sister's name is never mentioned in Cefn Court, but I often walked in on my mother crying when I was younger. She still visits the grave every day.'

Annie swallowed and thought about visiting the churchyard to leave flowers at the simple wooden cross which marked her mam's grave where she was buried with her still-born son. She took Edmund's hand and pulled him towards her. She realised there were tears in his eyes.

'I'm sure your mam doesn't love you any less, Edmund. No mother should have to lose a child.'

Edmund inhaled deeply. 'I'm sure you're right. I can't imagine what she went through. But … come on, don't let's get maudlin. Let's unpack Cook's picnic. I'll get the hamper.' He sprang into action.

Annie opened the double doors and bright sunshine bathed the room in pale gold. A fold-up wooden table and two chairs rested on the wall by the doors. Annie assembled them and placed them on the veranda. Edmund returned carrying a wicker lidded basket with leather buckles.

'By the weight of this, I think Cook must have thought she was feeding an army.' Edmund laughed and the sparkle was back in his pale grey eyes. He placed the basket down and handed Annie an embroidered white tablecloth and matching napkins for the table on the veranda. Then he joined her, carrying cutlery, plates and two crystal wineglasses, helping to lay the table in readiness for their special picnic. This was all new for Annie. Her stomach fluttered with excitement. Edmund went back into the kitchen and returned with a bottle of white wine.

'We don't need to eat yet,' he said, pouring the wine and handing her a glass. 'If that's all right with you. Let's sit and admire the view over the lake. We can talk here without any interruptions.'

They clinked glasses and Annie took a sip. It was the first time she'd tasted wine. Her mam's sweet sherry was the only alcohol she'd been allowed to sample at home, just to taste it, and that was only at Christmas.

'I hope it's not too dry for you, my love. I tried to pick more of a fruity one.'

Annie sipped from her glass again. She had nothing to compare it with, so it could be "dry" for all she knew. A light breeze from the water cooled her cheeks. 'Are you looking forward to the training, Edmund?' Annie realised that this might be the last time she'd see him for a very long time. She hadn't had time to regret Reggie going. He just announced it one evening, and within days he was gone. She'd known about Edmund leaving for weeks, and her heart ached with each passing day. She stifled a sob, dreading the moment.

'Don't get upset, my love. I want to do my bit for the country, so it's a mixture of excitement at the prospect of doing that … and regret.' There was a pause. He looked across at Annie. 'Regret that we didn't admit our love for one another until now. I feel we've wasted all this time when we could have spent time together as a couple rather than just as friends.'

Annie's eyes welled with tears. His thoughts were matched by hers exactly. They had fought so hard to keep things as employee and employer, as friends, but to know he loved her as much as she loved him filled her with intense joy. Yet there was also a profound sadness that maybe Edmund didn't share. As well as the understandable anxiety that he could be killed at any time once he left to fly planes over France, there was the additional sense that their love was doomed. *You only read about peasant girls marrying members of the landed gentry in books, my girl.* And that's what she was. A mere peasant girl from a poor family.

Edmund squeezed her hand. 'Whatever happens, Mary-Ann. You will be my love until the end. Will you write to me? I shall write with my address as soon as I can. From what I can gather, things are pretty tough there for the pilots. I don't have to tell you that, my love. It may be a time before you hear from me.'

'It's the same in the army. That's why my father was so upset about Reggie going. Even after what's happened to his brothers, he still signed up. He had no need to go.'

They both sat for a minute in silence.

'Come on, let's eat our picnic.'

Chapter Twelve

After finishing the food, Edmund took Annie's hand and led her inside the boathouse. They sat together on the tweed sofa opposite the open doors. Edmund pulled Annie into his arms and they began kissing. Familiar sensations returned to Annie's insides. As the passion in the kisses increased, so did Annie's desire. She knew it was wrong but she wanted to experience complete lovemaking with the man she adored before he left for war. She realised it might be their only chance. Edmund's lips were soft and moist, and he gently probed her mouth with his tongue. Heart racing, she returned his kiss, her insides melting.

'I love you so much, Edmund. I didn't think love would feel like this. How am I going to cope without you?' Annie knew this was how thousands of girls felt when their lovers left for war. She resolved to be brave and not to spoil the moment.

Edmund pulled her to him and kissed the top of her head. He stroked her hair, soothing her. She tilted her head up to him, seeking out his lips and they kissed again. She felt his warm breath move down to her neck, and he nibbled on her earlobe.

'You will, my love. You must remember that once this awful war is over, I will come back and make you my wife.' He hesitated before continuing. 'If the worst happens, I want you to promise me you'll find someone else to bring you the happiness you deserve. You must get married and have beautiful children – you'll be a wonderful mother. And just sometimes, in your quieter moments, you will think of your first love.'

Tears streamed down Annie's face, and she clung to

Edmund as if he was about to leave there and then. He pulled away and took a small plum-coloured velvet box from his breeches pocket.

'Here,' he said. 'I want you to have this.'

Annie's hand shook as she opened the box, flipping the clasp. Inside was an exquisite oval locket, fashioned in rose-gold and intricately engraved with leaf patterns. She gasped. 'It's beautiful,' she said, suspending it from her fingers. 'I can't accept this, Edmund. It looks far too expensive.'

'Nonsense. It has always been handed down through the family to the eldest girl on their twenty-first birthday. When I became twenty-one, my mother gave it to me. After what happened with my sister ... well, she and my father wanted me to have it in readiness for when I find myself a wife. I've found her, Mary-Ann.'

'I don't know what to say,' she said.

'Say nothing, my love. Please wear it every day as a good luck talisman for my safe return. May I?' He reached behind her and placed the locket around her neck. Once he'd fastened the clasp, he kissed the nape of her neck before turning her to face him. 'There. A Pryce family heirloom where it belongs. I *will* marry you, Mary-Ann. Please wait for me.'

Annie's hand strayed to touch the locket, and she knew this would have to stay their secret. Reaching up her arms, she pulled him towards her and kissed him, tears still pricking at her eyes. Their kisses became more passionate, more urgent. Edmund undid some buttons on her dress and slid in his hand to touch her breast. She gasped.

'Is this what you want, Mary-Ann? I can stop if I'm being too forward.'

She wanted it more than anything in the world, but she became shy and felt her cheeks flush. She simply nodded and Edmund continued to undo the row of covered buttons that ran down the front of her dress, revealing an ivory cotton camisole. The locket that meant so much to both of them rested between her small breasts. Edmund ran his hands over her and she gasped with pleasure, bashful at the intensity of her feelings. He smiled at her reaction.

'Let's go somewhere a little more comfortable,' he said. He led the way to a tiny bedroom up in the eaves where a soft feather bed, covered in an embroidered counterpane, almost filled the room.

Edmund pulled Annie down on to the bed. They undressed each other slowly until they lay naked in each other's arms. Their kissing and caressing becoming more and more intense. Annie had never experienced such pleasure as they made love. She realised that whatever the future held, she would never regret that moment. They lay there for a while, alone with their thoughts. Edmund was the first to break the silence.

'I shall remember this moment forever,' Edmund said. 'Wherever I end up, seeing your face and its look of pleasure will be what will keep me going through the bad times. And there will be bad times. I have no doubts about what's ahead.'

'I shall pray for you, Edmund. Come back to me safe and sound,' Annie said, but she knew, deep down, that was out of her hands. Too many young couples had had their dreams dashed in the cruellest of ways. A feeling of apprehension washed over her, and she sat up and began to dress.

'Yes,' he said. 'We must get back. We don't want people asking why two friends have taken so long over their picnic. Perhaps a stroll over to the waterfall as I promised, just so that you can say you've been there?'

They cleared the boathouse and packed the hamper to put back in the carriage. After locking up, Edmund showed her where the family rowing boat was housed to the side of the house, and then they walked in the direction of the waterfall. The sky was pale lemon at the horizon. The footpath was slatted with bars of sunlight, and the young foliage dappled the rest in circles of shadow. Primroses and white woodland anemones were dotted under hedges and in the grass verges. It was silent apart from birdsong. Holding hands, there was an unspoken closeness between them now. Their special moment was their secret. The precious locket a symbol of what their relationship had become. Annie wanted to shout it from the top of the hills around her, but she knew she would not tell a soul.

'There we are,' said Edmund. 'The famous Rhaeadr Pen-y-rhos falls. In the summer months, after a long spell of dry weather, you can walk behind the waterfall and feel the spray on your cheeks. It's too dangerous to get that close this early in the year. See how muddy it is down there,' he said, pointing.

Annie squeezed his hand. 'Thank you for bringing me here, Edmund. And for telling me how much the boathouse means to your family. I'm ... I'm glad we got to make our love special here.'

They kissed again before returning to the boathouse. As they were leaving the lake, the sound of a motorbike came from the woodland. Fred Rhys, with Harry riding as pillion, blasted on his horn and rose his hand. The look of glee on his face suggested to Annie that what he had seen would be the topic of gossip in the village in the morning.

'Oh no,' she muttered. 'That Fred Rhys gets everywhere!'

'We haven't done anything wrong. Everyone knew I

was taking you for a picnic as a thank you for helping get Ebony back for my father. All we were doing was coming back from a walk. Now what can be wrong with that?' Edmund smiled that charming smile of his that made her heart sing.

Chapter Thirteen

Annie never saw Edmund again after he dropped her home. That night, she relived every minute of the day and held her locket as she dropped off to sleep. In the early hours of the morning she awoke, bathed in perspiration with her heart racing. She had welcomed Edmund's lovemaking with all her heart, reasoning that it might be the only time that she'd experience such joy. But what if …? Panic took over as questions began flooding into her mind. Girls in school had always said you couldn't get a baby if you only did it once. Was that definitely true? But then others always said that if the man really loved you, he wouldn't let you. He'd take care of things and use protection … whatever that was. And Edmund *did* love her. She was sure of that. *Oh, Mam, I wish you'd stayed long enough to tell me things about love and babies. I can't ask Dada, can I?* She remembered how frightened she'd been when she'd started her monthlies. All that blood. She'd thought there was something seriously wrong with her. It wasn't until Gwennie in school told her about a conversation she'd had with her mam that she realised it was perfectly normal.

No, she'd be all right. She took down the blackout card and stood by the window. The night sky was velvety black and dotted with stars shining like diamonds in the moonlight. She touched the locket and felt the pattern that had been carved on its surface. The rim that went around the outside suggested it could be opened like her mam's could. It would be in two halves clipped together. She slid a nail into the groove and the locket clicked open. In the bright moonlight, she could see a portrait of Edmund; his fair hair falling to one side and his characteristic grin beaming up at her. Her throat tightened. How she was going to miss that handsome face over the next months ... or even years. Who really knew? On the other side was a piece of paper, folded to fit under the rim. She opened it and read the message. *To my dearest Mary-Ann, All my love until the end of time, Your own, Edmund x.* She held the message to her chest and looked up at the sky.

'Wherever you'll be, *cariad*, we shall be looking at the same sky, the same stars.'

Folding the paper and placing it back in the locket, she climbed back into bed, vowing that she would never take the locket off and also not let anyone see it. It was their secret. Hers and Edmund's.

As she rode her bike to the stables the next morning, she knew that Edmund would be long gone. He'd mentioned that Pearson would be taking him at seven o'clock, so they'd be well on their way to the RAF base now. There would be plenty to do and by keeping busy with Kenna, Annie would stop herself from fretting over Edmund.

'Did you enjoy your day off, Annie?' Frank Baker was mucking out the stable.

Annie's heart raced. 'Yes, thank you, Frank. It was a real treat and very kind of Sir Charles.' She tried to keep her voice steady and hoped that her flushed skin wouldn't give any clues as to how much of a treat it really was. 'Mr Edmund showed me the family's boathouse up at the lake, and then after a picnic, we walked to the Pen-y-rhos waterfalls. What are they doing for you to say thank you?' Frank had been promised a special reward for his part in bringing Arthur Phillips to justice as well.

'I know you won't approve, but Sir Charles is taking me on the next hunt, and I've got the privilege of riding Ebony. Drinks and lunch at the manor afterwards too.'

'I thought all hunts had stopped during the war,' said Annie.

'They have. This isn't an official one. Just between a few of his hunting friends.'

'You'll love that, won't you?' Annie smiled. She'd really enjoyed working with Frank, especially after the horrible start she'd had with Fred and Harry. A ripple of anxiety unnerved her. She'd forgotten the smug look on Fred Rhys's face up at the boathouse. She was being silly. What trouble could he cause for her? As Edmund had said, they weren't doing anything wrong.

'Fancy a canter over the meadows?' asked Frank. 'Ebony and Kenna could do with some exercise.'

They saddled up the horses and led them outside. Soon the wind was blowing Annie's long hair out behind her as she urged Kenna to gallop faster. The mare wasn't as long in the leg as Ebony, but thanks to the condition Annie kept her in, she always gave the black stallion a good run for his money. She was closing the gap, and soon Annie brought Kenna alongside Frank and the bigger horse.

'Ebony, my black beauty, we can't have this.' She heard Frank's booming voice as he prodded the horse's belly and increased the pace further. Both horses rounded the top field and then carried on the homeward sprint back to the paddocks, Ebony was the clear winner.

Annie and Frank dismounted and both bent over, completely out of breath.

'A good run, Miss Beynon.' Frank straightened up and offered his hand.

Annie grinned. 'I'll get you next time.'

Neither of them had noticed Fred Rhys standing astride his motorbike, his hands on the handlebars as he revved the engine. His partner in crime was sitting pillion again. 'Didn't take long to get over steady Eddie then, Annie

Beynon? All over him up in the woods yesterday, but less than twenty-four hours later, it's Baker boy here's turn. Think what we wrote on the wall was just about right, eh, Harry?'

Before either Annie or Frank could say anything, the bike was gone, shrinking to a dot along the lane. 'How dare they?' The threatened tears spilled down her cheeks. Frank put his arm around her shoulders.

'Don't take any notice. They're not worth it.'

But Annie knew that what she'd dreaded was about to come true. Fred Rhys was going to spread rumours about her and Edmund, and cause trouble for both the Beynons and the Pryce family.

Annie dried her tears on the sleeve of her jacket and took a deep breath. There was nothing she could do about it now. Life would go on, and soon they'd have somebody else to gossip about ... she hoped.

Later that day, Sir Charles paid them a visit. 'Good afternoon, both. I'm sure you'll be pleased to know that Edmund got off safely this morning. I understand you enjoyed the picnic yesterday, Mary-Ann. Just my way of saying thank you for what you and Frank did. I hear he took you to the lake and showed you the boathouse.' He hesitated. 'So many happy memories for our family there.'

Annie hoped he couldn't hear the drum of her heartbeat.

'Thank you, sir. It was wonderful. Something I'll never forget.'

Sir Charles walked over to Ebony, who was safely back in his stall after the long ride. 'Hello, boy,' he said, stroking the horse's head before turning back around. 'Frank, I came to see if you'd get the horse box ready for a visit to a farm in Credenford tomorrow morning? I'm collecting a new addition to the stables. After that awful business with Phillips, I'm a bit wary now. However, I've already been to see the horse; a beautiful dappled grey. A mare. She looks a bit like Silver Shadow, but this time I've seen the paperwork and everything is above board. She's called Arianwen.'

'What a pretty Welsh name!' cried Annie.

'It means "white silver". And she is too. Pale silver grey with slightly darker dapples. I've wanted another horse for a while. And even though Lady Delia doesn't want to ride any more, I've bought Arianwen for her in the hope of getting her out and about … stop her fretting over Edmund all the time. In fact, my wife was a very accomplished horse-woman before she had a serious fall.'

After what Edmund had told her at the boathouse, Annie now understood that Edmund would be very precious to his mother, even if he didn't think so. She couldn't imagine how it must feel to lose a child. *Not the right order of things*, her mam was fond of saying. It was happening all the time in this awful war. At least her mam had not been there to know that Alf and Jimmy had been lost in action in France. The image of her father's face when he'd read the telegrams would haunt her forever. She swallowed down the lump that had formed in her throat.

'Mary-Ann, I was saying to Frank. To start with, before I can find a suitable groom, you will share the responsibility of looking after Arianwen. I thought perhaps that stall in the corner would suit her. There's plenty of light and she's far enough away from the others to settle in.'

'That's fine, sir. I shall look forward to having extra responsibility.' Annie smiled.

'Yes, and I'm hoping I can persuade Lady Delia to at least come and meet her new mare. If anyone can coax her back to riding, it will be you, my dear. She always thought so much of your mother. The whole Beynon family, in fact.'

Annie blushed, remembering how many times her mam had complained about the extra jobs she's been given by her ladyship. 'I'll see you in the morning at eight o'clock sharp, Frank. As Pearson's had such a long journey today, you can drive the horsebox for me tomorrow. It will be good practice for when you take over from him in future. I do forget how old he's getting ...'

With that, Sir Charles left. *Frank's face is a picture*, thought Annie.

'Who's the blue-eyed boy then, Mr Baker?' Annie loved the banter between them. She and Frank gave as good as they got from each other, and he never made her feel inferior because she was a girl doing a lad's job. He laughed and threw a handful of dry straw at her.

Chapter Fourteen

Annie found her father already home from work when she arrived at the cottage. He was sitting in his armchair by the range, still in his work clothes with his eyes closed. He didn't stir. She was shocked by how old he suddenly looked, and she stood for a moment, watching the rise and fall of his chest. Her throat tightened. How hadn't she seen what working on the land in all weathers was doing to him?

His eyelids flickered, and for a moment he seemed disorientated before opening his eyes fully and noticing her.

'Oh, hello, *bach*. I must have dozed off.' He went to stand. Annie took his arm and helped him sit back down on the chair.

'No, Dada. You stay there. You look worn out. I'll make you a mug of tea.'

For once, he didn't argue and let Annie wait on him. 'You're a good girl. Just like your mam.'

She brought her father a mug of strong, sweet tea and began to prepare their evening meal.

'I hear that Fred Rhys's been causing trouble again.' Annie stopped peeling the potato, heart thumping. It was only a matter of time before her father heard the rumours.

'Oh. What's he done now?' she asked, trying to stop her voice from shaking.

'Tom the Bryn said he'd been cutting up all them fields behind the manor 'ouse. That simple 'arry lad sitting behind him like Lord Muck. Using them meadows like a dirt track. Should have signed up like our Reggie. Th' army'd sort 'em out. Ruddy menaces, the two of 'em.'

After the meal, they sat together and listened to the wireless. Getting updates on the war was a daily occurrence in the Beynon family now Reggie had enlisted, but Annie soon got up and turned it off. 'That's enough about that. Let's have some good news for a change. What if I put some Glenn Miller on for you? You and Mam loved the dances in the Rock Park Pavilion, didn't you?'

He smiled. 'Never missed a Saturday night. Your mam was so light on her feet. She even taught me how to dance. Oh, I forgot, *bach*. There's an envelope arrived this morning. My specs were upstairs and I didn't have the strength to get 'em. I put it behind the clock on the dresser. Be a good girl and read it, will you?'

Annie jumped up, her heart racing. 'Why didn't you say, Dada? It may be from Reggie.'

At least, it wasn't another telegram. Young as she was, she still remembered the anguish in her father's face and her own howl when they received the telegram informing them that Alf had lost his life. *Alfred Edward Beynon 1923–1940. Killed in action*. The second one just a few months later informed them that Jimmy was missing, presumed dead, too.

Annie had written to Reggie as her father suggested and had kept the tone of her letter light, telling him all about Kenna. She'd asked him about the training and whether he'd made any friends.

Her hand shook as she slid her nail under the gummed seal. Neat copperplate handwriting jumped up at her. Her brother's handwriting was meticulous.

Dear Dada and our Annie,

Thanks for your letter.
 Well. I'm on my way to another barracks. I won't be sorry I can tell you. The training base was awful. Freezing cold out in the middle of the Lincolnshire

back o' beyond. I thought Radnorshire was bad but this is flat. The greyness goes on for miles. Biting east winds, huts with cracked and missing windows and rats. Lots of rats. Had to make sure we tied legs of our breeches tight with string.

I can hear you now, Dada. "Serve the blighter right. He wanted to go."

In spite of all that, I'm proud to have signed up. I'm going to do my bit. The other boys all feel the same. We're ready to stop the Jerries. I'm officially Gunner Reginald Beynon 864499. They've trained us hard, how to use guns of all sorts. We started with rifle shooting and moved on to shell guns. Another six weeks more training at this new place before they post us abroad. It'll be the Middle East most probably.

Once I get my new address, please, please write and tell me what's going on at Cefn Court. Has Eddie boy left for his training yet?

Your ever loving son and brother, Reggie.

Ted Beynon took in a deep breath and stood up from his chair. Annie watched as he went to the sink and looked out of the window.

'He'll be all right, Da,' she said, not believing her own words. It was the luck of the draw, she knew that. Another person's face came into her head. Edmund Pryce was now training to fly fighter planes and, for a few weeks at least, he was safe.

She folded the letter and placed it back on the dresser.

'I need to get our ration of stewing beef from Sid the Meat, Da. If he's got a couple of kidneys, how do you fancy that tomorrow? Your favourite.' Her dad's eyes lit up, and for the moment all maudlin thoughts had receded.

*

The air was fresh and clear as she walked down the lane into the village. The verges were quite low at this time of year, but soon they would be full of a myriad of colours from a variety of wild flowers, attracting bees and butterflies. Each day there were more leaves on the trees, bursting with luminous greens and glowing in the late spring sunshine. New growth, new life and new birth. Lambs gambolled around the ewes in fields belonging to the Pryce family. How she loved this time of year.

As she neared the main street, she saw a few villagers; young mothers pushing prams, old gentlemen hunched over walking sticks and women hurrying with wicker baskets on their arms, probably collecting the weekly rations like her.

Annie turned the corner and spotted Fred Rhys's motorbike parked outside the village shop. She felt a sinking feeling in the pit of her stomach. *I wonder what lies he's spreading now*, she wondered. She went to the butcher's first and hoped he'd be gone by the time she came out.

'Hello, *bach*,' said Sid Jones. 'How's your da?'

'He's fine, thank you. Working hard as always.'

The butcher smiled. 'He's lucky to have you, *bach*. Must be hard with all the lads of his gone.'

The butcher was talking as if Reggie was dead too! 'Reggie's fine, Mr Jones. In fact, a letter arrived from him this morning.' She didn't tell him that both she and her father were worried sick for his safety. 'Could I have a pound of stewing beef, please?'

The butcher weighed out the meat on the ancient metal scales and wrapped it in greaseproof paper. Annie slid the buff-coloured ration book across the counter for him to stamp.

'Also, have you got any lambs' kidneys? Thought I'd make Da's favourite.'

'I'm sorry, *bach*. Ma Bowen had the last not two hours ago. If you like, I'll put a few away for you next week. That do you?'

Annie thanked him and paid for the beef. But Sid had one more thing to say before she left.

'I hear you're getting on with that Baker lad now the master's gone off to war.' The middle-aged man winked and Annie blushed, furious at herself. There was nothing to feel embarrassed about ... but she could kill Fred Rhys. It had to be him spreading the rumours.

Chapter Fifteen

Life settled into a normal routine for Annie. Every time she visited the village, she braced herself for more gossip, but nothing more was said – at least not in her hearing. Arianwen had arrived at the stables, and both she and Frank loved sharing her grooming duties.

'A big day for us today, Annie. Lady Delia's agreed to come and see her at last,' said Frank. 'Around two o'clock, Sir Charles said.'

'I wonder if she'll ever ride her. It seems a shame if she doesn't. Apparently, she was a marvellous horsewoman in her younger days,' commented Annie.

Deep down, Annie found it difficult to think of Edmund's mother as a young woman, let alone mounting a horse to ride. For as long as she could remember, she had dressed in sombre colours with her fair hair dragged back into a severe chignon. Her mouth tended to be in a permanent straight line. Annie had always felt intimidated by her.

By the time Edmund's parents arrived at the stables, Arianwen was ready. Her dappled coat looked like polished silver. Her new saddle, reins and bridle gleamed.

Annie brought her out from her stall and led her into the stable yard where everyone was waiting. Lady Delia's face instantly changed. The pinched expression softened, and for the first time Annie saw a glimpse of the young woman she once was. She tentatively put her hand out to the horse and Arianwen nuzzled into her. Lady Delia smiled and turned to her husband.

'Charles, she's beautiful. Doesn't she remind you of a young Smoky? A lighter silver, of course. I can see why they named her Arianwen.'

Her husband beamed. 'I knew you'd love her, my dear.' He turned to Annie and Frank. 'Smoky was an old pony we bought for Edmund when he was learning to ride.'

At the mention of Edmund, Annie stopped short. There'd still been no word from him, and although she couldn't stop thinking about his handsome face, she worried that she'd have to get used to the idea of life without him.

'I shall have to write to him and tell him all about her,' Lady Delia said.

Annie felt her blood pound in her veins. 'You've heard from him already?' she blurted out.

'Of course. He's coming to the end of his training and is being shipped off to another airfield on the south coast next Monday.' Sir Charles cast a look of concern over at his wife.

Annie felt light-headed but determined to keep her feelings to herself. 'I thought I may have heard from him … to check on Kenna,' she added quickly.

'Oh no, dear. No need. I told him you were looking after her and all was well. Lady Arabella was asking about him too.' Lady Delia exchanged a glance with her husband.

Annie's neck flushed, knowing the comment was for her benefit. Perhaps Edmund's mother suspected that there was more to their relationship than friendship. She moved back into the stables and saw to Kenna. Frank was there if the Pryces needed anything.

A few minutes later, Sir Charles appeared at her side. 'Thank you, Mary-Ann. Lady Delia says she's not quite ready for riding yet, but she will call up to see Arianwen regularly.' He placed a hand on her arm. 'Try not to worry about Edmund, my dear. I know how much you and your brother think of him. We don't know what the future holds, but he will have been extremely well trained to keep himself and his men as safe as possible. He'll be one of Britain's finest squadron leaders, I'm sure. We must all pray for their safe return.'

Once he'd gone, her hand strayed to feel the outline of the secret locket inside her jumper. It seemed the slightest thing made her tearful lately. *Pull yourself together, bach*, her father would say. She took in a deep breath, determined to do just that.

She saddled up Kenna and led her outside into the yard to join Frank and Arianwen.

'I think you could say this beautiful girl was a big success with her ladyship. She's just got to get her confidence back and she'll be riding in no time.' He patted Arianwen's hind quarters gently, and she whinnied as if in agreement. 'Are you all right, Annie? You look a bit peaky. Have done for a few days, if I'm honest.'

'I'm fine. Nothing that a brisk canter on this one won't cure,' she said, stroking Kenna. 'Fancy a ride?'

She led the horse through the gate into the paddock, with Frank following on Lady Delia's grey mare. To start, they gently trotted side by side.

'There's a social in Pen-y-rhos tonight. Do you fancy coming along?' Frank asked. 'Should be a bit of fun. It'll be a full moon, so we won't need any lights on the bikes.'

Annie hesitated. It would be good to meet up with girls from school. She'd been neglecting them lately. Perhaps Gwennie would be there.

'I'm not sure. Da may be going to the whist drive up at the Reading Room and I said I'd go as his partner. I'll let you know, but thanks.'

That way, there'd be no one to spread rumours about her and Frank.

'I'll see you there if you change your mind. There'll be plenty of us to get you home safely, tell your da. Race you

82

to the far end of the field. Come on, Arianwen.' And he was off.

Ted Beynon didn't feel like going to the whist drive that night. He was tired after a long day repairing the hedges around the bottom field.

'All I want to do tonight, *bach*, is sit here in the warm and listen to the wireless. *It's That Man Again* is on, and it'll do me good to have a bit o' a chuckle. Mind, I don't know what Tommy Handley's saying half the time, his accent's so broad.'

Annie laughed. 'If you're sure, Da. Frank says there's a social over in Pen-y-rhos tonight. It'd be good to catch up with some of them. Like Gwennie Probert. Haven't seen much of her since I started at the stables. There'll be plenty of people coming back to the village at the end. Oh, by the way, there hasn't been any post for me, has there?' she asked hopefully.

Her father's expression changed. He fidgeted in his chair. 'No. Why? You expecting a letter then?' *Was it her imagination that his face had reddened?*

'I thought Mr Edmund would have written to see how Kenna was getting on, that's all. They've heard from him down at the Court.'

Her father avoided eye contact, adding to her sense of uneasiness.

'You don't want to be worrying about him now, *bach*. You and that Frank are managing just fine.'

He leaned back in his chair and closed his eyes. The conversation was over. A worrying thought crossed her mind. *He wouldn't ... would he?*

She pushed the thought away and kissed his cheek, before going upstairs to change.

*

The hall was full when she got there, and Annie scanned the room for anyone she knew.

A voice shrieked from the corner, 'Annie Beynon, I don't believe it.' Gwennie Probert rushed across to her. 'We all thought you'd emigrated or got buried in horse muck in them stables you work at.'

Annie laughed. Gwennie and the others had all gone into service straight from school a few years ago, but Gwennie hadn't settled and had returned home within weeks. She'd been helping out at the farms with seasonal work since then.

'Can't understand what you see in those dumb animals. I s'pose they don't answer you back. Mind you, the girls think it could be to do with the handsome lord and master.' She playfully pushed Annie's shoulder and gave an exaggerated wink.

Annoyed at herself, Annie felt herself reddening. 'Those beautiful creatures I look after are not dumb, Gwennie Probert. You should see the latest arrival. A gift for her ladyship.'

She didn't comment on the "lord and master" bit. She became aware of the heavy gold locket nestling between her breasts and wondered what Edmund was doing.

'Here,' said Gwennie, thrusting a full glass of an amber liquid into Annie's hand. 'Have this. It's shandy.'

Before Annie could protest that she didn't know if she liked shandy, they were joined by Frank Baker. 'You came then.'

Annie had only seen him in his work jodhpurs, but standing there in a shirt and tie, it dawned on her how attractive he was. He wasn't as traditionally handsome as Edmund, but more rugged and masculine. His dark hair was Brylcreemed to tame the natural waves, and his complexion was swarthy and tanned from working outside.

'Da wanted to stay in. Said I should catch up with all this lot.' Annie pointed at Gwennie and her friends who had gathered around them.

'Come on, then. First dance is on me.'

Annie handed her drink to Gwennie and allowed herself to be dragged through the crowd on to the dance floor by Frank. The band, consisting of local lads she knew vaguely from school, played music that was just the right tempo for the *twmpath*. A caller she recognised as the Welsh teacher shouted instructions as the dancers moved around to different partners. She watched Frank's animated expressions as he interpreted the moves and finally ended back with her again. The sensation of his arm around her waist felt strange. Work colleague and work colleague. That was it. But there was something else. She was enjoying herself but felt she was somehow being disloyal to Edmund. *Edmund, who hasn't bothered to write to you after all he promised.*

'Let's get back ...' Suddenly she was feeling very light-headed, and Frank caught her before she fainted to the floor.

'Wha... what happened?' she said, her voice weak. 'I was fine ... then it went black.' She felt clammy and shivered as an unwanted thought entered her head. She dismissed it immediately.

'Somebody get Annie a chair, please,' called Frank, who had obviously carried her through the crowd after she'd collapsed. In a flash, a chair was placed at the edge of the room. 'Place your head down to your knees,' he instructed.

By then, Gwennie and her friend Phyllis had seen the commotion and rushed to find out what was wrong. Annie started to feel better but couldn't avoid a searching look from Gwennie. Again, she dismissed it.

'I'll just sit here for a while. I'm feeling fine now. Must have rushed my tea. I don't want to spoil your evening.'

Frank pulled up another chair and sat down beside her. 'Just as well I brought the motorbike. I'll take you home on the back of that so you've no need to worry. You can collect your push bike tomorrow.'

She looked at his profile as he sat watching the dancers in the *twmpath*. His nose was perfectly proportioned. His jaw was chiselled and newly shaved. As well as being the kindest and most easy-going person she knew, he really was attractive, she thought for the second time that evening. It would have been so much more sensible to fall in love with someone like Frank, whose family was more like hers. But she hadn't. Love was something you couldn't make happen. She had fallen for the son of the local squire, and there was nothing she could do about it.

There were no further fainting incidents, and Annie relaxed and fell back into the routine of her work at the stables. She and Frank worked well together and began seeing each other in the evenings as friends. He started calling at the house to help Ted Beynon with the vegetable patch. Frank was young and strong and dug over the new beds in half the time it would have taken the older man to do it.

One morning, Annie was cooking breakfast and her father was singing Frank's praises. 'You couldn't do better than that young man, Annie. 'e'd make a good son-in-law, I reckon.' Annie's father winked at her. 'Near as dammit told me in 'is own words.'

Annie coloured. 'We're just good friends, Da. He'll be courting someone else before you know it.' She knew that what her father was implying was true, even though

Frank hadn't told her in so many words. But if what *she* suspected were true, it wouldn't be fair.

Her father raised one eyebrow and the two of them ate their breakfasts in silence.

Annie spent the morning mucking out the stables. Afterwards, one by one, she took the horses out for exercise, making sure that Ebony had a good hard run. At first, she'd been scared of the stallion's sheer size, but now that she had been at the stables for a while, she found him to be a thrilling ride. When she returned, she heard a female voice in the stables. Lady Delia was talking to Arianwen and didn't realise she had company. Annie listened more intently when she heard her own name.

'I miss him so much, *cariad*. It was different when he was at boarding school or university. Even when he was away studying in France, I knew he'd be home at the end of each term then. But this ... it's the uncertainty. Not knowing if I'll ever see him again. I couldn't bear it. What if he doesn't survive? Two children in the graveyard? No, I couldn't bear it. All he talks about in his letters is the Beynon girl. Her employer and nothing else. That's what he is.'

Arianwen snuffled and snorted. It was Annie's cue to enter the stable area.

'Oh, hello, Mary-Ann,' the older woman said. 'I ... I didn't see you there.'

No, thought Annie. *That's obvious.*

Lady Delia's cheeks flushed. She was dressed in a beautiful violet riding jacket and tight black jodhpurs. Her hair, still blonde like Edmund's, was held back in a finely crocheted purple snood. Her knee-length riding boots clung to her calves, and for the first time Annie saw where Edmund had inherited his stunning looks. Instead of her frumpy long dresses that skimmed her ankles, worn under shapeless knitted cardigans, Lady Pryce looked ten – even twenty years younger.

'I've come for my first refresher riding lesson, my dear. It's such a waste that this beautiful girl here is not being ridden as she was intended. I want to surprise Sir Charles.'

Annie didn't have the heart to tell her that Arianwen was ridden every day.

'That's wonderful news, your ladyship. I'll get her saddled up for you.'

The next hour was spent refreshing Lady Delia's skills, and it was soon obvious to Annie that she really was an extremely accomplished horsewoman.

'Thank you, Mary-Ann. I enjoyed getting back on the saddle. I don't know if my husband told you that I used to compete in horse trials before I married him and was quite successful at it, though I say it myself. One year, I sustained a fall that was so serious that they feared I may never walk again. All those years ago … and I'd never mounted a horse and ridden since. This is a big day for me today, my dear, and you helped with your patience and encouragement.'

'It was a pleasure, your ladyship.' Annie was determined to stress she knew her place.

'I don't know how much you heard earlier … it was nothing personal. But I can't allow my son to become too friendly with the workers. Nothing can come of it, my dear. That's all I'm saying. I shall see you again tomorrow afternoon. Please have Arianwen ready for me.'

Annie was left open-mouthed as Lady Delia strode away.

Chapter Sixteen

Ted Beynon was in the kitchen when Annie got home. A lamb stew made from the bones that Sid the Meat gave away for nothing was bubbling in the blackened pot hanging over the fire.

'Something smells good, Da. You made use of the bones like you said.'

Her father nodded and gave the pot another stir with the enormous ladle. 'Your mam used to say there was as much goodness in them bones as the meat. Mind, p'raps she was convincing herself of that when we'd run out of money for the meat.'

Annie went to wash and change out of her work clothes. She sat down with her father and they ate the meal in silence.

'This is good. I didn't realise how hungry I was,' she said. 'Fresh air makes both of us ready for this, I think.'

'You're right there, *bach*. Seeing young Frank tonight?'

Annie sighed. 'You've got to stop this, Da. I told you there's nothing going on. And, actually, I'm going to see Gwennie.'

Annie walked slowly into the village, enjoying having the time to collect her thoughts and reflect on the day. The evening air was cool and still. She pulled up her collar and placed each gloved hand in her pockets. The sky was pale lemon above surrounding hills and memories of the picnic at the boathouse flooded into her mind. *Oh, Edmund. Where are you? Why haven't you written?* Inside her pocket, she moved her hand to her stomach.

The lane snaked into the village and soon she reached

St Mary's Church, the stone wall boundary separating the churchyard from the edge of the road. As if drawn there by an invisible thread, she opened the kissing gates flanked by large yew trees and walked to her mother's grave. A plain wooden cross on which had been burned the initials *EMB* and the date *15-11-36* stood on a mound of earth alongside a plaque with the words *Born Sleeping* and the same date. Next to it was a weedless bed and a container holding late spring flowers. No elaborate marble or stone headstone for Eleanor Mary Beynon. This was all Annie's father had been able to afford, but she remembered him carving both the cross and plaque and burning the inscriptions with such care.

Annie knelt down on the damp grass and began to sob. 'I wish you were still with us, Mam. I'm so frightened. I can't imagine what it will do to Da.' She placed her hand on the wooden cross and got up. She heard people talking at the side of the church. She dried her eyes on her sleeve and went to leave.

'Good evening, Mary-Ann,' a voice called. It was Mrs Morgan from the shop. Annie remembered it was choir practice on a Wednesday night. She rose her hand and continued on her way to Gwennie's house.

Gwennie's family lived in Pryce Street; a long cobbled road of identical grey-stoned terraced dwellings. Her father had told her that the cottages were built by the Pryce family in the late 1800s for the workers at the local quarry that they owned. The numbers had depleted and the quarry employed far fewer men. Not all the occupants were quarrymen now. The light had almost gone when Annie entered the street. Shadows gave the whole place a mysterious air. Silhouetted crows lined up on the telephone wires that criss-crossed the road, even though no one living there could afford a private telephone. Their haunting caws made Annie shiver as she knocked on the door of number 13.

The door opened and a slit of light from the hallway pierced the space in front of Annie. A small girl eyed her with suspicion.

'Megan, who is it?' called a woman's voice.

'Dunno,' said the little girl.

The door opened and a woman stood there with a cigarette hanging from her lips. Annie had only seen Gwennie's mother in the street, pushing the latest baby in a dilapidated pram and always in a hurry.

'Yes?' she said, turning to the side to blow a circle of smoke away. 'Our Gwennie's not 'ere, if that's who you want. Don't spend much time 'ere, truth be told.'

'Hello, Mrs Probert. Do you have any idea where she may be?' said Annie.

'Off with some boy, no doubt. Try behind the Reading Room. Tha's where they all meet up, so I do 'ear.'

The door was closed before Annie could say more. Turning, she went back into the village and walked up the lane opposite the church. The noise and laughter coming from behind the Reading Room confirmed what Mrs Probert had said. Before the war, the young people of the village would have been members of the local Young Farmers, but all that had stopped.

Annie watched from the side of the building, but Gwennie soon caught sight of her and came across. 'Annie! What are you doing here?'

Annie took her friend's arm and led her to the wooden bench positioned against the building. 'I just wanted to see you, that's all ...'

'And to tell me you're walking out with the handsome Frank Baker. I knew it. As plain as the nose on your face.' Gwennie laughed.

'No-oo,' said Annie. She felt her cheeks redden. 'Nothing like that.' Her heart sank. She desperately wanted to tell Gwennie what she suspected and ask for her advice, but it was no good; she couldn't go through with it. It was better if no one knew about what she was going to do. 'Why don't I call for you when you're on your own?'

Gwennie returned to the others, and Annie made her way home in the dark. The full moon, high in the indigo sky and surrounded by stars sparkling like tiny diamonds, illuminated the lane ... so why did she feel uneasy? If her suspicions were correct, she had decisions to make. She just hoped she could make the best ones for everyone involved. Gwennie's teasing about Frank Baker came back to her. She knew her friend was right. He *was* sweet on her, even though he hadn't said it in so many words – and she *did* love being with him. Could that be the answer? She'd not be the first or the last, she was sure. She stopped in her tracks, shocked that she could even consider deceiving her friend. No, it was her problem and she had to see to it. Her steps gathered speed and soon she saw Beech Cottage in the distance. No warm orange lights on in the downstairs rooms as there had been before the war. All in darkness now and the familiar smell of wood smoke as she got nearer. *Home*!

Chapter Seventeen

A few mornings later, the sun was shining and there wasn't a cloud in the sky. As she cycled to the Court, the pale silver sky gradually became a deep powder blue. In the parts of the hedgerows still in shadow, spiders' webs glistened with droplets of condensing dew. *Whatever happens*, she thought, *living here in all this beauty is something to treasure when others are in the midst of the horrors of war.* She thought of Reggie. Then she thought of Edmund and hoped again that the lack of contact didn't mean he'd forgotten her. She dismounted her bike, placing it against the wall of the stable. Her hand felt for the gold locket inside her jacket.

'Here she is.' Frank walked out into the stable yard. 'All ready for exercising our three beauties today. It's a great day for a ride. How are you getting on with Lady Delia, by the way?'

Annie smiled and entered the stables. 'She was up here all afternoon yesterday, confronting her fear of riding. She really is a superb horsewoman. You know the story, don't you?'

Annie proceeded to tell Frank everything Lady Delia had told her. She was very conscious that when she was telling him, his eyes watched her intently and she felt herself blushing. It would be so simple if she could respond in the way he obviously wanted. *Could you grow to love someone?* No, it would be cruel to try, and deceit was not something she would ever forgive herself for.

'Come on, let's get those horses saddled up.' As she turned to leave the office, she was overcome by dizziness and grabbed the doorpost.

'That's the second time now, Annie. Don't you think you should have these turns checked by the doctor? You've gone as white as a sheet. And don't think I haven't heard you retching outside the stables.'

The blood raced through her veins and her heart drummed in her chest. Her monthlies had disappeared and she knew exactly why she felt the way she did. A visit to Dr Jenkins who'd seen to the last few generations of Beynons was the last thing she needed. No, this was something she'd deal with herself. *And she'd already decided how she was going to do it ...*

'I'll be fine,' she said. 'You go ahead. Isn't Sir Charles bringing the new groom up to look around today? You'd better be back by then.' Annie smiled, willing Frank to ride away. Her stomach was churning and she knew she was going to be sick.

'Mary-Ann, Frank. I'd like you to meet Brian Davies, our new groom. Now that Lady Delia is riding Arianwen regularly, we both decided we needed someone to look after her mare exclusively. Brian, this is Mary-Ann Beynon who is in charge of looking after my son's mare, Kenna, and Frank Baker who's the groom for my horse, Ebony. He's also responsible for the carriage horses. These two have had extra work since Arianwen arrived.'

'Pleased to meet you both.' Brian Davies shook each of their hands in turn. 'I'm looking forward to working with you.'

'And you. Please call me Annie.'

Sir Charles looked at Annie. 'Of course, it means that if anyone is not well, we now have another pair of hands to cover. Before this awful war, Lady Delia and I employed four grooms. Are you all right, Mary-Ann? I must say you look even more off-colour today. I was only saying to my wife that you seem to have lost that bloom in your cheeks you had from being out in this wonderful countryside of ours.'

'I'm fine, sir. I think I must be sickening for something.' She tried to change the subject and turned again to Brian. 'Welcome to Cefn Court Stables, Brian. It will be good to have another pair of hands.'

But she still felt all eyes on her, and her skin prickled. *Could they tell?* She remembered her mam had always been able to tell before it became public knowledge.

'I'm glad. My wife thought you were just worrying about Reggie. Only natural of course, as you two were so close. Have you heard how he's getting on?'

Annie told him about the latest letter they'd received and how his regiment was being prepared to be moved out to North Africa.

'Well, Brian, let Annie and I show you around. Then you can get to know that beautiful grey mare who'll be your responsibility,' said Frank.

Sir Charles left the three of them in the stables, and the rest of the day was spent getting to know each other and allocating who was responsible for what. Annie had a good feeling about the new arrangements.

Once it was time to finish for the day, she collected her bicycle and said goodbye to the lads. She was pleased for Frank to have male company, and perhaps having Brian around would distract him from noticing what was going on with her so much. She would go home and think up excuses as to why she had to catch the bus into Pen-y-rhos later for the second time in a week. Much as it would break her heart, she'd made up her mind. There was no other way. She remembered Gwennie and her friends talking about it in school. Others had solved their problems that way, so now she had to do the same. Best for her da, best for Edmund wherever he was, best for the Pryce family.

Tears formed along her eyelids. No, not best for her ... but there was nothing else she could do.

Griffith Avenue was a bleak run-down area of Pen-y-rhos. *Avenue? That's a joke*, thought Annie. *Not a tree in sight and there never has been by the look of it*. The narrow street was deserted in the gloom of late evening. Glass from many of the unlit streetlamps lay smashed on the wet cobbles. Shadowy doorways hid secrets and gave the whole place a sense of mystery. Annie had a secret of her own; one she was determined never to divulge. A black cat darting from behind an overturned bin where litter was strewn over the pavement made her jump.

Annie knocked on the door of the run-down cottage where generations of girls had gone before her. Old Maggie would sort things if you were ever in trouble. She's heard about the way things would go from other girls in the past. Maggie would offer her a mug of strong, sweet tea while she braced herself for what was to come. Annie heard footsteps thump along bare floorboards in the hallway inside. Her heart drummed in time to the steps, and it was all she could do not to run away. The door opened a fraction and the same smell of boiled cabbage filled Annie's nostrils as it had done when she first came to find out if Maggie would help her.

'Come in, dearie,' said the florid-faced woman, who was dressed in a grubby floral overall. 'Good to see you again. You've seen sense then. Got the cash?'

Annie nodded and followed the woman through to the back where she handed over the money into an outstretched hand.

'Nothing to fear, dearie. This little problem of yours will soon be done and dusted.' Maggie smiled a toothless grin at Annie.

Her stomach churned. Nobody had told her it would be as bad as this. *It's your own doing*, a stern voice in her head told her. *Are you sure there isn't another way, cariad?* That was a different voice; the soft Welsh lilt belonging to her mam. No, she'd gone over and over this. It would break her da. Her thoughts were interrupted. Old Maggie was talking to her.

'I said, a nice cup of tea to begin with, I think.'

Annie took one look at the dirty couch, the untidy room, and knew she couldn't go through with it.

Her heart thumping, she turned to leave.

'No. I can't. I have to go.'

She dashed outside into the damp evening air, leaving the front door wide open behind her. She bent down and was violently sick.

It was a few weeks since Annie had visited old Maggie. She shuddered every time she thought of it and how close she'd been to making the worst mistake of her life. She stood by her bedroom window, looking out on the patchwork of green and umber ploughed fields, edged with the immaculate hedges her father was so proud of. A gentle flutter inside her reminded her that, in spite of what was ahead, a tiny life depended on her and the decision she'd made. No one would ever know the sacrifice she was going to make in a few months' time.

She washed, dressed and joined her father downstairs. He sat next to the range, holding a thick slice of bread on an ancient toasting fork close to the fire. The smell of fresh toast filled the kitchen.

'Help yourself, *bach*. Them on the plate haven't been done long, so the butter'll still melt as you like it.'

The morning nausea had stopped and her hearty

appetite had returned. Her da joined her at the table and placed the last piece of toast in the rack.

'You need more than a bit of toast if you're off out hedging, Da.'

He sighed. 'I'll be fine, *bach*. Did I tell you there's a new lad started with me? He thinks he's an 'edger but I has to go round after 'im weaving in all the branches he's missed.' Her father laughed. 'The gaffer will miss me when I finish. Not that I'm planning to go anytime soon. We'd lose this place straight away. You realise that, don't you?'

Annie looked at her father. 'I know, Da.'

Ted Beynon sighed. 'I'll keep going. Rubbing plenty of liniment will sort out these ol' joints.

Chapter Eighteen

January, 1942

Weeks had turned into months, and Annie found it harder and harder to keep her condition a secret. Life carried on as normal. She worked each day at the stables, exercising Kenna every morning and doing all the jobs expected of her. Frank and Brian seemed oblivious to the fact that she was finding it harder and harder to complete the physical work. They were forever reminiscing about nights out and the pretty girls they'd been seeing at village socials. She found that she was far more afraid of falling when she was out on a ride now, and she'd lost that natural rhythm and poise she'd learned from a young age, keeping herself stiff and awkward.

'You should have come to the *twmpath* last night, Annie. There were people there from Brynderi, weren't there, Brian?' Frank pushed Brian's shoulder and they began a mock fight. 'A certain young lady took a shine to our friend here and left me all on my lonesome.'

Brian laughed. 'You should have joined us, Annie. Your friend Gwennie was asking about you. Said she hasn't seen you in ages.'

'I stayed in and kept my Da company. He's still gets worried about Reggie when he hears the news.'

She left the two lads and went to get Kenna ready for her ride, lifting the saddle onto her back.

Annie had twisted the truth. She did stay in, intending to keep him company but Ted Beynon had gone to the weekly whist drive in the Reading Room. He was in a much better mood since the arrival of another long letter from her brother that morning after weeks of no contact. He was in Egypt with the Royal Artillery driving vehicles and towing 25-pounder guns on carriages in sweltering heat. For now, he was safe.

Annie had taken advantage of the empty cottage, relieved to unroll the tight rubber corset that was keeping her true body shape a secret. She'd enjoyed lying in the tin bath in front of the fire. She'd boiled some kettles for hot water and used some of the precious soap she'd had from under the counter in the village shop; her secret, as she knew her dad wouldn't approve of the hard-earned money going on such luxuries. It was such a lovely change from the strong-smelling Lifebuoy soap they usually had.

Annie smiled as she remembered being fascinated to watch the ripples in her stomach as a tiny foot or arm moved position. There was a strong bond between the baby and her already. She dreaded the moment she'd have to do what she planned. She counted back the months to the time of the special picnic and when she'd last seen Edmund. She didn't know how much longer she could keep working at the stables without Frank and Brian suspecting that something was wrong, but what she did know was that she would meet Edmund's child soon. Just as she was thinking this, a searing cramp tore through her and she doubled over.

Niggly stomach cramps like the one she experienced in Kenna's stall continued for a number of days, and although she couldn't tell a soul about them, she guessed it wouldn't be long until the baby arrived. If only things could have been different. If she'd fallen in love with one of the local farm boys, they could have been open about how they felt about one another. Her father would have been upset at first that she didn't have a ring on her finger before getting in the family way, but she wouldn't have been the first and she certainly wouldn't have been the last. He would have seen that she had a nice village wedding and let her and her new husband move into Beech Cottage with him until the baby arrived. But in order not to break his heart, she would break her own. Falling for Edmund Pryce had been the best and the worst thing she'd ever done. She remembered the snatched moments and his tender lovemaking in the boathouse when every fibre of her body had come alive. And then he was gone. Her hand touched the locket she'd never taken off since the moment he gave it to her. Gone to war, and then who knew where he was now? Perhaps he'd been one of those brave fighter pilots flying their Spitfires over France she'd heard about on the radio.

It was when the pains started that she had to plan where she could give birth. At home was out of the question. To Annie, there was only one place. From there, she could put her plan into action.

Since Christmas, the weather had turned very cold. Every morning, filigree patterns of ice coated the inside of her bedroom window at Beech Cottage, and it was a struggle to keep warm both inside and out in the fresh air. Wrapping herself in as many layers as she could find, Annie arrived at the stables early as soon as her father had left. She checked that the place was empty and walked up the stairs into the hayloft. She'd been secreting blankets, muslin nappies and towels up there for the past few weeks and had hidden them under a piece of tarpaulin in the farthest corner. As she put her foot on the final step, a wave of pain seared through her as her stomach contracted. She held onto the handrail, gripping it tightly. *My God, that nearly cut me in half.*

She remembered being in the bedroom with the village

midwife when her mam was giving birth to her brother; the one who had not made it. *Please God, don't let that happen to me and my baby too.* She remembered Bertha Thomas telling her mam to take a deep breath and then pant every time a pain came. Annie's stomach tightened again and the pain was more intense this time. She followed the midwife's advice.

'Not yet, baby. I need to get more stuff up here.'

She walked over to the corner of the loft and peeled back the tarpaulin. She sat down on the wooden stool she'd brought up from Kenna's stall and rubbed her stomach as the baby moved from one side to the middle, its little heel pointing outwards. She opened the small suitcase that she'd disguised in one of the hessian sacks that had once contained hay. In it were some baby clothes and a shawl that once belonged to her little brother. She's found them in the attic and they were more yellow than white after so long. On the top of the clothes was her mam's dressmaking shears.

'Ow!' Annie clutched her stomach and doubled over.

A pile of newspapers was placed to the side of the haybed and rug where she and Edmund had once sat and talked. It seemed ironic that soon she'd be lying there, all alone, bringing his baby into the world and he might never know. Her throat tightened and tears pricked along her eyelids. Of all the times, this was when she wished her mam could still be here to help. *Stop being silly. Women are having babies every minute of every day. You just have to get on with it.*

The baby didn't arrive then; it was a false alarm and Annie got the time she needed to be fully prepared. That night, alone in her bedroom, she wrote the most heartbreaking note she would ever write in her life.

*

When eventually her time came, it was a clear January night when pink dusk descended and frost glistened in the moonlight. She'd watched Frank and Brian leave and then found the spare key to open up the stables, locking the door behind her. She'd prepared the loft for the night ahead. She'd told her father that she was staying with Gwennie in the village. She hated lying to him, but she didn't want to risk going into labour at home. After checking the shutters were closed and the hatch over the stairs was secured, she settled down for the night.

She woke with a start later. It was pitch black in the loft. Excruciating pain ripped through her body, and her stomach was hard and rigid. Alone and frightened, she knew it was the start of the real thing and the pains could go on for hours. Each time, the pain intensified and was like nothing Annie had ever experienced before. In the darkness, she writhed around on her bed of straw and began to cry. *Please God, let my baby be all right. This is something I have to do for myself, for Edmund.*

As she got to her feet to light the gas lamp, she felt a sharp pain like a knife cutting through her and warm liquid gushed out. She placed layers of newspaper on the wet straw to soak it up. She grabbed her stomach, put down towels and lay back down. She felt the need to push and remembered Bertha's instructions to her mother.

Now, Nell, you are ready to deliver your baby. When you're able to, push as hard as you can.

The pain came in waves and Annie was desperate for the labour to be over.

I can see the head, Nell. One more push for me, Bertha had said. *Come on, one big push.*

And that is what Annie did as she felt her baby enter the world. She looked down at the little slimy body covered in blood, its arms flaying in the air. As she cleaned the baby's skin, she gasped as she spotted a tiny heart-shaped birthmark near its left wrist. Her heart stirred as she remembered where she'd seen an identical one before ...

The sound she was waiting for soon came – a strong, lusty cry that told Annie all was well. She wrapped the baby in one of the clean towels and laying her down, carefully cut the umbilical cord with the dressmaking shears. She bound the baby's abdomen with the strips of old sheeting she'd found at the cottage, and dressed her in a clean nappy and the baby clothes.

She began shaking and her teeth chattered as she bound herself tightly to stem the bleeding. This changed to wracking sobs, and Annie wept until she had no more tears left. *A daughter, a beautiful little girl.* She looked down on her newborn baby and marvelled at the mop of fine golden hair, so like Edmund's. She was beautiful just like him, and a surge of love consumed Annie. *Please forgive me for what I have to do, my angel. If there was any other way, I would do it like a shot.* The love she felt when she held her baby for those precious moments in the hayloft consumed her again and new tears trickled down her face

Annie wrapped up her little daughter in the hand-knitted shawl and lined the suitcase with a soft blanket. She took the note she'd written for whoever found her baby from her pocket and tucked it underneath. She tidied away all evidence of giving birth in the hayloft and replaced the tarpaulin in the corner. Feeling unsteady on her feet, she sat for a moment and drank tea from the flask that had long since gone cold. She unlocked the hatch door over the stairs, closed the suitcase and picked up the baby. Checking that no one was around, Annie walked towards the main door of Cefn Court. The previous frosty day had continued into a clear, crisp night, and the full moon was still visible in the sky as dawn was breaking. Weak, pale light bathed the shrubs and trees in an ethereal silver. The servants would already be up, lighting fires and getting breakfast ready.

Annie walked up the three stone steps. She held her baby tightly to her and kissed her forehead. She opened the case and laid the baby in the base and placed another blanket over her so that only her little face was visible. Annie looked down and stifled a sob.

'Goodbye, *cariad*. Please forgive me.'

She pressed the bell and moved away to stand hidden behind a rhododendron bush.

Please hurry. Please take my baby and give her the life I would never be able to.

It seemed an age to Annie before the front door opened. It was Elsie who helped in the kitchen. She looked down at the baby lying in the suitcase and gasped. She picked up Annie's baby daughter and held the bundle close.

'Mrs Elias. Come quick,' she yelled.

Cook was beside her in minutes. 'Left on the doorstep? Poor little mite. Here, give it to me, Elsie. Go and see if you can find who has done such a thing. Oh my, I shall have to tell her ladyship.'

Annie froze and hoped that her dark clothing would disguise her presence behind the bush. Doing as the cook had asked, Elsie hurried in the opposite direction, to Annie's relief, and she began walking a little way along to the stables. The house was all in darkness, but Annie knew that behind the shutters every light in the place would have been switched on. She could hear voices shouting as the news spread through the household. Her baby would be safe.

She ran the rest of the way back to the stables and locked herself in the loft. Once she knew she was not going to be discovered, she sobbed again until there weren't any tears left to fall. She needed to rest before gaining the strength to walk back to the cottage. She knew she'd have to wait until her father left for work, so she lay down on the haybed and wrapped herself in a woollen rug like the one she and Edmund had covered themselves with in the carriage on their way to the boathouse. Every time she closed her eyes, she saw him as she imagined he'd look, standing proud in his air force blue uniform.

His mother wouldn't have wanted her as a daughter-in-law. No, the beautiful young ladies of the county set were more suitable wife material. Her father would have been the same if he knew. 'Likes of us should know our place, *bach*.' In an ideal world, her place would be with Edmund and their baby, but it was not to be. She'd done the right thing. Lady Delia would see to it, she was sure.

She must have dozed, but she woke up when she heard voices downstairs in the stables. It was Frank and Brian.

'The gaffer says we gotta take the horses out for a really long ride today. He wants 'em fighting fit, he said. You get Ebony all saddled up and I'll see to the new one he bought for his missus. 'arry ... something Welshy, I think he calls her,' said Brian.

'Don't you know her bleeding name yet? Don't let the gaffer know. He expects us to treat 'em like our own kids. It's Arianwen.'

Annie tiptoed to the shutters and opened them a fraction to see the young men lead the two horses outside.

Kenna neighed from her stall and the two looked back into the stables.

'Wonder if Annie will make an appearance today. She's been neglecting the poor old girl lately. Mr Edmund wouldn't be very 'appy if he knew his beloved Kenna hadn't had proper exercise.' Brian nodded in the direction of Kenna.

'She'll be back once she's recovered, you watch,' said Frank. 'She loves that horse. She can't ride her with a bad back, can she? It was so unlike Kenna to throw her the way she did, mind.'

The boys mounted the horses and cantered away.

They were right. She'd let Edmund down and, most of all, she'd let Kenna down. She gathered up her things and placed them in her basket. Knowing Frank and Brian were well away from the stables, she walked down the stairs and made sure the loft hatch was secure. Before leaving for home, she went to see Kenna. She took a grooming brush from the tack shed and spent time getting the horse's coat into tip-top condition once more. She made sure the straw in her stall was clean and topped up the trough with clean water.

'There you are, my girl. The boys will be back to ride you soon.'

Kenna nestled into her neck, and Annie felt positive about the future for the first time in a while. She'd managed to keep working and coming to the stables up until a few weeks ago. She was young and healthy and had hidden the baby well under her riding clothes and overalls. She'd been convincing when she'd told Sir Charles that she'd strained her back. Many a boss would have dismissed her, but he promised the job was still hers when she was well enough.

'Edmund would insist on it, my dear,' he'd said. 'He's moved to another airbase now, you know. Still on the south coast. The sorties over France are relentless and he's lost quite a number of men in his squadron. We just have to hope and pray...'

Annie led Kenna out into the paddock and locked the gate behind her. Telling her father about her imaginary back problem had been harder. Lying didn't come easy to Annie. She'd often found him looking at her intently, and she was afraid he'd guess her true condition. If he did, he never discussed it. Annie's heart pounded as she got nearer the cottage, hoping he'd be out on the fields. Feeling teary again, she realised her da would never know his granddaughter.

A plume of smoke curled from the chimney of the cottage, and Annie was relieved that she could burn all evidence of what had happened the night before. It was over. Her baby was safe and she would get back to how things were. She fumbled around the back of the terracotta flowerpot for the key. It was in its usual place and she let herself in.

Her father had left the place clean and tidy as he always did. There was a note left for her on the scrubbed kitchen table. For some reason, seeing her father's handwriting brought a lump to her throat.

Annie

I've left you some cold mutton on the stone in the pantry. The bread may be a bit stale so put loads of dripping on it. I hope you enjoyed staying over with Gwennie and that your back is holding up well.

Should be home about six.

See you tonight.

Your Da.

She sat back into her father's armchair and promptly fell asleep.

'That you, Da?' Annie heard the creak of the back door opening. The sound of her father scraping his boots and then water running as he washed in the scullery interrupted her thoughts about her baby and what would be happening at the Court.

'Hello, *bach*,' said Ted Beynon. 'Had a good day? I hear there's all hell to play down at the Court. I saw that Elsie. Someone only went and left a newborn on the steps just as it was getting light this morning. How could someone do such a thing? Can't be right in the head. Elsie don't know what them at the top'll do. Thinks Lady Delia will give it to the authorities and it may end up in the orphanage in Brecon. Poor little blighter.

Annie gripped the edge of the sink. *That wasn't what was supposed to happen. She can't go to an orphanage. Oh God, what have I done?*

Chapter Nineteen

A few days later, Annie was still feeling weak and tearful, so she'd told her dad she must have caught the flu.

'A lot of it about, *bach*. Here, drink this. Hot and sweet. I've been saving the coupons for you. Sugar, butter. Don't know what'll be next. This damn war. So much for folks saying it'll all be over soon enough.'

She sipped the tea, warming her hands on the sides of the enamel mug. 'Thanks, Da. I'll be up and going before you know it.'

Her father looked directly into her eyes and Annie's heart drummed in her chest. It was a knowing look, and she was sure he suspected there was something more amiss than influenza. How could she tell him about the emptiness inside her where her heart had been broken in two? First a bad back, then it was flu. What could she think up next to explain why all she wanted to do was curl up in bed and shut out the rest of the world? The last time she'd felt like that was when her mam died, but then she'd had to get up and going to look after herself and Reggie and check they were both ready for school. Now Reggie was away fighting and she'd given away her beautiful baby.

'In fact, I think I'll wander down to the village and get some fresh air.' Annie stood up and took her mug to the sink in the scullery. 'Is it just bread we're out of, Da?'

Her father was out by the back door and putting on his boots. He'd called in to see how Annie was on his way from one field to the other. He'd finished the top field and the gaffer had said there was a hedge that needed mending in the field behind the cottage where some sheep had been straying into the lane.

'Yes, I think we're all right for everything else. Better get back to it. Otherwise, it'll be mutton for tea again if them ewes get run over.' He chuckled as he left the door open for Annie to close after him.

The air was cold in the winter sunshine. The days were beginning to lengthen. In a month or so, everything would be bursting into life. The hedges were still bare enough to see evidence of her father's skill, with branches neatly and evenly woven into a solid boundary. Soon, the hedges would be full and green, impenetrable by the farm stock housed in the fields. What a lot had happened in a year.

Annie reached the corner at the top of the hill. Below her was the village that had always been her home. The church spire rose from its centre and Annie smiled when she thought of her childhood before the war. Carefree days when she'd played outside all day, calling on friends on neighbouring farms. The church bells had been her clock. When the bells struck six o'clock, that was when she had to return home.

She walked down into the village and made her way to Morgan's corner shop. She stopped and looked at the noticeboard in the window. It was plastered with adverts and items for sale but one notice jumped out at her. Beautifully printed in black ink was notification of a post for nanny to Clara Delia Pryce of Cefn Court. Annie began to shake and held onto the window ledge to steady herself. Was Lady Delia really already advertising for someone to help look after the newborn baby? *Her baby.* Despite Annie's anguish, she still managed to feel some relief that perhaps this meant that Lady Delia would not send her daughter to an orphanage after all.

Annie entered the shop and stood at the back of a short queue. Talk between the two women in front of her was all about the baby. She felt her pulse race, and she moved closer to listen.

'Seems her ladyship's had a change of heart in just a matter of days. You know the girl from Aberithon farm who works in the kitchen, Elsie Pugh? Well, she said Lady Delia wouldn't have anything to do with the little 'un, at first. Wouldn't even look at her. Elsie was nursing her yesterday, and Lady Delia came down, took one look and gasped. Her ladyship told her the baby was the image of Miss Marjorie, the little girl who died.'

'Never. I knew they had another child. Buried in the churchyard, she is.'

Annie felt the hairs on the back of her neck stand on end. *What if Edmund's mother realises whose baby she is?*

'Come on, ladies. Less gossiping. There's others waiting to be served you know,' an elderly gentleman called out.

'Sorry. It's just all this talk about the new baby. Who could have been as wicked as that to abandon her own daughter like that?'

Annie felt a flush creep along her neck. *Please God, don't let them look in my direction.*

'I'll serve Annie if you don't mind. She's been waiting patiently.'

'Just a tin loaf, please, Mrs Morgan.'

Annie offered her coupons, paid for her bread and left the shop. Overcome with emotion, she suddenly felt her breasts tingling. Milk was seeping into her undergarments again, reminding her of what could have been if situations had been different. She imagined what it would be like to sit with her blonde-haired baby daughter in her arms. *Clara.* She liked that. The name reflected the type of family she'd been born to – on her father's side. No children's home or orphanage for the granddaughter of Lady Delia.

*

Beech Cottage was empty when she got home. She peeled some potatoes and set them to boil. As she was doing so, she made a decision. She'd go and see Lady Delia. She'd say that her back was still not right. Certainly not well enough to ride Kenna, anyway. She'd continue to work for the family, and if they didn't have anyone else in mind she'd offer to look after baby Clara.

She heard her father come in and wash his hands in the scullery.

'That you, Da?' she called.

Her father appeared holding a joint of ham. 'A gift from Parry Penybryn for my help on the farm last autumn.' He placed it on a board on the scrubbed wooden table, then took down the long carving knife and sharpening iron. It was a ritual with him. As he sharpened the knife, he whistled his unrecognisable tune in concentration, and finally tested it on his thumb. 'Perfect,' he said. 'Just see how thin I can get these slices now.'

He filled a dish with wafer thin slices of meat and then returned the rest of the ham to its hook in the larder. Annie wiped down the table and covered it with a white damask tablecloth. When her father had returned to the room, she'd laid it with two place settings, a salt and pepper set and a bowl of home-made piccalilli – her da's favourite.

Annie and her father sat down together and enjoyed the meal as they did every evening. But there were four places not laid and four chairs were empty. She wondered if her da was thinking the same as her. She felt her throat tighten. Her father slid his hand along the table and patted hers.

'Yes, *bach*, I know it's hard. We've got to pray that Reggie'll come back in one piece. Gotta believe that he'll stay safe. Why don't you write him a letter after supper?

He'd like that. Tell him all about that mare of his. Well, not *his* exactly. But you know what I mean. He'd walk on hot coals for that little 'orse.'

'I'm going to see Lady Delia tomorrow, Da.'

'Oh. Not going back to work yet, are you? Mind, you seem to have a bit more colour in your cheeks after going down to Morgan's to get the bread. Feeling a bit better, then? I thought you had the flu.'

'Yes. I do feel better so I thought I'd go and see if there are any jobs in the house going,' said Annie. 'I don't think I can go back to the stables. I seem to have lost my nerve.'

'Well, only if you feel up to it, *bach*.'

That night in bed, Annie heard the grandfather clock strike each hour through to dawn. In her mind, she went over what she had to say to Lady Delia. She knew the questions she'd have to answer. Why did a young girl with no experience of babies want to become a nanny? How would she stop the baby girl from crying? What would she do if the baby was running a temperature? Did she even know how to make up a bottle, change a nappy? But she did know those things. Helping out Auntie Pat with her newborns last year, she'd learned everything from watching her. Annie rubbed her eyes and hoped she knew enough for Lady Delia to give her the job. She just wanted to see baby Clara each day.

She got out of bed and unbound her chest. The smell of stale milk hit her nostrils, and she wound up the torn strips of sheet ready to burn on the fire. Clara would be a week old in a few days and the milk would get less in time, but Annie still had to tiptoe downstairs to wash it from her skin every morning. She bound herself tightly as she'd heard somewhere that this would help it dry up.

As Annie looked down on her heavy breasts, tears formed in her eyes. How could they be so full yet she felt so empty? Perhaps becoming Clara's nanny would be the only way she'd ever feel complete again. She swung from one decision to the other. *What am I going to do?*

Chapter Twenty

'Oh, hello, Annie. Everything all right now? How's your back? I bet you can't wait to get back to the stables.' Elsie led Annie into the large kitchen. 'I'll go and see if her ladyship can see you now. Coming back to work, is it?'

Annie smiled, deciding to stay quiet and not give Elsie any more information to spread around. She liked the kitchen maid, but she'd learned a long time ago not to divulge anything she didn't want to be common knowledge.

The kitchen was warm and smelled of home cooking. It made Annie reminisce of the times she'd come home after school and their cottage kitchen had smelled just the same. An image of her mam standing at the table in her floral wrap-around pinafore, brushing down her floury hand to give Annie a welcome home *cwtch*, entered her head. But her thoughts were interrupted by Elsie barging into the kitchen.

'She says to go on up to the drawing room. She'll see you now but she can't be long. Members of the WVS committee are arriving to talk about how they can help the war effort.'

Annie thought of Edmund and wondered again where he was. 'Thanks.'

The wide sweeping staircase led from the vast square hallway to the first floor. This was where the living quarters of the Pryce family were situated. She'd only been up once before when she'd come to beg Sir Charles to be allowed to look after Edmund's mare, and now here she was asking to give up the job she'd loved so much and offer her services for a position far more precious to her. She knocked on the oak door, touched her hair and tucked away a tendril that had escaped from under her cloche hat.

'Come in.'

Annie took a deep breath. She opened the door and entered the huge high-ceilinged room. Whereas in the rest of the house, the drapes, rugs and furniture seemed dark and gloomy, the soft furnishings in this room were in coordinating shades of pale teal and gold, giving it an air of opulence and calm. *To think that her daughter would grow up in surroundings like this rather than in the shabby cottage she called home ...*

'Mary-Ann, what can I do for you? I trust you are feeling better.'

'Yes, thank you, your ladyship. My back is better, but I don't feel I'm ready to ride the master's mare again. I seem to have lost my confidence after she threw me.'

'That's understandable. I heard that it was a nasty fall,' said Lady Delia. 'My husband will be sorry to hear that.'

'I was wondering if I could offer my services for another post at the Court? I saw the notice in Morgan's shop that you need a nanny for the little one.' Inside her chest, Annie's heart beat like a drum. Her hands grew clammy and she willed herself not to show the emotion she was feeling.

'Oh, that was very quick. I only instructed the notice to be put up a few days ago. I was rather hoping for an older person, my dear. Preferably someone who's brought up children of her own, and ideally someone who was still feeding a baby and could act as a wet-nurse.'

Annie felt her heart plummet. If only she could tell her employer that she could do that. Her milk was still there. At the thought, her breasts tingled, and she hoped that there would not be tell-tale leaks on her bodice.

'I may not have had children of my own, your ladyship, but I know how to look after a baby. I helped my aunt when she had twins last year. My da said I could stay with her until she got into a routine, what with her already

117

having two an' all. I know how to boil up the water to sterilise the bottles; they had them boat shape ones. You know with a teat one end and a rubber valve on the other? I changed their nappies, measured out the powdered milk to make up bottles—'

'I'm going to stop you there, Mary-Ann. I can see that you desperately want the job, and I'm sure, from what you say, you'd do very well. But I have to go with my instincts. An older, wiser head is what I've set my heart on, and I really want Clara to be breast fed. I want to do the very best for the little one after her awful start in life. Do you know that callous birth mother of hers left her at six o'clock in the morning in a battered old suitcase on a freezing cold doorstep?' Tears filled her eyes. 'Anything could have happened. It doesn't bear thinking about.'

Annie wrung her hands and made a silent promise to Clara that she would do everything in her power to make right the dreadful wrong she had done.

'I won't let you down, your ladyship. Or baby Clara.'

She could do no more. It was up to Lady Delia. What Annie *did* know was that the woman facing her had the best interests for her daughter at heart, and Clara would have a far better life with the Pryce family than the meagre upbringing that she'd have been able to offer. Heart-wrenching as it was, she believed she'd done the right thing.

'Now, you'll have to excuse me. The ladies from the committee will be here soon. I'll ring for Elsie to show you out.'

Annie thanked her, but as she walked away with Elsie, it was an effort to lift one foot after the other. It had been her one chance to spend more time with her daughter, and Lady Delia had made it very clear that it wasn't going to happen.

'You all right, Annie? You look a bit flushed. Not some sort of row with her ladyship, I hope.'

'No, I'm fine. Just the remnants of that old flu bug.'

They walked along the passageway from the drawing room in silence. Then Elsie looked in all directions, checking no one was around.

'You want a peek at the baby?'

The comment came out of the blue. She hadn't mentioned the baby. Had Elsie been eavesdropping outside the drawing room?

'I'd better not. Lady Delia might not approve of you showing her to me.'

Elsie tapped the side of her nose. 'What her ladyship don't know won't hurt her, will it? She's in here.'

They entered a small-ish room that led off landing. Light from the floor-to-ceiling windows flooded the space, and an ornately carved hooded crib with white *broderie anglaise* drapes stood at the far end. A large rocking horse took pride of place in the middle of the room.

Annie and Elsie tip-toed over to the crib. Annie felt her eyes prick with tears as she looked at the sleeping baby. Clara had grown so much, even in a week. Her skin was like porcelain, a tiny dimple visible on one cheek. The golden hair on her head was thicker, so like Edmund's. She wanted to reach out and touch her. Dressed in white, Clara resembled a sleeping cherub. Annie turned away and walked to the door, not wanting Elsie to see the effect the baby had had on her.

'Babies always get to me like that too. So innocent, so perfect. Too perfect for this world anyway … when there are monsters like her real mam about.'

Annie strode out of the door down the stairs and out into the fresh air. She didn't care if she'd been rude to Elsie. She needed to be on her own.

Chapter Twenty-One

Annie fumbled behind the plant pot by the front door to retrieve the door key. The sun was low in the sky and shadows from the lane opposite cast tall gloomy shapes on to the wall of the cottage. The clocks would be going forward in just over a month, and Annie was looking forward to the longer days. Silhouettes of crows that had gathered on the lowest branch of the tallest tree gave the place an eerie feel, and she remembered how her mam had told her that they always gathered when there was bad news.

She let herself into the hallway of the cottage. Preparing the evening meal would help to take her mind away from Clara and the disappointing result of that afternoon's visit to the Court. *It's for the best*, she thought. She'd done what she had for Clara's sake and she had to live with her loss.

Later that evening, the back door opened and she heard her father washing in the scullery. 'Whatever it is, that smells good, *bach*. Had a good day?'

How could she tell her father that she'd been close to tears for most of it and had to listen to cruel comments about what she'd done to her baby daughter. 'Not bad,' she lied. She suddenly ran to her father and gave him a *cwtch*, wrapping her arms tightly around him.

That night, she thought about other jobs she could do. Her father was out all day, and it didn't take long to run the cottage now it was just the two of them. She'd go down to Morgan's the next day and look on the board again. With any luck, there'd be something at another stables, far away from the Court.

She closed her eyes and drifted off to sleep, ignoring

the noise of the crows in the tree opposite. They hadn't brought bad news earlier so she dismissed the old wives' tale.

The next morning, Annie didn't pass a soul on her way into the village. She felt stronger with every day that passed and decided that she *would* try and get a position at another stable.

The shop bell rang as she opened the door and Mrs Morgan emerged from the back.

'Twice in one week, Annie Beynon. What can we get you today, *bach?*'

Annie walked over to the notice board. 'I've come to see what work is going. I've decided not to go back to the Court.'

Mrs Morgan raised one eyebrow quizzically.

'I've lost my nerve a bit after that fall and injuring my back.' She didn't tell her that she would jump at the chance of working with horses on another farm. Severing all links with her past at the Court was what she had to do.

'That's understandable. It wasn't the right job for a girl anyway, was it?'

Annie clenched her fists, feeling her nails dig into her palms. *And why not, Mrs "know-it-all" Morgan?* It was then she noticed. There was a gap where the advert for Clara's nanny had been. Her heart thumped.

'Has that nanny position already been filled?'

Mrs Morgan walked over to stand beside Annie. 'Yes, *bach*. Elsie Pugh came in this morning and said Lady Delia had found someone and I was to take it down. Wouldn't have been any good for you, though. A young slip of a lass like you. What would you know about babies?'

It was all Annie could do than to shout at the woman, but instead she kept her eyes fixed to the board to see if there was anything suitable. There wasn't, so she left.

As soon as she got outside, tears fell. That was it. Lady Delia had got someone already to look after her precious girl. Someone experienced, no doubt, like she'd wanted.

Chapter Twenty-Two

The afternoon sun filtered into the cottage. The showers that had dampened the garden that morning made the crocuses and daffodils all the more vibrant. Annie was still without a job but it wasn't for the want of trying.

There might be no work and no money coming in, but Annie made sure she was never idle. It was baking day in the Beynon household and Annie had made several fruit cakes, eking out the rations and making savings where she could. Her last task was to make a batch of her father's favourite Welsh cakes. She was just flipping the last few when the door knocker clattered. She took the bakestone off the range and quickly placed the Welsh cakes on the rack to cool. The door knocker rapped again, this time more loudly.

Annie wiped her hands on a teacloth and rushed through the hallway to answer 'All right, I'm coming as fast as I can,' she called.

Standing on the doorstep was Lady Delia, dressed in a smart plaid overcoat with her fair hair dragged back into her customary chignon.

'Oh. Lady Delia, I'm sorry. I didn't know it was you. I didn't want the Welsh cakes to catch.'

'They smell delicious. May I come in?'

'Of course.'

Annie led the older woman into the parlour and went to turn on the fire.

'No need for you to take me in there, Mary-Ann. The kitchen will be fine. And I may get to sample one of your Welsh cakes?' Lady Delia gave a warm smile and followed Annie through to where she'd been busy baking.

'It's a bit of a mess, I'm sorry. Please sit down. Can I get you a cup of tea, your ladyship?'

'I'd love one.'

Annie made sure she used her mam's best bone china, hidden away in the cupboard of the dresser, and spooned the loose tea into the floral teapot. A bit different to the giant brown earthenware pot she and her dad had stewing permanently and the large enamel mugs they drank from. *Always create a good impression when you have to, cariad*, her mam would say.

Annie placed a few Welsh cakes on a plate and poured two cups of tea. Lady Delia didn't take sugar either, and Annie was glad as she'd used the last of the week's sugar ration to dust the Welsh cakes.

'I expect you're wondering why I've called on you.'

Annie nodded and sipped her tea.

Lady Delia nibbled delicately at a Welsh cake before continuing. 'Well, I've been giving your offer to become Clara's nanny some thought. As you know, I had my heart set on someone with more experience and ideally someone who is still nursing their own child.'

Annie's pulse raced. Her hand shook and she placed her cup back in its saucer.

'I've interviewed a number of women over the last few weeks. I even employed someone on a trial basis but it didn't work out. The longer it goes on with the kitchen girls taking it in turns to stay with Clara, the longer she gets used to being bottle fed and most likely wouldn't take to a wet nurse now anyway.'

Annie's hands became clammy, and she hoped Lady Delia wouldn't notice the flush she was sure was creeping along her neck. *Please, your ladyship, just say it.*

'So, I've come to offer you the post if you still want it. I'd like you, with all your youth and enthusiasm, to look after baby Clara. If you're as good as you say you are, you'll soon gain the experience.'

Annie stood up. It was all she could do not to hug Lady Delia. 'Oh, yes, your ladyship. I do. I promise you I'll look after her ...' She stopped herself before she said *like my own*.

'I'd like you to come up to the Court at eight o'clock in the morning. I'll go through Clara's routine with you and we'll discuss money then.'

Annie shook her hand, and she sensed Lady Delia pulling away for fear of having her hand shaken off. She laughed. 'I take it you're pleased, then?'

'Oh, yes. You won't regret it, I promise.'

'Good girl, and thank you for the tea and Welsh cakes. Your mother taught you well. Until the morning, then.'

Annie saw her ladyship out and closed the door behind her. She leant back against the cool wood, slid down onto the tiled floor and burst into tears. *My baby. It's going to be all right after all*.

Annie was unable to sleep the night before she started her new job at the Court. She tossed and turned, talking in a whisper to Edmund. She told him what baby Clara looked like, and how she was so like him that it hurt. She wondered what he'd say if he'd been around when she'd first found out. It would have been good to share her news with someone even if, like her, he'd been horrified at the result of the single time they'd made love properly. Babies weren't part of the picture then. Annie dressed and went downstairs to wash in the scullery. Her father was still there in the kitchen, packing the tin box she'd filled with sandwiches for his lunch into his canvas knapsack. He filled the thermos with strong brown tea.

'It don't seem right you looking after that little 'un some

mother just went and abandoned. I can't understand her ladyship taking her in. Should have got the authorities involved. What do she want with a babby at her age anyway? More the age of its grandmother, I'd say.'

Annie felt her cheeks burn. What if people put two and two together? 'It's not the baby's fault, is it, Da? Pretty little thing. Elsie showed me when I went up to ask for the job.'

'Ah, well. If that's what you want to do. I 'spose it'll be good practice for when you have babbies of your own. Seen any more of that Frank from the stables?'

Annie sighed. 'Not that again, Da. Plenty of time for that when this war is over.'

Annie was glad when her father left and she was able to compose her thoughts before leaving to start her new job. She willed herself to remain aloof and not succumb to her emotions when she handled baby Clara for the first time. If she didn't, it could be over before it started. She couldn't risk anyone guessing her secret. She was the only one who knew the truth and that was the way it was going to stay.

The sun shone high in the sky as she cycled along the lane from her cottage to the Court. The dappled shade from the leaves overhead made patterns on the stony surface, and the hedgerows were beginning to fill out. When she got to the top, she stopped for a moment to admire the view. A patchwork of green and brown fields stretched out behind the grey stone building, all belonging to the Pryce estate. *Imagine owning all that*, she thought. The Beynon family didn't even own their cottage and Sir Charles had every right to evict them at any time. It seemed so wrong somehow that some folks had so much and others, like her da, had so little. *All the luck of the draw*, he used to tell her when she asked why they didn't live in a big house like her friend, Edmund Pryce.

Annie got back on her bike and free-wheeled down the slope, cycling into the drive leading to Cefn Court. She went around to the servants' entrance at the back of the house and left her bicycle propped against the stone wall. She dusted down her skirt, smoothed her hair back from her face and pulled on the bell. It was Elsie who answered.

'Come in, Annie. We're all so excited you're going to be joining us. Didn't like the look of them others who came for the nanny's job at all. Mouths turned down, beady eyes ...'

Annie grinned. 'They can't all have been like that, Elsie.'

'Well, p'raps I'm exaggerating a bit but I've got real fond of that little girl. I didn't want them being all strict with her.'

'I'm sure whoever gets the job has to bring baby Clara up as her ladyship wants. It's not up to us, is it?'

Elsie led the way into the large kitchen and showed Annie where to hang her coat. She handed her a pile of neatly pressed clothes.

'Her ladyship says these are for you to wear as Clara's nanny.' Annie unfolded them and held up a pale lemon dress made from thick cotton, a starched apron and a matching cap. Elsie carried on talking. 'I said to the others, "You should see the way that girl looked at the baby. She couldn't have looked at her with more care than if it was her own child".'

Annie's heart drummed in her chest as she asked if there was somewhere she could change. Elsie took her to a small cloakroom leading off the scullery.

A little while later, Annie emerged from the cloakroom in her uniform.

'You do look the part. Come on. I'll take you up to her ladyship.'

Annie's stomach somersaulted with each step she took

up the stairs, and not for the first time she wondered if she was doing the right thing.

Elsie knocked the door. 'Annie Beynon is here, your ladyship.'

'Thank you, Elsie. You may leave now. Come in, Mary-Ann. Please sit down.'

In her arms, Lady Delia was holding a sleeping Clara, wrapped in a beautiful hand-crocheted shawl. She stood up, rocking the baby gently so that she didn't wake her, and laid her in Annie's arms. Annie's heart skipped a beat and she bit her lip, determined not to show what she was actually feeling.

'There you are, baby Clara. Meet Nanny Mary-Ann. She's going to be looking after you now.'

The baby stirred but didn't wake. Annie looked down at her in awe. Her plump pink cheeks were just visible in the shawl and long, silky eyelashes curled up from her closed lids. Blonde hair formed a small curl on her forehead. *She's even more beautiful than I remember.* Annie pulled the baby close. Looking at Lady Delia, she beamed.

'Thank you, your ladyship. I won't let you down. Or baby Clara.'

Chapter Twenty-Three

✢ ODILE ✢

June 1943, Normandy

Odile entered the stone farmhouse she shared with her parents. It was just the three of them now. *Well, four if you counted …*

'*Ça va*, Maman? Something smells good.'

Monique Lefèvre looked up at her daughter as she entered the large family kitchen and smiled.

'I have to eke out every bit of meat I can now. The butcher's window in Ville de Roi has been empty for weeks. He's keeping any little he gets under the counter for his regulars.'

'It's a good job we still have a few chickens left then, for the pot and for eggs.'

Odile took off her coat and went through to the dark passageway behind the family room to hang up her coat. Checking she was alone, she took the new bundle of leaflets, tied in string, that she'd collected and went up to her bedroom. The room was set under the eaves of the cottage and overlooked the yard.

She knew what she had to do and hid the leaflets under her mattress until she was ready to do the leaflet drop. Odile looked around the small space which allowed her some privacy away from the bustle of family life. With three brothers, it had always been important to her. How she would give anything to have that noisy, argumentative family back together again. The house was always eerily silent now. Two of the boys had enlisted to fight for France and were somewhere with their regiments. But it was

Pierre who had been in even more danger; he'd left to go underground and actively fight for the *résistance*. He'd told them on his last secret visit to see his parents that his group were making inroads behind the German lines and if there was any risk of being discovered, they had been instructed to shoot and kill on sight. News that he had met his death that way had devastated the family.

When Odile had finished upstairs, she joined her parents in the kitchen where her mother ladled out the chicken broth.

'*Coq-au-vin* without much chicken, eh, Monique?' Odile's father laughed and winked at her. The three of them sat down together and sipped the thin stew. It was hot and tasty and her mother had used the last of the flour to make some bread rolls. Odile managed to secrete half of hers into her napkin without her parents seeing. She offered to wash up and sent her parents to sit down. With them out of the way, she poured the broth she had left in her bowl into a covered ceramic pot to take to her airman later.

When she returned to the living room, her father was already asleep, his gentle rhythmic snoring breaking the silence.

'No wireless for you tonight, *Maman*?'

'No, it's all bad news. The Nazis are everywhere in Sainte Marie-Hélène. It is only a matter of time before they come here to Collinac. I fear for your brothers, especially after what happened to Pierre. At least the other two are following orders with officers making the decisions. But Pierre, pah! He was headstrong. He died in the name of the *résistance* and now Colette and my lovely granddaughter are without a husband and father.'

Anything rather than let the Germans win. Odile knew he had given up his own life for the cause. That was why she felt she had to do her bit too …

'Try not to worry, *Maman*,' she said weakly.

'I hear the Nazis shot down an Allied fighter plane yesterday. Not far from here. Wreckage of the plane was seen in the field behind the village. There was no sign of the pilot. Poor man. Gone to meet his maker, no doubt.'

Odile thought of her secret in the barn and the wound on the airman's head that he must have sustained when he'd bailed out with his parachute. She excused herself and went upstairs. She found an old crocheted blanket at the back of her wardrobe and wrapped it around her like a cloak. Next, she packed a bag with some of her brothers' clothes and everything she could find to help the man clean up and dress his wound. She waited until her parents had gone to bed.

When all was quiet, she tiptoed downstairs with only an oil lamp to help her find her way. It was the first clear night after a week of rain and dense cloud, and once outside, moonlight bathed the stone cottage in silver. The poplar trees edging the yard looked like silhouetted guards in columns, standing to attention. Odile hoped that her new-found British friend would be safe here until his wounds had healed.

She placed the bag and oil lamp on the ground, and with her one hand she eased up the wooden bar that slotted over both doors. She held the pot containing the broth steady in her other hand. She entered the barn and lit the oil lamp.

'Hello,' she called.

A tall figure appeared cautiously at the top of the stairs, but then beamed down at her.

'I thought you weren't coming back. Here, let me.' He descended a little way and took the bag of clothes from her.

'I waited until my parents were asleep. I have to hope they do not wake up.'

Once they got back into the hayloft, Odile opened the wooden shutter wide enough to let in the moonlight and turned off the lamp.

She took the pot of broth and ladled it into a large enamel mug. Handing it to the man, she said, 'I hope it is still hot. Perhaps warm. It is very cold here.'

The pilot sat back down on a pile of hay he'd made into a bed and cupped his hand around the mug. He brought it to his lips and sipped.

'This is so good. Thank you. You must not go without yourself, though. I have read how difficult it is to get enough food.' He snatched at the bread Odile had placed next to him and chewed it hungrily. 'You've probably guessed that I haven't eaten since the crash. I cannot thank you enough.'

For the next few minutes, there was silence as he ate. Odile watched and took in every detail about the visitor. She wondered where he lived in Britain. His fine features with his sculpted cheekbones and fair colouring made him appear aloof at first, but on that second meeting, she realised it might be shyness. He seemed quiet; a true British gentleman, and much more refined than her brothers and their friends. *And Antoine.* When she'd shaken his hand earlier, she'd noticed how this man's hands with their long, slim fingers were soft and smooth. It was obvious he'd never had to do any heavy manual work.

She smiled and took the mug from him. Their skin touched and a tingle of excitement fizzled inside her. She felt herself redden, her pulse racing. Why did this stranger have such an effect on her? She tried to distract herself by showing him what she'd brought. 'In here you have some clean clothes. There is a towel and some soap. I will leave you now. Oh, and maybe you'd like a shave, eh? There is one of Papa's straight blade razors. The sink and cold-water tap are at the far end of the barn. Downstairs. I'll bolt the door when I leave you.'

'I won't forget this, Odile. *Merci.*'

Chapter Twenty-Four

The airman had been hiding in the barn for over two weeks, and it was getting harder and harder for Odile to make excuses for leaving some food on her plate.

'It is not like you to leave anything, *chérie*. You are not going down with something, are you? You are working very hard to help Papa on the farm. You must eat,' said her mother at breakfast one morning. 'Don't you agree, Henri?'

Her father peered around the edge of the paper he was reading. 'What's that?' He didn't wait for an answer. He was so preoccupied with what he was reading. 'It says in here that we must expect the worst. The Nazi army is advancing in greater numbers far more quickly than was thought possible.' He held open the paper for them to see the full page spread of the German army, soldiers with grim, determined faces with their bayonets, each one at exactly the same angle.

Seeing the grainy images of the men who regularly cat-called after her whenever she ventured into Ville de Roi was almost as bad as seeing them face to face. She shuddered as the enormity of what she had done, and continued to do, hit her. What if the Nazis raided the farm and searched the barn? It wasn't fair to put her parents in any more danger than they already were.

'Are you all right, Odile? You've gone very pale.'

'I'm fine. It's just there's no doubt now it's really happening. It's here in our own community. That is what scares me.'

Her father put down his paper and held out his arms to his daughter. Odile bent over him and hugged him.

'We will be ready, *chérie*. We must be on our guard and do nothing to draw attention to ourselves. We are simple country folk going about our business, trying to eke out a living.'

Odile's heart drummed against her rib cage. *An active member of the résistance, dropping propaganda leaflets at every home in Ville de Roi, attending meetings, hiding a British pilot. If I'm found out ...* Her thoughts were interrupted by her mother.

'Will you take the coupons and try to get some sugar when you go into town? Try Jean at the bakery for me as well, please. If the reports are true, I think we need to stock up all we can. Chantelle said that when they invade your farm, they take all the livestock – chickens, goats, everything. Her parents were left with nothing when they arrived in Ville-des-Champs. They even stripped the garden of all the vegetables.' Her mother stood and went to the large oak dresser on the far wall. From the top shelf, she stood on tiptoe and took down the old tin where she kept the sheets of coupons for rationing. 'Here. Look after them safely until you get there.'

Odile took them from her mother and tucked them in the inside pocket of her coat with her *carte d'identité* that went everywhere with her.

It was what her father said next that made her stop in her tracks.

'A good idea, Monique. I think we need to find a place to store everything where the Nazis won't find it. If my old hips will allow, I'm going to go up into the hayloft and clear a space up there. It needs a clear out anyway, judging by the noises the floorboards are making. I'll take some traps up with me and get rid of the rats. Any food will need to be in metal boxes so that it stays fresh and no vermin can get at it.'

Trickles of sweat formed inside her collar and on her palms as she clenched her fists. She'd have to warn the airman that every movement he made was heard in the barn below. He'd need to be more careful and check if he heard anyone enter the barn. She realised she had to get him away. But how? And she had no idea where she could take him …

'I can do that, Papa. I'll go and get what *Maman* wants now and you have the boxes ready for me when I get back. The metal crates and buckets will be fine for what we want. The sooner I go, the sooner I get back.'

She dashed out of the cottage and called in the barn on the pretence of collecting her bicycle which was already outside resting against the wall. She wheeled it inside and shut the door behind her. She ran up the stone steps to the loft where her secret British man was huddled on a hay bale, trying to keep himself warm. He had one of her brother's overcoats on and the crocheted blanket wrapped around his shoulders. His face was flushed and his eyes were sunken deep into their sockets.

'Odile. You do not normally come here in daylight.' His teeth chattered so loudly that the noise echoed in the empty space.

'*Monsieur*. You look very ill. You were all right last night.'

She felt his forehead. It was burning and damp with sweat. The skin around the wounds on his head was hot and angry red. There was no way she could move him. She'd have to keep the secret a while longer.

'It came on all of a sudden.'

Odile poured him a drink of water and led him to lie down on his makeshift bed of hay. As soon as his head rested on the hay, he closed his eyes. 'Thank you, Odile. What would I do without you?' he whispered.

She placed the jug of water by him. 'I have to go into town now but I will be back. Keep drinking this. I will try and get something to bring your fever down while I'm there.'

She wheeled her bike out of the barn and made sure the wooden latch was securely fastened over the two wide doors. There was no time to waste. It was only a matter of time before her father, always so independent and stubborn, would insist on clearing the loft himself. And that must never happen. If the airman was to stay hidden and have time to recover, her parents must never know about her secret guest.

Odile rushed around Ville de Roi getting the provisions her mother wanted. She picked up what she needed from the pharmacy. Memories of the taste of the viscous pink medicine filled her mouth and almost made her gag. *It will do the trick*, her mother always said. And it did. After the deliriums and watching the red and green monsters crawl up the bedroom wall, her temperature would always return to normal and she'd soon be on the mend. Odile hoped that that the same would be the case for the airman, and that the medicine would act fast.

In her rush to get out of the shop, she didn't notice two German soldiers walking towards her and almost bumped into them.

'The pretty *fräulein* seems in a great hurry, Hans. Perhaps we should escort her to her home so that she doesn't get lost.'

Hans laughed. '*Ja*, she is a very pretty *fräulein*, Jakob.' He sneered and snatched the paper bag that contained the bottle of medicine, reading the label. 'Someone is not well, I think.'

Odile felt her pulse race. 'That is why I rush. I am sorry.

My father, he is ill and has the fever. Please let me pass.' Saying the words so politely nearly forced Odile to retch. What she really wanted to do was to scream in defiance at them but she knew she had to get back. Don't draw attention to yourself. Wasn't that what her papa had said?

'Let her go, Hans,' said the tall one called Jakob. 'I'm sure we will see the pretty *fräulein* again.'

Hans handed the medicine back to Odile and the two soldiers stood to one side and let her through.

She pedalled as fast as she could and was soon travelling down the gravelly lane to the farmhouse at speed. She entered the yard and, to her horror, the barn doors were wide open.

She dismounted her bike and threw it on the yard, running into the barn.

'Papa, what are you doing?' Her father had one foot on the bottom step leading up to the hayloft. 'I told you I'd do it. And I will. Now please go back in the warm.'

Henri Lefèvre took a step backwards. 'I know what you said but it's no job for a young girl. What sort of papa leaves the hard work to his daughter? It would be different if your brothers were here ...' Odile placed an arm around her father who was now visibly upset.

'I know, Papa.'

Monique Lefèvre appeared at the door. 'I couldn't stop him. He can hardly walk now because of the pain, and all I got was him shouting, telling me it was nothing to do with me.'

Odile gave her mother the sugar and bread she'd bought in Ville de Roi. She watched as she led her husband away, leaving Odile alone to deal with the airman. As she turned back into the barn, a loud rasping cough came from above, followed by a moan. Moments earlier and the pilot's cover would have been blown. With her hand on the bottle of "pink magic", as her mother called it, Odile went up the stone steps.

The airman raised himself up to sitting and attempted to smile at Odile.

'You came. I could hear voices down in the barn. I was so afraid whoever it was would come up here.'

Odile knelt down beside him and unscrewed the bottle. She poured the medicine onto a spoon and put it to his lips.

'Here, sip this. It should bring your temperature down.'

The airman did as she said, and the grimace he pulled on sipping the liquid made her smile as she remembered the taste.

'Awful, eh? But it will do the trick. I have brought you more water too, so keep drinking. The sooner you are well again, the sooner we can find you somewhere safer to hide. The Nazis are everywhere. It is only a matter of time until they come to the farm.'

The airman nodded. 'I know. And I must not put you and your family in danger. I'll be gone as soon as I gain my strength. How can I ever repay you, Odile?'

He took her hand and brought it to his lips. His hot lips on her skin made her jump.

Chapter Twenty-Five

Odile awoke to shouting and hammering on the back door. The thin, watery light of dawn trickled into the room. Odile rushed to the window and saw the yard behind the farmhouse filled with armoured vehicles and German soldiers.

'All right, I'm coming,' her father said as his footsteps clattered on the uncarpeted wooden stairs.

'We are here to search.' Several men, with guns poised, stood behind the soldier shouting his intentions at her father.

'Search for what? We have nothing for you here.'

The men barged into the house and Odile heard heavy footsteps coming up the stairs. She grabbed the coverlet and wrapped it around her. They spoke to each other in rapid German and one word jumped out at her. *Gefangene.* Prisoner. She became fixed to the spot and her heart hammered in her chest. How did they know about the airman? No one had been to the farm, and it was clear her father had no idea why they'd arrived there.

One soldier pushed open her bedroom door and she faced the end of a rifle. She screamed. 'What do you want?'

The man smirked at her and pulled away her coverlet. Odile felt exposed standing there in front of a total stranger in her flimsy chemise. She wrapped her arms around herself in an attempt to protect her modesty. The German sneered again. '*Schönes mädchen.*'

'Get out,' she said, her voice rising to a screech. 'Get out!'

The soldier opened the wardrobe, prodding the butt of the rifle through the hanging clothes. Next, he knelt to look under the bed. Odile's heart hammered in her chest as she prayed the bundle of leaflets would not be visible through the bed springs.

'*Nichts*!' he shouted.

He picked up the coverlet from the floor and threw it at Odile. Leaving the room, he slammed the door behind him so that it rattled in its doorframe. The other soldiers had searched the other rooms and, from the sound of it, marched down the stairs one after the other. They'd found nothing, but Odile watched in terror as they made their way to the barn. She knew it was only a matter of minutes before the airman would be found. As she got dressed, she could hardly bear to think about what lay ahead for him if the stories of what the Nazis did to their prisoners of war were correct.

The double doors of the barn were wide open when Odile joined her parents in the yard.

'I don't know what they expect to find in there,' her father said.

Grey figures were turning everything over and the hay cart trailer was cleared of all the hay that Odile had helped pile carefully. Chickens flapped their wings in terror as they were disturbed from roosting on their perches, and the cacophony of noise seemed to spread panic all over the farm. The horses in the outhouses alongside the barn became unsettled and Odile rushed to talk soothingly to the two mares.

'It's all right, Chantilly, Fleur. *Restez calmes*.' She stroked both horses, one with each hand and, although her voice was soft, she felt the creatures' pulses racing and increasing. 'Papa, tell them to stop. The horses are terrified.'

Henri Lefèvre looked at his daughter, helpless and frightened for his family's safety as well as that of his animals. He shook his head. 'There is nothing in the barn,' he said.

The German, who appeared to be in charge and was referred to as Kurt by his fellow soldiers, began to walk up the stone steps to the loft.

'No!' Odile shouted. 'There is nothing up there either.'

Her father looked at her in dismay. Her outburst was enough to suggest that there was, and three other soldiers ran up the stairs to follow Kurt. The floorboards creaked their presence and Odile knew that her secret airman was done for.

She fell to her knees and placed her hands over her eyes. But then she heard the German voices begin shouting and ranting, understanding some of the angry words. It became obvious that the soldiers had found nothing and were frustrated that they'd been led on a wild goose chase. Her heartbeat slowed back down but she was also confused – *how had he managed to get away?*

The German in charge approached her, his eyes blazing. 'We will be back,' he said, spitting out the words like venom.

Odile backed away and turned her head. If only they knew how she and her *résistance* friends were foiling every plan these men were making. They would never give up. She would find the airman and persuade him to join them once he was well enough. It was only when she heard the sound of the Nazi vehicles' tyres crunching on the gravel yard as they reversed in haste that she went to her father.

He stood, clearly traumatised by what had just happened. 'You must tell me what all this is about. What were they looking for, Odile? They seemed convinced that something was in the hayloft. *Je ne comprends pas.*'

She knew that the time had come to confide in her parents that they were harbouring a British airman on their land. She didn't know how he had got away with it but she would look for him later; she just hoped he was somewhere safe. She led her father back into the farmhouse where her mother was looking out of the window, wringing her hands.

'*Maman*, Papa, there is something I have to tell you. You

know you have been hearing things coming from up in the hayloft, Papa? Well, there is a young airman up there. He is badly injured. He was in the plane that was shot down near Collinac you heard about, *Maman*. He did not die but now he has a fever.'

Monique Lefèvre gasped. 'But you have put us in danger, Odile. If the Germans find out we have been helping the enemy, we will be shot. I heard how angry they were just now. You must tell him he cannot stay.' Odile's mother started pacing back and forth. 'Henri, you agree with me, surely? He cannot be found here.'

Her father shook his head. 'The British are our allies, *chérie*. We cannot turn him over to the Nazis ...wherever he is.'

Odile's father hated the Germans. Until he had become too frail to go out on night raids for the *résistance*, he had been an active member. She knew he would never turn the British pilot in.

'Papa's right. We have to help him. You've heard what the camps are like, *Maman*,' she said. 'I have to go and find him. He can't have moved far. They didn't find him in the hayloft so he managed to stay hidden somewhere. I bought some of that awful pink medicine you used to give me, so let's hope it's started to work.'

She left her parents in the kitchen and began to look in the out-buildings, searching each one in turn. Nothing. It was obvious from the discarded and untidy array of implements and brushes the German soldiers had searched each one before her. Odile re-entered the barn and crept up the stone stairs to the hayloft. The door at the top of the steps was partially closed and she pushed it gently with her foot. There was no resistance, so she entered. Pale grey light bathed the loft space in silver and the door slammed behind her. She turned on her heel.

'*Monsieur*!' She ran over to him. He was leaning on an upside-down broom, which was acting as a crutch, and sweating profusely from the effort. Leading him back to the hay mattress, she felt the heat from his body against hers. The fever was still raging. 'Where did you hide? I thought they'd captured you,' she said, her voice shaking.

The young airman pointed at the far corner where the tarpaulin normally was piled. 'I'd noticed the wooden panels by the window were a different colour to the rest. I worked out that because the eaves didn't go right down to the floor there must be a sort of cupboard or storage either side of the window seat. When I checked the boards were loose and by removing five of the boards, I could squeeze into a hidden space. I just had to hope I could secure them and replace them from inside. And I could. I had hidden evidence of my airman's clothes in there so when I heard the commotion outside, I disappeared in case they came up here.'

'You're a genius. But what if you'd started coughing?'

'I'd be on my way to one of their camps, I should think.' The airman looked up at the ceiling. 'I think the Lord up there is looking out for me. I meant what I said, Odile. Once I can get this leg mended and get rid of the fever, I'll be gone. It's not fair to put you and your family in danger.'

Odile thought of her mother's words and pushed them to the back of her mind. 'You must stay as long as it takes for you to get well. My parents know about you now.'

'That is so kind.' He touched her cheek, tracing a finger along her jawline. She felt herself redden and tilted her head up towards his. They moved together as if to kiss, but then the British man pulled away.

'I'm so sorry, Odile. That was unforgivable. Taking advantage of your generosity. You look so beautiful when you show concern for me. Please forgive me for doing that.'

Odile touched his arm. 'There is nothing to forgive, Monsieur. I'll go now. I do not want Papa to look for me. I'll come back. You stay warm and try to keep drinking water.'

Back in her bedroom, Odile took a long time to drop off to sleep. She thought about the young airman and the feelings he'd stirred within her. She had wanted him to kiss her. Before Antoine, she'd only ever kissed one boy. During harvest time, Étienne from the neighbouring farm had chased her and a friend into the barn. It had been her he'd wanted, and he'd pinned her against the stone wall separating the horse's stalls. He'd kissed her so hard that her lips hurt and then he'd tried to force his tongue in. She'd vowed then that boys were not for her. She'd work hard and stay on the farm helping her papa. But all her friends talked about were boys; who they liked and what they wanted to do with them. Many of those boys were fighting for their country and some, she knew already, would not be returning home ... ever.

Antoine had changed all that. Like the handsome airman, he was not immature like they had been. He'd made a woman of her and when he'd kissed her, she'd wanted it to go on for ever. She knew it would be the same with the young pilot hiding in her barn. She closed her eyes and saw the airman's fair skin, his grey eyes and straight blond hair that had grown to reach his collar. How different he looked now from the dirty stranger hiding in the corner of the loft when she'd first set eyes on him. Two men, so contrasting to look at, who made her heart race in different ways. Antoine, with the smouldering brown eyes and black curls, and now the British man, with the blond hair and unusual shade of grey eyes.

Chapter Twenty-Six

As the weeks passed, Odile and her parents cared for the British airman. His leg improved, not as serious as they first thought, and the wounds on his face and head had healed. He had even started to help Odile with the running of the farm. He was particularly fond of rounding up the animals on horseback.

'You are a very good horseman,' said Odile, when he returned from one ride. 'You must have owned one yourself before the war, I think.'

The young man put his hand to his head, clearly trying to force himself to remember.

'Perhaps. I love being with Fleur and Chantilly. I always feel calm after being with them. Often at night in the darkness, I wake up terrified, soaked in sweat and my heart hammering from horrible nightmares. Once awake, I can't remember what happened ...'

Odile reached over to him and touched his arm.

'I do remember bailing out of a plane. I had this searing pain on the side of my head. I was surrounded in parachute silk. For a moment, I thought it was a shroud and I was dead.' His laugh was hollow.

'You must not joke about this, *mon ami*.'

His face became serious.

'You are a British airman, *bien sûr*. News of the crash reached the village. A Spitfire fighter. Maurice, my neighbour, was on the scene very quickly. He saw you drop from the sky. He drove over the field to see if he could help but he could do nothing. You had disappeared.'

He proceeded to tell her what he could remember, about hiding in the wood surrounding the farm until it got dark, how he befriended the farm dog, coaxing him not to bark and give him away when he approached the farmhouse.

'I remember squeezing in through the barn doors. The smell of cows and cow dung told me it was a cowshed too. I felt the side wall with my hand. In the darkness, I was relieved to find steps. Something told me if I could only get up to the top there may be a loft to hide in, a hayloft maybe.'

Odile squeezed his arm. 'And you were right. We will get you well, and when it is safe, we will get you back home. Someone is probably very worried about you.'

Odile and her *résistance* friends had repatriated a number of servicemen from the Allied Forces. But not one with no memory ... and not one as handsome as him. She dismissed the thought as selfish. He was someone's son, someone's brother, someone's friend. But what if he was also someone's lover?

Although he was getting stronger by the day, even a short ride over the fields exhausted him. He went up the stone steps in the barn and lay on his mattress to recover. Odile had told him that her parents had said he was welcome to join them in the house, but he didn't want to put them in any more danger than they already were, he'd said.

'But you are happy to work on the land for us,' Odile protested.

'Yes, but to *live* in the house is not what a casual worker would do, is it?'

Instead, she and her father had moved the cows to another cowshed and used the barn for farm machinery now. The barn had been cleaned and upstairs swept of years of dust and sawdust. They'd supplied him with thick blankets and bolsters after padding a mattress with extra hay.

'Papa says you are to have this.' Odile handed him a small bedside table and an oil lamp. 'And this is from me. My friend, Lucien, gave it to me to learn some English words if we help the Allies. There is a section about how we say things in Normandy and Brittany. Perhaps it will help you sound more like us.'

The airman's face broke into a smile. 'I don't know how I can thank you. This is getting more like my home every day ... or what I imagine to be my home. And this book is so helpful. I will be talking like a local in no time.' He chuckled but then his face changed.

Odile sat beside him on the bed. 'What is it? You look as if you have seen a ghost?'

'It's nothing. It's just ... this image of sitting in rows in a huge hall lined with wood panelling looking at a book full of French words flashed into my head. French poetry, I think. Baudelaire. It's gone now. I don't think French poetry will help convince the Boche I am a local farmer hand, do you?'

They both laughed. Odile was fascinated by this man and wanted to know more about him.

'I will leave you now. I'm going to cycle into Ville de Roi. You know the *résistance* group I talk to you about? I'm meeting them to arrange a leaflet drop this evening. We know now that the Boche is going to all the farms. They're looking for prisoners like you so we must stay ahead of the game. I'm going to tell them about you. Will you be happy about this?'

He nodded. 'Yes, of course. I just wish this leg would let me join you. Anything I can do to help the movement, please let me know. I will study your book when you are away.'

'*Au revoir, mon ami.* Perhaps we should give you a French name and once you've worked on your French accent, not even the German soldiers will guess our new farm hand is not from Normandy. We can get you a forged identity card. No one can go anywhere without one.'

'A brilliant idea. I'm not leaving anytime soon. From now on I shall be ... Charles.'

Odile smiled. 'Why Charles?'

'It was the first name that popped into my head.'

Odile stood and kissed him on both cheeks. 'Charles Lefèvre. My cousin from Brittany. Come to join us on the farm to help his sick uncle Henri. How does that sound? See you soon. *À bientôt.*'

Odile began the cycle ride into Ville de Roi. She enjoyed the time alone to sort out her thoughts. It was good the airman now had a name. Much as she was enjoying helping Charles back to health, she knew she was taking a great risk and putting the whole family in danger. Since Pierre had been killed, she knew first-hand the brutality that could be inflicted at the hands of the Boche.

Tears filled her eyes when she thought of her handsome brother and how much in love he and Colette had been before this awful war had come to wreck their lives. He'd been fearless in the *résistance*, but it had cost him his life. She smiled when she thought of their little daughter, now six years old and living in safety in Switzerland with her other grandparents. Away from the danger in the north of France where the atrocities had shocked the French people.

The morning air was cool and fresh as she cycled along the narrow road into open countryside. Today she couldn't see the landmark castle standing proud on the water's edge. A shimmery mist over the sea gave an ethereal character to the vista that became the horizon. So many ghosts of people lost in this senseless war. She swallowed a lump that had formed in her throat. It didn't discriminate between different nations, different religions or those in different classes of society; all had lost loved ones in the trail of one man's blitz on society to achieve his ambition. She increased her pedalling. *Well, he's not going to invade this corner of France.*

Odile looked at the pretty Norman town as she cycled up the hill. The river that played an important part in the comings and goings of the *résistance* emptied into the bay below Ville de Roi. In the dead of night, small groups would travel to land further upstream, planting mines and explosives near where the Germans had taken over farm after farm in the French countryside. Once the *résistance* fighters knew all the French were well away from the farms they'd once owned, they carried out a reign of terror on the Germans. They threw grenades into barns, burned down hayricks and set alight vehicles parked in the lanes outside. The roads were searched after every incident but the *résistance* had slipped back safely and secretly to their own homes.

On the edge of the town, there was a cobbled walkway dotted with benches, where people used to watch the world go by. It was here that she'd said a last goodbye to Antoine. She remembered the passion in the way he kissed her as if he knew he wouldn't see her again. It was on one of the raids that he was shot by a Nazi as he fled from a farmhouse near Collinac. News had travelled fast and she remembered being woken in the dead of night to be told of her lover's death.

Chapter Twenty-Seven

'*Guten morgen, fräulein.*' A deep voice brought Odile out of her thoughts. The German she now knew was called Kurt stood astride his motorbike. 'You don't have work on the farm today? You seemed a little flustered when we called.'

Odile had dismounted her bicycle so she could walk the rest of the way up the road. Now she tightened her grip on the handlebars. 'I have shopping to do for my father,' she said. 'I don't remember being flustered. Being raided by you and your soldiers is becoming a regular occurrence round here.' She glared at the tall blond man with the piercing blue eyes. He seemed to get the message and carried on his way.

Her pulse raced as she hurried on to the main square and found a place to park her bike. As with many towns in this area of France, stylishly sculpted statues of French generals adorned the well-kept gardens which were central to the town. Shops with large display windows were tucked under apartments built from grey stone. Buildings with turrets and spires, clad in charcoal-grey slate, edged the central square. One building in the centre of the row had two Nazi swastika flags flying where the French *Tricolores* had once been.

The meeting room for the *résistance* members was down a narrow street off to the left. Odile looked around her to check that she wasn't being followed, but Kurt the Nazi was nowhere to be seen. The wooden doorway showed signs of neglect; paint was peeling away where sun and rain had left their marks. She pressed her finger on the brass doorbell, and a voice came across the intercom.

'*Oui?*'

'*Cygne noir*. Odile.'

The door buzzer told her she could enter.

Her footsteps echoed as she walked up the steps. She tapped on the door at the top of the stairs. '*Entrez*.' The voice was Lucien's, the leader of the local group there in Ville de Roi.

The air was heavy with the smell of strong *Gauloises* cigarettes.

'Sit down, *chérie*. Do you have them?'

Odile nodded. She undid the buttons on her dark green serge coat and brought out a thick pile of leaflets she'd secreted in the large hidden pocket sewn into the lining.

'Five hundred, like you said,' she said. 'You know I found a British airman hiding in the barn?'

The rest of the men around the table had obviously not heard by the way they started commenting amongst themselves.

'*Silence*!' said Lucien.

You could hear a pin drop. 'That is why I haven't been here for a while,' explained Odile. 'I wanted to check no Germans were watching the farm. They seem to have been satisfied by the raid when the pilot hid in a secret cupboard in the hayloft. But we know they are not to be trusted. The good news is that he is much recovered and has started helping on the farm. He speaks some French and is now called Charles Lefèvre, my cousin from Brittany.'

There was laughter from around the table.

'Are you sure you can rely on him, Odile? We cannot risk this raid that is coming up next week. It cannot fail. Reports are that more Germans are progressing across the north of France. It's just a matter of time and the Boche will be ruling us completely here. This has to work.'

Odile's throat constricted.

'I give you my word, Monsieur Lucien. I need you to get a *carte d'identité* for Charles. I will do it for Antoine.'

With that, all the men around the table stood and clapped. '*Bravo. Pour Antoine.*'

Odile smiled through a mist of hot tears. She had no option but to continue her part in resisting the Germans.

'*Au revoir.*'

Odile completed her shopping and filled the pannier on her bike with groceries, so that if she met the slimy Kurt on her journey back, he would have no reason to be suspicious. She thought of Charles, still hidden away on the farm and lucky not to have been discovered. It felt strange calling him that, but it would be better to get used to it sooner than later. What would he think about what she was going to do? More appeasing the Boche.

Her stomach churned when she thought about it. *But if it saved this little corner of France, it would be worth it*, she reasoned.

Charles was waiting for Odile when she returned. She could tell by the way that he was pacing the floor of the barn that something had happened. 'What is it?' she said.

'The German. Kurt. He returned. He was shouting at your father and I heard your mother scream. I kept hidden in the loft. I did not want to make it worse for them. It doesn't feel right that I couldn't help.' His face was white.

'You did the right thing. If the Nazis had found you here, they would have killed everyone. Stay here and I'll see to my parents.'

She dashed across to the farmhouse and saw that the front door panels were splintered and entry had been forced. Her mother's sobs echoed into the hallway, and when she entered the main living room her mother held the lifeless looking body of her father in her arms. Blood from a wound on his temple dripped down, pooling to make a large stain on his waistcoat.

'*Maman*!' Odile screamed, rushing over and feeling her father's neck for a pulse. 'What happened? Charles said it was the big Nazi, Kurt.'

Her mother helped Odile lay her father on the floor, placing a cushion under his head.

'It was terrible. He broke in and started beating your father. He hit him there with the butt of his rifle,' she said, pointing to her father's temple from where the blood was seeping. 'He said he had proof we were helping the *résistance*. Said we would be punished for not giving in to the German rule.'

Odile's arms puckered in goosebumps as she realised it was *her* not the British airman who was the cause of such brutality.

Henri Lefèvre moaned. He was coming round.

'*Dieu merci!*' Odile's mother grabbed her daughter's arm. 'Henri, you are safe now. Odile is back.'

Odile asked her father if he was feeling all right to sit up and then stand. She led him to the armchair next to the open fireplace. 'Sit quietly, Papa. *Maman*, please get Papa a small glass of cognac for the shock.'

Odile bathed the wound on the side of her father's head. It was not as serious as she thought but the bruising was already starting to show. The damage that could have been done did not bear thinking about

'There. Does that feel better? *Merci, Maman*. Sip this, Papa, and sit there. You must not try to get up. That monster could have killed you.'

She pushed a clenched fist into an open palm. It was clear she had to be more careful. Kurt must have followed her and then driven straight to the farm to terrorise her parents. Did the German know that she did more than help deliver leaflets? Her *maman* and papa must never know the secret she shared only with Lucien, the *résistance* leader.

Each Thursday night she attended the *danse sociale*, at the aptly named *Club Jeudi*. Dressed in a blonde wig, she became Babette and entertained the German soldiers who packed the bar. Her time was bought by officers who, when well plied with red wine, would be happy to tell her their plans for the coming weeks. Her job then was to report to Lucien. Usually, it was nothing more than sitting on an officer's knee and, asking the right questions, to listen when his tongue loosened and gave away German secrets.

She thought back to the one time when it nearly all went wrong. An officer, Gustav, became very familiar and his hands started to wander. His breath smelt of garlic and red wine and he forced his mouth onto hers. She bit down hard on his bottom lip. He yelled as she pulled away, leaving him holding his face. He slapped her hard and dragged her out into the street. Not one of the other soldiers came to her aid. The music played on, the raucous laughter became more shrill and the thick *Gauloises* cigarette smoke followed them out into the night air. He brought his mouth down onto hers again, forcing his tongue between her lips. Odile struggled and tried to push him away. He grabbed her red satin dress and tore it off her shoulder, exposing bare skin. Then he flung her against the wall of the building. She felt the stone scrape her flesh. She dug her nails into his cheeks as hard as she could and dragged them down causing him to release his grip.

'*Aidez-moi*. Someone help!'

'No one will hear you, you bitch. You might as well give me what I want,' said Gustav, wiping the blood from his face. 'I can tell you want it too. Just playing hard to get.'

He ripped the front of her dress and forced himself on her there in the street.

Part of her died that night and she hadn't returned to the group for several months afterwards. Every night she relived the pain, the humiliation and above all what she felt was a betrayal of Antoine.

Why had she started again? Why had she ever rejoined the *résistance*? When news came through about Antoine's death, she knew she had to fight in his name. She made sure she never got too close to individuals from then on. She sang on the small raised stage and sat with groups of soldiers, choosing different tables to sit at each week. She reported any information she picked up from the German soldiers' drunken loose talk to Lucien at their next meeting and she never had to endure what she'd experienced with Gustav again.

Charles became stronger each day and, with the help of Odile, his French accent continued to improve in leaps and bounds.

'I know you can't remember, Charles, but you must have studied French in your past life to learn the language so quickly, bien sûr. You speak very fast. Very correct. We just need to work on those Normandy and Brittany sayings now. To sound like a local man.'

Before the crash was now referred to as a "past life" and a little joke between them. He had begun working regularly on the farm and had ventured into Ville de Roi, too. He would act as a look-out for the grey uniforms of the Germans and let Odile know when it was safe to walk down the street to the meeting room.

Although she wanted more than friendship, and she was convinced that he did too, she knew that they could only ever be friends; each one helping the other. It would not be long before Charles left, but until then he would continue to be part of the *résistance* cause. He was accepted by Lucien and the group while they planned his safe return to Britain. For now, she would enjoy his company and fight the cause that meant so much to them both.

Chapter Twenty-Eight

1963, Rural mid-Wales

'Is that better, Mother?'

I drew the heavy brocade drapes partly across the bay window as she'd requested. It made the bedroom cool and gloomy, even though it was a sunny day outside. I poured a glass of water from the jug on her bedside table and held the crystal tumbler to her parched lips. Her snow-white hair appeared to merge into the starched *broderie anglaise* pillowcase so that all I saw lying propped up against the padded headboard was a grey, gaunt face, with hollow eyes staring back at me. A lump formed in my throat and my eyes burned as I tried to stop the tears from falling. She didn't look like my mother at all. Gone were the plump cheeks on which she'd always dabbed on her powdered rouge, and her lavender-grey eyes no longer twinkled.

'Thank you, my dear.' Her voice was weak and barely audible. 'You've been such a good daughter to me.'

'There now, don't try to talk.'

I took my mother's bony hand and stroked it gently, tracing the raised blue-grey veins with my fingers. Poor Mother. I was the only child she had left now. I glanced over at the photograph of the brother I never knew. From an ornate silver frame on the bedside table, a proud smiling man in uniform with light-coloured hair and pale eyes remained forever young.

Edmund was my older brother. Like me, he'd studied French at university and would have stayed in academia if war had not been declared. He'd wanted to fight for his country and left for RAF training before I was born. My mother had been informed that his plane had been shot down somewhere over northern France, but his body had never been found. All I knew of him was from this photo and other sepia and black-and-white photographs displayed around the house; him as a baby, him as a young boy playing with Nanny M. and her brother, and photos of him as a very handsome and dashing young man. I often used to daydream about the young debutantes all falling for him. After that telegram arrived, they said Mother was never the same.

I didn't understand what she meant when she sometimes referred to me as her third child. But then M. took me to one side and told me about Marjorie and how she'd died in the nursery where I'd been brought up after contracting scarlet fever.

I knew that my mother's life was almost at an end; they'd called me home from university to be with her. I'd made arrangements to defer the rest of the term until next year when my head would be in a better place to take my finals. M. had summoned the doctor and Mother had taken to her bed.

Now, her eyes were closed and a faint smile crept along her thin lips. 'It's time for me to meet ... Edmund and Charles ... again. And baby Marjorie.' A silent tear escaped from the corner of her eye and trickled on to the pillow, forming a damp spot on the starched cotton.

'No, Mother. Please. I still need you. You can't go. You'll get better. I know you will.'

But deep down, I knew she wouldn't. Her time had come and I felt bereft, panicking that the parent who'd always been there for me was dying.

She squeezed my hand, and with her other she beckoned me to come closer, her voice now barely a whisper.

'It's all yours … you'll be looked after. Don't listen to …'

But with that, my mother took her last breath. I was alone. I buried my head in the counterpane beside her and sobbed. When I'd composed myself, I rang the bell and the portly Elsie Pugh, who had worked at the Court since before I was born, entered the room, followed by the young kitchen maid, Sara. They gently pulled me away.

'It's all right, Miss Clara. We'll see to her ladyship now. You go downstairs. I'll get someone to call Nanny M. for you.'

Sara led me away, and I took one last glance behind me. Elsie was pulling up the sheet to cover my mother's face. She was gone in my eyes, replaced by a corpse resting under a shroud.

A howl from deep inside me shattered the air, and the young maid put her arm around me as we descended the stairs into the kitchen where she made me a cup of hot, sweet tea.

'For the shock, Miss Clara,' said Sara. 'My mam always says you must have tea when summ'at like this 'appens.'

I needed Nanny M.

I heard Elsie's voice echo in the hallway as she made a vital telephone call.

'Yes, Doctor. Her daughter, Clara, was with her when she passed but she's been failing for days as you know. Yes, if you could. We can then inform the undertakers. Thank you. No, just young Miss Clara.'

Elsie entered the kitchen and sat beside me at the table. 'Are you feeling a bit better after the tea, Miss Clara? I know you've had a terrible shock but your mother is at peace now, in a better place.'

She patted my hand and I drew it away. *How did she know that? How could my mother leave me all alone?*

'The doctor is on his way. Once he signs a death

certificate and gives the cause of death, you can start to plan the funeral.'

'How can I do that? I don't know what to do!'

'I know it's hard, my dear. But we'll help you. I'm sure Nanny M. will get here soon. I've sent Sara to get her.'

I closed my eyes, but all I saw was my mother's face draining of colour and her lips becoming an ink-blue. I'd never seen a dead body before.

The door burst open and Nanny M. rushed over to me, pulling me up and hugging me tight.

'Oh, my poor baby. I'm so sorry you were all alone when she passed, cariad.'

The warmth of her *cwtch* reassured me that maybe I would be all right after all.

M. looked at Elsie. 'I don't suppose anyone has informed Mr Edgar that his sister has passed away. He should be told. Thank you, Elsie.'

It was M. I wanted, not some cold-hearted distant uncle I'd only just met.

I didn't realise how much I'd miss my mother. After all, Nanny M. had brought me up and done all the things like bedtimes and bath times when I was little. I can remember her being more of a mother to me than a nanny. She'd been there in the night when I'd had bad dreams about monsters and bogeymen, and it was her I went to when I fell over and cut my knees when out playing. Her magic cream always worked wonders. But Mother was always there in the background, and when I'd gone to boarding school and spoken to my friends there, I came to realise that she was no different to their mothers. It was just the way it was. I considered myself lucky; I had two mothers.

Before the funeral, I started to spend hours alone in Mother's bedroom. It reminded me of the evenings when

I was a little girl, when I'd spent an hour with her before Nanny M. took over the bedtime routine. Sometimes when I was up there, a waft of strong rose perfume would fill my nostrils, and I'd turn expecting to see her standing behind me in her immaculately cut suit ready to go to a Rotary Ladies' event in the nearby town, her fair hair expertly coiffed and her lavender-grey eyes twinkling. And then my spirits would sink, knowing that I'd never see her again.

One afternoon, I was sorting through some of her things. The antique chest of drawers was pushed against the far wall opposite the window. Mother had told me that the chest was mid-Victorian, and the servants were instructed to polish it with a lavender wax polish which they rubbed in as a ritual every Tuesday morning. It had been crafted in a beautiful rosewood, and marquetry inlays added to the edges of each drawer gave the piece an added sense of opulence. I also recalled Mother telling me it was a family heirloom that had been passed on to the eldest daughter of each generation, so now, I supposed, the chest was mine. Each drawer was lined with paper, and my mother's clothes lay on top, neatly folded; one with her underclothes, another with her signature fine silk blouses. The bottom drawer was full of unopened toiletries, and tucked at the back was a small jewellery box.

I picked up the ornate silver box, placed it on the table by the bay window and sat on the chair. When I opened the lid, music tinkled a familiar tune that brought a lump to my throat. It was a lullaby my mother used to sing to me. I took out each piece of jewellery and laid them all on the table – rings, bracelets, strings of pearls, brooches and an exquisite gold wristwatch. I turned the watch over and read the message inscribed on the back. *With much love, Charles, 1925.*

My father had died when I was three years old. My

mother had told me stories about him, and I'd seen many photos, but for all of the life I could remember, it had just been Mother and me. And M., of course.

I started to put the jewellery back in the box when I noticed a tiny loop on one side of the plum-coloured velvet base. I pulled it up to reveal a secret compartment, and inside was a folded handwritten note. *Please look after her. I know you will do the right thing. I love her so much.* The handwriting looked vaguely familiar, but I couldn't think where I'd seen it before ...

Chapter Twenty-Nine

I returned the note to the compartment in the box. *What could that be about?* I was distracted from my thoughts by a knock at the door. It was Elsie.

'Miss Clara, there's someone to see you.'

I quickly put everything back in the jewellery box, leaving it on the chest of drawers.

It was the undertaker and his assistant. Elsie had taken them into the drawing room, and they turned to face me when I entered.

'Thank you, Elsie. Perhaps you'd kindly bring some tea for my guests?'

'Right you are, Miss Clara.' She left the room closing the door behind her.

'Good morning, Miss Pryce. Or perhaps I should call you Lady Clara now.' The tone of his voice appeared to be more of a sneer than a genuine inquiry.

'Good morning, Mr Owen. I haven't met with my mother's solicitors yet to discuss anything. In any case, I won't inherit her title.'

The tall, thin man opposite me pursed his lips as if he didn't approve of the possibility of having to call somebody like me "her ladyship" in future. 'I'm sorry for your loss. Your dear late mother instructed us to conduct her funeral in the same manner she arranged for Sir Charles, so it's all arranged.'

How dare he? What if I want to have a say in the funeral I have for my own mother? Oh, I wish M. was here. I glared at the man. 'Please sit down. Ah … here's the tea now. Thank you, Elsie.'

As I saw Elsie back to the door, I asked her quietly to get Nanny M. to come to the drawing room.

'Mr Owen. I'd like to go over the details with you myself. My father's funeral was eighteen years ago. I was very young, so obviously I know nothing about that.' My heart raced, and I hoped that I sounded more composed than I felt. I'd never even been to a funeral, let alone arranged one. 'I want this funeral to reflect the wonderful woman my mother was, not be a replica of the one held for a man I hardly knew.'

Mr Owen's mouth dropped open and he glanced at his companion. 'I'm afraid your mother gave specific instructions when I visited her just a few weeks ago. She was very ill then and knew it had to be organised before she deteriorated further.'

I felt tears welling in my eyes.

'I think she was trying to spare you all this, Miss Pryce,' said the assistant. He, at least, had kind eyes and looked at me with sympathy.

That did sound like my mother, but I needed to know the funeral would be right for her and reflect the type of person she really was; the good she did in the village community, how kind she was and how I idolised her. I'd already started looking at readings and poems together with favourite hymns.

There was a knock at the door. It was then that Elsie led Nanny M. into the room, and I immediately felt better and more confident.

'Mr Owen. This is Miss Mary-Ann Beynon, and I'd like her to be here when we discuss the funeral I want for my mother. First of all, let's look at dates.'

A slate-grey sky greeted me and the rest of the mourners as we emerged from Cefn Court. The weather definitely seemed to reflect the feelings of the funeral party. I was dressed head to toe in mourning black as Nanny M. had advised and felt very strange.

'But it doesn't feel right, M. Of late, Mother had come to love brighter colours,' I'd told her.

'I know, *cariad*. But it wouldn't be right. It's what everyone expects. Tradition, like.'

I knew she had a point so, after my initial protest, I'd gone to Credenford with her to buy my first black coat and chosen a black corduroy Baker Boy hat; a style I knew was now very fashionable in London. I appraised myself in the long cheval mirror in my mother's bedroom before joining the rest of the family and was taken aback by how old I looked. *At least you look as if you could run the manor now. No longer a slip of a girl still in university.* I thought of the fun my friend Diana and I had shopping for trendy, bright-coloured clothes in the King's Road boutiques. We'd go in the evenings when the main shops had closed, listen to the loud music and sip the free drinks.

Everyone was at the funeral, including a lot of people I'd never seen before; long-lost relatives coming out of the woodwork, all hoping for a slice of the family fortune no doubt.

My mother's brother, Edgar, was waiting for me at the base of the steps. Along with my aunt Eliza, I'd only met him in the recent weeks when he'd suddenly started visiting my mother. He'd always insisted on speaking with his sister alone, leaving me with that awful woman. Mother had always appeared distressed after his visits and I could understand why after speaking with him.

'It's time, Clara. Come with me to the funeral car. Aunt Eliza and your cousin Georgina are waiting for you. I shall walk behind the coffin with the other gentlemen,' he said, in a cold, matter-of-fact manner.

'Where's Nanny M.?'

'She'll be somewhere with the rest of the estate workers, I presume. That's one of the things that's going to change around here. Now come along, my dear. We don't want to be late.' He sighed impatiently and pulled out his gold pocket watch from his waistcoat.

My heart raced. *What could he mean?* Nanny M. *had* to be with me. I hardly knew these people. I scanned the servants lined up along the drive and couldn't see her anywhere. I got into the back seat of a gleaming black limousine courtesy of the funeral directors.

Cousin Georgina hardly acknowledged me and Aunt Eliza just nodded. If not M., how I wished Diana could have been there with me for support. We'd met the first term in university in the same halls of residence. She was a year ahead of me and we'd been inseparable ever since.

The cortège moved slowly along the long drive, down to the lane which led from the Court to St Mary's Church. I could see the hearse in front of the group of men, every one of them dressed in black overcoats and wearing black bowler hats, all marching solemnly. It was as if they were in uniform and belonged to a mysterious sect dragged in to perform their duties. The mahogany coffin, a deep red-brown wood with brass handles, was as Nanny M. and I had chosen. In every window of the hearse was a wreath of flowers. I'd chosen deep red roses because I knew how much my mother loved their heady perfume.

We arrived, and I watched as six of the procession moved forward and raised the coffin onto their shoulders before walking slowly through the open doors of the village church.

Be careful, I wanted to shout as we followed, with me leading the mourners. *My mother is in that box.*

And that was when it hit me. Inside that wooden coffin lay my mother's lifeless body. I began to sob. Aunt Eliza gripped my elbow a little too firmly. 'Pull yourself together, for goodness sake. The likes of our family don't make a spectacle of themselves.' This woman I hardly knew glared at me, and I took out my lace handkerchief and dabbed my eyes before I reached the chancel steps.

Georgina looked my way and rolled her eyes, leaving me in no doubt that my reaction was not the done thing. As I neared the front of the congregation, I saw Nanny M. sitting with Elsie and the rest of the staff from Cefn Court. She smiled as I looked at her, and I knew then she'd be with me every step of the way.

When we emerged from the church for the burial, rain was falling in torrents. The mourners were shielded by big black umbrellas, resembling an army of mysterious shelled insects moving slowly in convoy towards a deep gaping hole in the churchyard.

By then, Nanny M. had joined me, and she stood by my side as I threw in a handful of earth before the rest of the family. *Ashes to ashes, dust to dust.* As I walked away, she placed an arm around my shoulder and I heard Uncle Edgar tut his disapproval as we passed.

'He hadn't been near for years. Until she was dying. He only came to see Mother, his *sister*, in the last month. Now he arrives and takes over. It's not what she would have wanted, Nanny M.'

'Don't upset yourself, *cariad*. He'll be gone soon and then you can get on with running the Court as your mother wanted you to.'

I thought for a moment and remembered something he'd said earlier about how there were going to be changes around here. I sensed the hairs on the back of my neck standing up and suddenly felt very uneasy. The reading of the will was organised to take place in a week's time. Mother had always said if anything happened to her, she'd leave everything in trust for me until I was twenty-one. I'd celebrated that milestone in January this year.

As we walked through the kissing gates back to the limousine, I spotted a woman I didn't recognise standing at the far side of the church tower. She was dressed head to toe in black, and her dark hair was dragged back into an elegant French pleat. When she saw me looking, she ducked out of sight.

'Who was that, M.?' For no reason, I shivered, not with cold but with something like foreboding.

'I've never seen her before. But she clearly didn't want us to see her,' said M., linking her arm through mine. 'Probably just somebody who came along with a family member for support. Nothing to worry about, I'm sure.'

But I couldn't. I knew the woman had been watching us in secret, and something about that didn't feel right.

Chapter Thirty

It was another gloomy, grey day when we assembled around the long mahogany dining table, awaiting the arrival of my mother's solicitor. Uncle Edgar and Aunt Eliza sat in silence opposite me and avoided eye contact. They'd been strangers for years, but in the last few weeks had invaded every area of my living and thinking. Never had I felt so alone. If only Nanny M. could have been with me, but that was out of the question according to my uncle.

There was a knock on the door.

'Enter.' My uncle's voice boomed before I had a chance to reply.

'Mr Gibson, Miss Clara,' said Elsie.

'Thank you, Elsie. Good morning, Mr Gib—'

Before I could greet the solicitor, my uncle had rushed to shake his hand. 'Please, Winston. I've put you at the head of the table.'

Mr Gibson made his way to his place before producing a pile of papers from his leather briefcase.

'Good morning. You all know the reason for my visit, and I shall not waste any time.'

Uncle Edgar exchanged glances with my aunt and smiled. There was something about the knowing look that made me feel uneasy. Surely, as I was her only surviving child, Mother's estate would be very clear-cut?

The solicitor continued. 'I have here the last will and testament of the deceased, Lady Delia Pryce. I shall read it to you:

I, Lady Delia Marjorie Pryce née Watkins, am of sound mind and leave Cefn Court and its surrounding estate to be shared equally between any surviving children, Edmund Charles Pryce, and my daughter, Clara Delia Pryce. Until such day that she is twenty-one years of age, Clara's part will be held in trust for her by the solicitors who are dealing with my affairs. At the time of writing, Edmund Charles Pryce is missing in action, feared dead. In the event that he is officially declared to be deceased, his part of the estate will be inherited by his sister, Clara Delia Pryce.

I leave the sum of £500 to Miss Mary-Ann Beynon for her services as nanny to my daughter and her continued support to me. I leave each member of staff—'

Before Mr Gibson could finish the reading, my uncle stood up and banged his hand of the table, causing everything to rattle from the force.

'That's not her *last* will. That is preposterous. My sister would not have left everything to *her*. As for her son, he's been dead for years! When was that dated? She assured me that the estate would be left to me! She's not even family.' He pointed at me, and for a moment I thought he was going to attack me. My aunt remonstrated with him to sit down. The venom in his words alone made me flinch.

The solicitor became flustered and assured my uncle that he had overseen the writing of the will himself and those were my mother's wishes.

'Huh! Haven't you received my sister's most recent will?' Uncle Edgar stood again, his voice raised. 'My solicitor was supposed to have sent it to you in time for today's meeting. He and I witnessed and dated it just a month ago. It overrules anything in that one you're holding, Gibson.'

I couldn't listen anymore. I rushed out of the room and nearly bumped into Elsie who had obviously been listening at the door.

'Where's Nanny M.?' I asked.

'I'm here, *cariad*. I made sure I was close by just in case that man caused any trouble. You said he'd been unkind to you since your mam died.'

The warmth of her *cwtch* was just what I needed.

'He claims Mother changed her will. She left everything to him! He said I wasn't family.' I noticed Nanny M. and Elsie exchange glances. 'He's lying. Baby Marjorie and Edmund are both dead, so I'm her only child.' I sobbed until there were no tears left.

The sound of voices in the hallway echoed. 'This isn't the end of it, my man. Call yourself a solicitor, ignoring a legal document just because a rival lawyer was the one called to draw up my sister's final will? I shall contest it and produce evidence in court. You mark my words! That bastard girl will be out of here, just you wait and see. Cefn Court will become the rightful home of the Watkins family. Good day.' My uncle's deep voice ensured I heard every word.

'Perhaps you'd better see Mr Gibson out, *cariad*. I'll come with you. Let's see what happens now,' said Nanny M., her gentle voice soothing my turbulent mind.

I composed myself and walked out into the hallway.

'Ah, Clara, my dear. I'm so sorry you had to endure the unpleasant outburst and bad language from your uncle. I've received no such document from any other solicitor. If you come to my office tomorrow morning, we'll decide how to proceed from here.' Winston Gibson shook my hand. 'Shall we say 11 o'clock? And perhaps you'd like to bring someone with you. I felt you were very much on your own in the meeting that's just taken place.' He gave me a sympathetic smile and then left.

Nanny M. held my arm. 'It will be all right, *cariad*. I'm sure of it. Would you like me to be the one to come with you?'

I nodded. Now Mother had passed on, there was no one else I felt close to. M. had been with me throughout my childhood, had written to me every week when I was at boarding school and, if I was honest, had been more of a mother to me than Mother herself on occasions. I'd loved and respected my mother, of course, but what we had together was different to the closeness and warmth that M. provided. I'd had the best of both worlds.

The next day, the chauffeur took M. and me into Pen-y-rhos. He parked the maroon Daimler on the corner between the main street and the narrow road that housed one of the largest hotels in the town. The solicitor's office was situated at the end of the street. The car got some attention from the passers-by and was in stark contrast to the more modest Ford Cortinas and Austin 1100s parked around it.

The receptionist told us that Winston Gibson was expecting us and took us along a narrow passageway into a bay-windowed room overlooking the street. The solicitor stood when we entered the room.

'Good morning, ladies. Clara, my dear, I hope you've got over that awful scene yesterday. Are you happy that Miss Beynon remains in the room? I have been giving some thought to what Mr Watkins claimed and personal matters concerning your mother's conversations with me will be aired. I wonder if you want those shared with an employee?'

M. went to stand and I told her to sit down. 'Whatever you have to say, I'm happy for Nanny M. to hear it.'

'Very well. I didn't say anything in front of Mr and Mrs Watkins, but your mother anticipated that her brother would react the way he did. However, when she wrote the letter I'm going to show you, she hadn't written another will. I've yet to receive that, of course. She told me in confidence that the reason she and her brother had been estranged for many years is that he contested her own father's will when money was left to her. As the male heir, he felt he should have had everything. He begrudged her the modest amount of land adjoining the Watkins estate surrounding the lake by Rhaeadr Pen-y-rhos falls and a small boathouse bequeathed to her.'

M. took in a deep breath and steadied her hands.

'Are you all right, M.?' I asked. She nodded without looking at me.

Winston Gibson continued. 'He never spoke to your mother again. Until, it seems, she became very ill. We may have a problem if there is a second will.'

I looked at M. who looked as puzzled as me. 'What do you mean? Surely, the will was clear. She wanted me to inherit. You haven't received another will, have you? I'd never met my uncle until he started arriving to see my mother as she lay dying. Always insisting I had to leave the room. On one occasion, she rang her bell for someone to go to her. He'd upset her so much I had to ask him to leave. And then he tried to take over the funeral arrangements. Awful man!' My voice cracked.

M. took my hand and stroked it. 'Try not to get upset, *cariad*. Let's hear what Mr Gibson has to say.' She handed me a handkerchief and I dabbed my eyes.

The grey-haired man opposite opened his file and took out a cream vellum envelope exactly like the one that had contained my mother's will the day before. 'As I said, your mother anticipated that Mr Watkins would cause trouble for you and instructed me to give you this if that was the case, and *only* if that was the case. I don't know what's written inside. She told me this explains the reason for his objection and she insisted that we, as her executors, are to do everything we can by law to see that her wishes are carried out.'

My hand shook as I took the envelope from him. I slid my nail under the gummed seal, unfolded the letter and began to read.

My dearest Clara, I want you to know that your father and I loved you very much, even though he only had three years with you. When news came of your brother, Edmund, being missing in action, it was you who saw me through it. I was so proud of you when you got into one of the top London universities and know you will graduate with the highest honours as your brother did. Another fluent French speaker in the family!

But there is something I should have told you many years ago. Your uncle Edgar is right when he says that you are not my next of kin, that you are not family. You are only reading this if he has done that as I suspect he will. You see, my dearest, I have brought you up as my daughter but I did not give birth to you. You were left as a gift to me to bring up as if you were my own ...

I couldn't believe what I'd just read, and I crumpled up the letter and threw it across the room.

'What? What does she mean "left as a gift"?' I screamed. There was an intake of breath from both the solicitor and M. 'Where was I left? Surely she doesn't mean literally left ...?' I noticed M. shifting in her chair and gasped. 'Did you know about this, M.?' Her face drained to the colour of milk and tears filled her eyes. 'You did!'

'We were all sworn to secrecy,' she whispered, not making eye contact with me.

'Well, that's it. My life's been a sham.' I had to get out of there. I dashed out of the office, leaving M. and Mr Gibson open-mouthed.

I got into the waiting car. 'Take me back, please.' I said, and the chauffeur drove me home. Once inside the car, the tears that had been burning along my eyelids spilled over into wracking sobs. *A gift*, she said. *What a joke*. Why couldn't my mother say what I really was? A foundling!

Chapter Thirty-One

That night I lay awake listening to the grandfather clock in the hall below me strike every hour. I went back over things that had happened in my life, searching for clues that I wasn't who I thought I was. I thought back to what my mother had told me about the night baby Marjorie died after the initial explanation from Nanny M. The anguish in the way she related what happened took me to the scene as if I was there too. She'd woken to a blood-curdling scream that echoed along the landing. Knowing where it came from, she dashed out of her bedroom and burst into the nursery. She found a sobbing Agnes, the nanny at the time, clutching a bundle of white to her chest and pacing the floor.

Snatching the infant from Agnes, Mother knew her baby daughter was dead. The baby's cheeks were blotched with an angry red rash but around her mouth, the skin was pale, the lips blue and her skin already cold.

She'd relived the moment as if she was experiencing it there and then, tears pouring down here face.

As a child, I'd often woken to the noise of the rocking horse that was positioned in the corner of the nursery moving on its own. More often, it was M. who arrived at my bedside to comfort and reassure me I was having a bad dream, but on one occasion my mother came and told me it was most likely Marjorie wanting to play. For some reason, instead of frightening me, it reassured me to think I had a special friend. She always said how much I looked like her and Edmund. But how could that be if I wasn't related at all? And, really, who could do that to her own child? Leave a baby on the front step? I'd plucked up courage to read the note again. Whoever my real mother was had simply left me and rung the bell.

In the moonlight seeping through the curtains, I got out of bed and went to my mother's bedroom to retrieve the jewellery box. I took the note from its compartment and re-read what it said. Now it made sense. It was from my birth mother. *Please look after her. I love her so much.*

I'd always been conscious that my mother seemed old. How stupid could you get? Everyone else had known who I was apart from me. *The girl who was dumped.* No wonder she packed me off to boarding school and never invited other children to the Court to play with me. Afraid they'd spill the beans, no doubt. Only M. arranged for her friend Gwennie's children to visit. Uncle Edgar was right all along. His furious red face came into my mind. No wonder he was angry at his sister; she was leaving everything to a stranger. How could someone have rejected me and left me like a parcel on a cold doorstep? I lay there as silent tears fell, until sleep eventually came.

It all happened very quickly after that. Mr Gibson called in to inform me that in spite of him fighting for my mother's wishes to be adhered to, Uncle Edgar was contesting the will in a probate court and claiming his sister had changed her mind in the last month of her life. If there was a more recent will, it would mean that my uncle would inherit Cefn Court and the estate. The solicitor explained that he was under no obligation to gift Nanny M. or the other members of staff the small legacies as directed by my mother in her original will.

'I shall strongly advise him to do so and provide for you, my dear, but it will be up to him. I'm so sorry, Miss Clara. Your mother was adamant that she wanted everything to go to you. And of course, until the case is proved, you are entitled to remain here.'

'I won't stay. I'll move out.' I couldn't stop shaking. *Where would I go? What was I going to do?* 'But if she did want that, why did she write the letter about me not being her daughter? She could have kept quiet.' I couldn't stop the angry outburst.

'I think she wanted to protect you from all this coming out in a court case, but it will now anyway, I'm afraid. She knew her brother would stop at nothing until he got what he wanted.'

I started to cry and rang the bell for Elsie to see Mr Gibson out. He looked at me sympathetically as he left.

'Like I said, I'm so sorry, Miss Clara. News of this more recent will is as much of a shock to me as it is to you. I will do everything in my power to fight your uncle's claim.'

I watched from the bay window as he drove away. My heartbeat drummed in my chest as another car drew up in front of the main steps. A chauffeur in full uniform walked around to open the door for my uncle and aunt to get out. They hadn't wasted any time.

Elsie knocked on the door and entered. 'Mr Edgar and Mrs Eliza Watkins are here, Miss Clara.'

'Thank you, Elsie. Please tell Nanny M. to come.'

'Leave us, woman,' my uncle boomed as he barged in behind Elsie.

Elsie's face blanched and she scurried from the room as she was told.

'I hear that the truth is out and you know that this barn of a place will soon be proved as rightfully and legally mine. That ridiculous idea of my sister's that everything was going to you will be thrown out of court. Quite rightly.'

I clenched my fists so hard that my nails dug into my palms. My voice rose to a screech. 'She may not have been my birth mother, but I was a loving daughter to her and looked after her. More than anything you did as her brother. I'd never seen you until you knew she was dying.'

My aunt glared. 'And why do you think that was, you stupid girl? She was afraid we'd tell you the truth about your dubious start in life. You've already had more than you deserve from this family. Full time nanny. Boarding school education. And now one of the top university educations in the country. The harlot who gave birth to you must be laughing ...'

Before she could finish her tirade of vitriol, the drawing room opened and Nanny M. rushed to my side.

'That's enough. Clara has had a huge shock, and you're making things ten times worse. Lady Delia could not have loved this young woman any more than if she had given birth to her.'

My uncle towered over to Nanny M. 'How dare you speak to my wife like that? And you—' he said, glaring at me '—you have a matter of weeks to clear your things from this house and find somewhere else to live. My wife and I need to look around to see what needs doing and to make an inventory of what's here, and we don't need either of you getting in the way. The latest will *will* be proved valid.'

That was the last straw for me. I ran out of the room and upstairs to my bedroom, closely followed by M. Once inside, she took me in her arms and let me sob until there were no more tears left.

'What am I going to do, M.?' I choked out.

'Well, first things first. You *do* have somewhere to live if you're sure you want to leave. You must come and stay with me. I know it's very poky, not what you're used to, but you'll have your own room.'

I hugged her. 'Oh, thank you, M. I don't know what I'd do without you. That's what Mother used to say too.'

M. had never married. A few years back, she told me that she had loved someone once but he'd died in the war. Her father had worked on the estate until he was too frail to work as a hedger. M. had said it was as if he gave up living once he couldn't work any longer … and after the awful row between them. She hadn't elaborated on what the row was about, but her eyes misted with tears when she was talking. She'd had to find somewhere to live after their tied cottage was needed by the young man and his family who replaced him. She'd earned enough at Cefn Court to afford a two-up-two-down terrace next to the corner shop in the village. Mother had kept her on as one of the housekeepers once she wasn't needed as my nanny.

'I don't know what I would have done without Nanny M., Clara,' my mother had said. 'She was here to take over when that awful telegram arrived about Edmund. I don't know who was the more distraught. Her or me. You were just a baby and she made sure you were her priority. No matter how much I withdrew into my shell, she never gave up on me. In the end, she got me back to health. And then again when your father passed away.'

I often reflected on those words – and here Nanny M. was again, sorting out another Pryce family problem.

Chapter Thirty-Two

Even though in the eyes of the law I didn't have to leave straight away, I couldn't bear to stay. So certain that the second will would be proved valid, my departure was my uncle's opportunity to move into the Court.

Moving to the village went as smoothly as it could have done. It was obvious my uncle would be successful, so why prolong the agony? He was already making his presence felt. His instructions made it clear that no belongings from the house were to be removed. I did, however, take personal papers belonging to my mother and asked the current groom to fetch my beloved rocking horse and take it to M.'s. Mother had always told me that she'd bought it for Marjorie before she was born, and because I reminded her of the daughter she lost, I was to call it my own. It seemed to me to be a bond to the sister I never knew, and I was sure that the occasional spontaneous rocking in the middle of the night was Marjorie letting me know she was there. It was a struggle to get the horse up the narrow stairs. It nearly filled the room, but it was a part of my former life that I needed at that moment.

I settled into M.'s quite quickly. She had left Cefn Court as soon as my uncle and aunt moved in, but most of the other members of staff had stayed. M. was lucky enough to quickly find work in the shop next door helping Mrs Howells, the new owner. My plan was to stay in the village until term started again in September.

When sorting through my mother's things, I found letters from my brother, Edmund, written when he first joined the RAF. He kept mentioning "Mary-Ann", and it took me a while to work out who he was referring to. *Of course, it's Nanny M.!* I was still so used to using my childhood name for her. I found it slightly puzzling that he talked about her so much in his letters, but I was more struck by what a lovely man my brother seemed to be. I found myself feeling sad I'd never met him. It was obvious that he was a passionate horseman and his love for the horses, especially his own mare, Kenna, came across. It made me pleased I'd kept the rocking horse. I would think of it as a replica of my brother's horse.

I told M. about finding the letters and was surprised when she immediately tried to change the subject.

'He was obviously a very good horseman. I found medals and rosettes. There's even a photo of you riding a horse too! I didn't know you could ride, M.'

M.'s expression changed and I noticed a gradual flush travel up her neck.

'Let's make some tea, and I'll tell you something I should have told you a long time ago.'

For some unknown reason, my stomach flipped with a sense of unease. I watched as M. warmed the floral china teapot before spooning in the tea and pouring in boiling water. She laid a tray with an embroidered tray cloth and placed two cups and saucers on the tray. She seemed to be taking her time to do everything, and I noticed her hand shook as she poured.

'Be careful, M. You'll spill it.'

I took the tray and carried it into the front room where we sat on the settee. M. took a sip of tea, but then quickly put her cup down and looked straight at me. 'Clara, I want you to hear me out. Edmund was a wonderful horseman. He lived for horses. And, yes, I could ride too. My brother, Reggie, was Edmund's groom, and when he went off to war, I became the groom instead of him.'

'I didn't know that. I didn't think women did that sort of work back in those days.'

'Your father thought that too, but in the end it was Edmund who convinced him to give me the job. What I'm going to tell you next, I want you to remain calm. Clara, Edmund Pryce wasn't your brother ...' M. hesitated. 'He was your father. That's why you look so like him and baby Marjorie.'

I felt my eyes widen. 'What?' I gasped. 'Why was I left on the doorstep then? Why didn't he own up?'

M. took my hand. 'Because he didn't know about you. He'd left for his training before ...' She tailed off.

My heart thumped. *So, I'd been brought up by my grandparents?* I couldn't take it in and didn't know whether to be pleased or angry. I realised M. was talking again and tried to focus on what she was saying.

'So, you see, Lady Delia *did* leave her estate to a rightful heir if that was your uncle's objection. You are a blood relative.'

'Why didn't you say something in the meeting? You let my uncle rant and rave and never corrected him once. I'm surprised at you.' My voice rose and M.'s face crumpled. I'd gone too far. She hung her head.

'That's because I'm your mother, *cariad*,' she whispered.

I dropped my cup back into its saucer, spilling the tea. 'I don't believe you.' M. tried to take my hand, but I snatched it away. '*You*! You were the heartless ... *bitch* that dumped me on that freezing doorstep in the dead of night?' I couldn't take it. I ran up to my room and flung myself on the bed, punching the pillow again and again. Rejected by the person I loved most in the world. M. and Edmund. My birth parents; one who didn't know I existed and the other so ashamed by me that she'd discarded me on a doorstep like I was nothing. What if no one had opened the door?

What if I'd died of the freezing cold? How would she have felt then?

I had to leave. I'd contact Diana in London. It was bad enough being apart from her anyway. It was easier to feel anonymous in London, and I needed to get away from this village and all the secrets and lies …

I looked over at the rocking horse. That thing could stay with my so-called mother. I'd had enough of horses. I stood on the narrow single bed and brought down the brown leather case that I'd stored on top of the wardrobe. I began to pack everything I'd brought with me. I wouldn't be coming back.

There was a knock at the door.

'Go away,' I said.

'Please, Clara. Let me explain. I *couldn't* tell you. No one knew it was me. Your mother warned me that if I breathed a word to you about how you'd been found, she'd find someone else to look after you. Being your nanny was the next best thing to bringing you up myself.' M.'s voice was calm and quiet through the door.

'Go away!' I shouted it this time.

'I did it because I loved you so much. Still love you.' I heard a sob. 'It was that or have you adopted by strangers.'

Footsteps echoed down the stairs and I put on my coat. I needed to get to the post office to ring Diana and withdraw money out of my account. There was nothing in Brynderi for me now.

Chapter Thirty-Three

MARY-ANN

Annie heard the door slam with such a force that she shuddered. Perhaps she should have kept the secret to herself until her dying day. She'd kept it for twenty-one years, and it was obvious Clara wanted nothing more to do with her. From being her daughter's most trusted ally, she'd become her worst enemy in a blink of an eye. Her hand felt for her gold locket. If only she'd started by showing Clara the family heirloom and Edmund's declaration of love in the note folded inside with his photograph. All she wanted was for Clara to have what was rightly hers. She was a blood relative of the Pryces, and it was up to her to prove it.

The front door creaked as it always did when it was opened and Annie heard Clara creep upstairs. She'd try one more time to explain.

'Would you like a cup of tea, *cariad*?' she called.

The bedroom door opened and Clara struggled down the stairs towards her carrying her case.

'Clara! Where are you going? There's no need for this. You have to let me explain. I can prove to the solicitor that you're Edmund's daughter and Cefn Court is rightfully yours. Please.'

Clara's mouth was pulled into a taut line and her lavender-grey eyes blazed. 'Out of my way. You wanted rid of me then so you're getting your wish. You'll never see me again. I'm leaving for good.'

She pushed past Annie and opened the door, leaving it wide open for Annie to see her leave.

Annie couldn't help it. She fell to her knees and howled. What have I done?

Annie couldn't face serving in the shop for some days after Clara had left. She made the excuse that she had a fever and didn't want to pass it on to her customers, but the real reason was that she wouldn't have coped with all the questions about Clara. There was nothing in Brynderi for her now, but she was at a loss about where to go and what to do. She thought back to the friends she'd had growing up. Friends like Gwennie, who she went to the dances with. She was married now and had a family of her own. And then there was Frank Baker. She could have easily become involved with him as he'd made it quite clear he wanted more than friendship, but she'd lost touch with him too. She had no family left now. Poor Reggie had survived the war. He'd come home victorious in his smart demob suit only to be killed in a tractor accident on the estate. She'd neglected everyone while she had devoted her life to her Clara and had never looked for love again. Now it seemed like she had lost Clara for good and she was totally alone. The only friends she had were employees at the Court, and she didn't want to go anywhere near that place. She wouldn't be surprised if they all ended up losing their jobs too.

A week after Clara had left, Annie woke up with a start. The sound of a van driver delivering goods to the shop next door and people's voices made her realise that life was going on regardless of how she felt. Her father's voice came into her head: *Pick yourself up, bach. Don't let things beat you.* She washed, dressed and reported for her duties behind the counter in the shop.

'Morning, Annie. It's good to see you back with a bit of colour in your cheeks. Feeling better, then?'

Annie smiled. 'Yes, thank you, Mrs Howells. That old bug really laid me low.'

'I hear Miss Clara's gone to London then. Pritchard the Post said she's taken her money from her post office account and left a forwarding address for any mail.'

Annie's heart raced. *Nothing was private in this place.*

'Said Powell the Garage took her into Pen-y-rhos to get the train. Told him she was going for good now her uncle was taking over the Court. Sad business that. Lady Delia will be spinning in her grave.'

Annie didn't comment and began to stack the shelves with tins that were waiting to be sorted.

Mrs Howells carried on with her gossiping. *Quizzing,* her da would say. *That woman has to know everything. Ruddy old busy body, as bad as old Mrs Morgan before her.*

While Annie was going about her chores in the shop, she had time to think. She may have lost Clara but that didn't mean she wouldn't stop fighting for what was right. She'd visit Winston Gibson in Pen-y-rhos and tell him what she'd told Clara. She'd show him the family heirloom of the locket and Edmund's note. Even if she never saw Clara again, at least she would have tried. She also made another decision. She'd write a letter to Clara and tell her all about how she and her father fell in love and how he'd asked her to be his wife when he returned from the war. She'd tell her about the locket and explain that she'd done everything out of love; she'd sacrificed her own happiness for hers. If Mr Pritchard had a forwarding address for her, she could at least let Clara know how much she meant to her.

That night, Annie sat at the table by the window in her sitting room and wrote down words that poured from her heart. They'd been stored there for over twenty years, and she'd never uttered them for fear of losing the most precious thing in her life. But now she had lost her. Perhaps by releasing the words into the open, she'd be able to reclaim her daughter's love.

My dearest Clara

I understand what a shock it must have been for you. Lady Delia, and she is still your mother, cariad, is the one who brought you up and loved you as much as if she had given birth to you. Deep down, I think she knew you were of Pryce blood. You look so like your father with the same eyes and blonde hair. We've both looked at the photos of baby Marjorie, and it could be you lying on the crocheted shawl, couldn't it? No wonder she loved you from the very beginning.

Your father and I were very much in love, and I have grieved for him from the day the telegram arrived to say his plane had been shot down over France. He'd promised that we'd be married after the war. I never heard from him again (even though I found out much later that he did write, but I didn't receive the letters) and could not tell him about you. He died not knowing he had a beautiful daughter who was the image of her handsome father.

It broke my heart to give you up, cariad, but if anyone had known that I was expecting, and especially if anyone had found out who the father was, my own father would have been so ashamed of me. It's possible he would have lost his job and our home. There would have been no money to live off. Girls like me were shunned by the village back then, and I might have ended up having to give you up to an orphanage to be adopted by strangers. You deserved better than that.

After giving birth to you alone in the loft at the stables, I was overwhelmed with such a feeling of love for you and knew that whatever happened, the bond between us could never be broken. I wrapped you up and placed you in an open suitcase on the manor steps and rang the bell. I was not far away and waited until you were taken into the warm and were safe. I didn't tell a soul until the moment I confessed to you. In time, I think no one ever thought of you as anything but the youngest child of Lady Delia and Sir Charles. You were the apple of their eyes.

I broke my silence because I think I can prove you are the right person to inherit the estate as your mother wished. Every single day since your father gave it to me, I have worn a beautiful gold locket. It's a family heirloom and he wanted me to wear it until he returned and we could get married. Inside is a picture of him and also a message where he declares his love for me. I'm going to take it to Winston Gibson as proof that you are Edmund's daughter. You have the same shaped birthmark on the inside of your wrist, and I'm sure Lady Delia would have recognised it too.

And so you see, dear Clara, I had to tell you the truth. If I can prove you are Edmund's daughter, there will be another reason for why your mother's wishes are perfectly understandable. It is breaking my heart with things as they are between us. I think about you every day. I hope you will forgive me and understand why I had to do what I did.

Your ever loving,
Nanny M.

Tears trickled down Annie's face as she re-read the letter and sealed the envelope. She would never stop until she got justice for her daughter. She could hear her father's voice in her head. *You never give up once you get a bee in your bonnet, do you, bach?* This news would have broken him. She remembered all the times he'd asked her why she wasn't "walking out" with a nice boy like Frank Baker. Every time her answer had been the same. *I'm happy with things the way they are, Da.* If only that had been true. All he'd ever wanted was to walk his only daughter down the aisle.

Annie folded the letter and placed it inside the envelope. Leaving the cottage to walk to the village post office, she had a spring in her step for the first time since Clara had left for London. Unleashing those pent-up feelings felt good. The bell at the top of the door tinkled to signal her entry into the narrow shop where the walls were lined with greetings cards on one side and magazines and newspapers on the other. She was pleased to be the only customer in there.

'Good morning, Mr Pritchard,' she said. 'I understand that you have a forwarding address in London for Miss Clara Pryce.'

Her pulse raced as she waited for the inevitable questions. Sure enough, they came quickly. Why hadn't Clara given it to her? Wasn't it a shock for the young lady to leave so quickly? Wasn't it sad that she'd been driven out of her own home?

Annie kept up a polite smile while the elderly postmaster retrieved it and gave it to her to copy down into the address book she'd remembered to bring with her.

'Thank you. She'll be wondering why I haven't written, I expect,' said Annie, knowing that was not true. Standing to the side of the glass screen, she carefully wrote the address, *c/o Miss Diana Knight*, on the envelope and left the shop to post it.

Outside in the fresh air, Annie took a deep breath. *It's up to you now, Clara, cariad.*

Chapter Thirty-Four

Annie got off the bus in Pen-y-rhos and walked over the railway footbridge. She looked over at the train tracks and thought of her daughter leaving on a train for London. Annie had only ever been there once herself. Lady Delia had thrown a party with her society friends for Clara before she went to university. As Annie had been her nanny for all the years before boarding school and remained her daughter's confidante ever since, Clara had insisted that she was invited. Wearing a new evening dress and jewelled sandals, she'd loved every minute of the evening. She'd been so pleased to see Clara dazzling everyone with her beauty and poise.

'I'm so pleased you decided to come, M.,' she'd said. 'You've done so much for me. I can't thank you enough.' The dimple that always appeared on the left-hand side of her face when she laughed was the only feature Annie had passed on to her daughter. She was Edmund's through and through, but seeing that dimple always gave Annie a warm feeling inside.

Annie carried on over the bridge, swallowing the lump that had filled her throat. She walked the length of the street until she came to the solicitor's offices, feeling the weight of the locket as she moved. The locket represented another weight too; the responsibility for proving that Clara was a true blood relative to the Pryce family, and that Lady Delia's decision to leave the estate to her was even more fitting than even her ladyship realised. Could she convince Winston Gibson of that?

She entered the office where a receptionist sat behind desk. She looked up. 'May I help you?'

Annie's heart raced. 'I've an appointment to see Mr Gibson. Mary-Ann Beynon.'

The young woman found her name and led the way down a long corridor of Victorian tiles. Her smart high-heeled shoes clattered and echoed in the empty space. They arrived at the last door on the left where the receptionist knocked before opening the door.

The smartly dressed man in a fine wool suit stood and offered Annie a seat opposite him at the desk. 'Miss Beynon. It's good to see you again. What can I do for you?'

Annie's hands shook as she reached for the fastening of the locket at the nape of her neck and laid it on the desk in from of them. 'I think this will prove that Miss Clara is a blood relative of Lady Delia – and that's another reason she has every right to inherit the Pryce estate,' she said.

The solicitor leaned forward and picked up the heavy gold locket, suspending it from his fingers. 'Welsh rose gold. An impressive piece ... but I don't understand. How will this prove anything? You know that Lady Delia wrote a letter to Miss Clara admitting she wasn't her birth mother?'

'Please open it. I was given that by Clara's father before he left.'

Mr Gibson slid his nail into the edge of the locket and clicked open the two oval halves.

'That's Mr Edmund, Lady Delia's son. Who does he look like?' said Annie.

The older man shifted in his seat. 'Well, he and Miss Clara are the image of each other.'

'Read the letter in the other half.' The solicitor unfolded the paper that was now yellowed with age. 'Look who he's writing it to.' Annie waited for the solicitor to read the note. 'Edmund Pryce and I loved each other and were going to get married. Clara is our daughter.' Annie felt her cheeks redden as Mr Gibson looked intently at her.

'Are you sure this isn't something you've thought up to try and help Clara?'

Annie stood up. 'Certainly not! If you knew what it's taken for me to admit this after all these years …'

'Sit back down, Miss Beynon. I didn't mean to insult you. But why now?'

Annie told him what she had told Clara about Lady Delia forbidding the staff from talking about the manner of the baby's arrival at the Court.

The solicitor handed the locket back to Annie, and she returned it to the place where it had been for the last twenty-one years.

'I'm afraid, even if it were true – and, for what it's worth, I do think you are telling the truth – it would not help Miss Clara. Lady Delia's wishes would be granted and there would be no need to prove that Miss Clara is a blood relative *if* it can be proved that this supposed second will is not valid. But it's a big *if*, I'm afraid.'

Annie's heart sank. 'But she is Lady Delia and Sir Charles's granddaughter. She *is* a Pryce!'

'As I said, what will help her is to prove that the will to which Mr Watkins is referring – if indeed there is such a will – is invalid. Now that Mr Watkins has contested the will I witnessed with my colleague, there is work to be done.' The solicitor suddenly looked uncomfortable. 'I don't know how to tell you this, especially given what you have just shared with me. The truth is … I needed to get in touch with Miss Clara anyway. There's another complication. It will come as a shock to you, I'm afraid. I've had a visit from someone claiming to have news of her brother, Edmund. In fact, *she* also claims to be his daughter.'

Annie's mouth gaped open and her pulse raced. *No! He would have come back to me. He promised.*

'There must be a mistake. He died in 1943. His plane was shot down. I was with his mother when the telegram came. It can't be right, surely. Who is she? She's lying!' Annie's voice rose and she couldn't stop shaking.

She was taken back to that awful day so long ago now, Lady Delia's piercing scream echoing in her ears. She'd rushed from the nursery to find her in the drawing room on her knees clutching the buff-coloured telegram that every mother dreaded, rocking back and forth.

'He's dead! His plane has been shot down. Edmund's dead!' the older woman had cried.

Instinct had made Annie get her ladyship to her feet, leading her to the sofa. Lady Delia had started to howl like an animal in pain. Soon, one of the kitchen maids arrived and Annie left the room. It was then that the shock and horror of what had happened to the man she loved took over. She'd became breathless and dizzy. Clutching Edmund's locket, her body had become wracked with sobs.

Back in the present, through her tears, she realised she was crying out as if she'd just found out the terrible news from twenty years before. '*Nooo!*'

Mr Gibson waited for Annie to calm herself, watching her sympathetically. 'I was as shocked as you. She was at the funeral apparently – didn't like to intrude, she said.'

Annie remembered the mysterious girl in black in the churchyard, watching the committal by the church tower; the one who appeared like she didn't want to be seen.

Mr Gibson passed over a sheet of paper which had lots of details written in type.

'Her name is Françoise Lefèvre. She says her father was taken in by her mother and grandparents and hidden from the Germans. Eventually, he and her mother fell in love and married. In order to integrate into the French community, he took the name Charles Lefèvre. She is their only child. Her father died last year but had no memory before the crash when his plane was brought down.'

Annie sat back in her chair, not able to take it all in. Edmund had married? Her voice cracked. 'This is such a shock … How do we know this young woman is genuine? Edmund's name is on the war memorial and on a commemorative stone in the family plot. It *can't* be him!'

'I agree, Miss Beynon. This will all have to be checked out, but the first thing I have to do is contact Miss Clara and inform her of this latest development. Do you have her address in London?'

Annie nodded. 'She left a forwarding address at the post office in Brynderi and I've sent a letter to her there.'

She rummaged in her handbag for her address book and handed it to the solicitor so he could copy from the page.

Winston Gibson stood as Annie went to leave. 'Thank you. I'm sorry I can't be more helpful, Miss Beynon. It is my duty as a solicitor to give you my professional opinion and to inform you that it is unlikely that the locket and letter alone could prove Miss Clara's birth right. The only person who could confirm that you were romantically involved is Mr Edmund Pryce himself. And he is now dead. Miss Clara is mentioned as a beneficiary in her mother's will but the problem, of course, is the other will. I bid you good morning.'

'Thank you for hearing me out, Mr Gibson.'

Outside in the fresh air, Annie burst into tears. Ignoring passers-by staring at her, she returned to the bus station and caught the next bus to Brynderi. Edmund had survived the crash and hadn't come back to her! How could he? Even if he'd lost his memory, surely he would have returned to Britain …? She stopped dead in her tracks. But what if he *had* written to tell her he was alive and, along with the others, that vital letter had been destroyed by her father? Her pulse raced as she remembered when she'd found out and her da had broken down, admitting what he'd done. They'd have lost the cottage if it ever got out, he'd said. The awful row echoed in her ears again, even after all this time.

Chapter Thirty-Five

Annie resumed her work in the shop, but no matter how hard she tried to push it from her mind, the idea that Edmund could have survived the war and made a new life in France constantly niggled at every waking thought. One minute she was angry that she'd sacrificed any chance of happiness and then felt guilty because, if all were true, he would have had no memory of her and so deserved to have moved on. If only Françoise Lefèvre had not disappeared after the funeral. Why had she not just spoken to them rather than gone straight to the solicitor? Perhaps if she spoke to the French girl, she could find out more than she'd been told by Winston Gibson.

One evening, after a long day unpacking boxes and filling shelves in the shop, Annie let herself into the house. Her heart thumped when she picked up the post scattered over the coir doormat. One letter stood out. Her handwriting on a cream vellum envelope. A black line crossed through the address. *RETURN TO SENDER*. Her eyes burned and she reproached herself for not telling Clara everything to start with. Perhaps Françoise Lefèvre *could* prove she was Edmund's daughter by showing the correct paperwork? It was only Annie's word that Clara was his daughter, an illegitimate one at that, whereas Françoise's mother had married Edmund according to the girl. A locket and a love letter were no good to anyone, and yet she'd lost the love of her daughter by thinking that they were.

After the despondency of receiving the returned letter, Annie didn't sleep much that night. She was fidgety and restless. When she closed her eyes, it was always Edmund's face she saw. It was as if he was willing her not to give up. As dawn broke, pale silver light seeped into her room, giving it an ethereal shimmer. A rhythmic knocking came from the bedroom across the landing. Getting out of bed to see what it was, she flinched as her feet touched the freezing lino. She lifted the latch and looked into the room. Clara's wooden rocking horse was rocking back and forth unaided as it used to do when her daughter had bad dreams all those years before at Cefn Court. There was never anyone in the room then and there was no one present now either. A shiver fizzled through Annie. A brief image of a smiling Edmund waved to her from the window and then vanished. Surely it was a sign that she had to do everything in her power to get Clara to see her and read the letter?

She went back to her bedroom. It was too early to get up, so she snuggled back under the candlewick bedspread, alone with her thoughts. The only sound was the birdsong. Clutching her locket, she made up her mind; she would travel to London and face her daughter and she would deliver the letter herself. If she refused to see her, at least Annie would have tried. She would also tell her about what the solicitor had divulged to her. But what would she say? *Oh, by the way, your father didn't die in 1943 and you might have a sister.* Would Clara be as sceptical as she was? Pangs of unease crept along her veins. If only Edmund could have let them know he'd survived. How could you carry on functioning as a human being with twenty years of your life wiped away?

Credenford railway station was busy as Annie made her way to the platform for the London train. She'd booked herself into a small boarding house not far from Paddington station and although she'd been to London once before, it felt very different to be travelling alone.

Every evening for the past week, she'd scoured the London street and Tube maps she'd got from the bookshop in Pen-y-rhos, and had meticulously worked out her route from the boarding house to where Clara was staying in a fashionable area of London.

A booming voice on a tannoy announced the arrival of her train on platform three. Annie stood back as a group of people, seeming to arrive from nowhere, pushed in front of her. The whistle blew and she boarded the train just in time. She walked along the narrow corridor to find an empty compartment. Sliding open the door, she found a seat next to the window. At last she could relax, and she watched as the countryside whizzed into a green blur. She opened her bag to check she had everything she needed for the journey – money, tickets, street maps, address book and, most importantly of all, the letter to Clara. Her throat tightened as she relived the last time they'd spoken and replayed the moment when she'd confessed to her daughter that she was her real mother. She questioned again whether it had been right to reveal the secret. It would have all been for nothing if the second will was valid anyway. And now there was another complication in the form of Françoise Lefèvre ...

At the next station, Annie's thoughts were interrupted by the sliding door opening.

'Is it all right if I sit in here? The other compartments are full.'

'Yes, of course,' said Annie.

Dressed very smartly in a boxy two piece suit the colour of wild heather, and wearing a matching Jackie Onassis style pillbox hat, the young woman struggled into the carriage with her suitcase to sit on the seat opposite. She took off a grape-coloured leather glove and offered her hand to Annie.

'Pamela. Pamela Parker-Jones.'

Annie coloured, suddenly feeling shabbily dressed in the young woman's company. She reached across to shake her hand.

'Mary-Ann Beynon. People call me Annie.'

The young woman smiled. Her ash-blonde hair was elegantly coiffed in the latest bouffant style, and tiny amethyst earrings twinkled as the morning sun flooded the carriage with warmth. She rummaged in her handbag and took out a file of foolscap paper.

'You'll have to excuse me, Annie. I've got to learn these darned lines by the time I get to Paddington. An audition with a theatre company. The director said to catch a cab to Viscount Theatre as soon as I arrive. My stomach is in knots, I can tell you. My first ever audition after leaving drama school.'

Annie assured her that it was fine, but instead of practising her lines as she said she was going to do, Pamela Parker-Jones did not stop talking. By the time the countryside had changed to buildings, factories and railway sidings, Annie had learned the minutiae of the life story of the woman sitting opposite her and couldn't get a word in edgeways. Whenever she tried, Pamela began another anecdote of what her dashing older brother said here and what her eminent father had done there. She hardly stopped to draw breath.

As the train drew into Paddington station, Pamela said, 'Well, Annie. That's enough about me. What about you?' She paused for breath. 'Oh, here we are. Another time, maybe.'

The smart young actress left Annie in the compartment, and she chuckled to herself. The journey from Credenford to Paddington had flown by thanks to her talkative companion, and she'd hardly had time to worry about the reception she'd get when she turned up at Clara's door the next day.

Annie found herself in the middle of Paddington station; a maze of confusing signs and exits and crowds of people. Her pulse raced. What had she got herself into? Everyone seemed to be in a hurry, heads down, scurrying to the platforms as if there was no time to lose. *Count to ten, Annie Beynon, she told herself*. You've got it all worked out. She found a bench by the waiting room and sat down to look at the street map and the address of her lodgings. *192 Newfoundland Road. Within walking distance*, her letter of confirmation said. *Exit the station at the north end*. Annie looked up at the signs and realised with relief that she was sitting opposite the exit she wanted.

'186, 188, 190.' Annie let out a long sigh. 'At last, 192 Newfoundland Road.'

The sign read *Heath Garden Villa*. The three-storey terraced house towered above her. Not a garden in sight and certainly no villa in its present state. With its generous bay windows and sandstone façade, it looked as if it had been quite grand in its day, but now it was rundown and shabby.

Annie walked up the stone steps to the front door of the boarding house and rang the bell. After what seemed like an age, a woman with hair dyed peroxide blonde and wearing heavy make-up opened the door a fraction. *Mutton dressed as lamb*, one of her father's sayings sprang to mind.

'Yes?'

'Mrs Brown? I've booked a room. Mary-Ann Beynon.'

'Ya betta' come in, luv.' The landlady led Annie into the hallway and took her to the top of the house where the small single room overlooked the backyards of the other houses in the road, as well as the ones in the street behind. The smell of cheap perfume filled the enclosed space. 'This do ya?' the woman asked.

'Yes, thank you,' said Annie, immediately missing the village.

'As I said in me letter, it's dosh up front. No smoking, no alcohol, no drugs and no men. Breakfast is eight o'clock sharp, and bathroom's on the first floor. There's a meter for hot water. Door's locked at half ten every night.'

The list of rules was uttered in a matter-of-fact manner that suggested they had been rehearsed many times before, and the woman's unsmiling expression did not waver.

Annie took out her purse and counted out the money onto Mrs Brown's open hand. The landlady turned and left Annie alone in the spartan room.

Chapter Thirty-Six

The sky was still dark outside when Annie awoke the next morning; not that this room could have ever been pitch-black like her bedroom back in Brynderi. The streetlight outside her window was still lit, filtering an orange glow through the worn paisley patterned curtains. It had taken her long enough to get to sleep with the continuous sound of traffic and trains as she watched the luminous hands on her travel alarm pass midnight, one o'clock, two o'clock ...

A thin tinkling accompanied by a soft whirring sound encouraged her out of bed, and she went to the window to draw back the curtains. The noise came from the glass bottles in crates that rattled as a milk float stopped and started. A man in a peaked cap delivered pints of milk to each house along the street. Annie put on her slippers and the dressing-gown she'd managed to squeeze into her case. Armed with her wash bag, she ventured along the landing and down the flight of stairs to the bathroom. The door was locked and she could hear water running inside. Rather than miss her turn by returning to her bedroom, she decided to wait. After what seemed an age, the door opened and a middle-aged man in a vest and braces hanging down from the waistband of his trousers emerged, freshly shaved with his hair Brylcreemed. He grinned at her.

'Should've knocked, darlin'. Would have let you in, no trouble.'

Annie's cheeks flushed and she quickly entered the bathroom, locking the door behind her.

Breakfast was served in the room overlooking the street and a table for one had been reserved for her in the bay window. The tablecloth was worn in places and could have done with a good iron.

'Full English, luv? Tea or coffee?' Mrs Brown's make-up appeared to be thicker than ever and accentuated the lines on her face. Her voice was gravelly and the smell of cigarette smoke mixed with her perfume suggested she was a heavy smoker.

'Yes, please. And tea,' said Annie.

She caught the eye of the man she's seen half-dressed earlier. He now wore a shiny dark blue suit with a white shirt and patterned tie. He nodded. The other tables were occupied by people looking all ready for work, mainly men in suits. *What did they all do?* she wondered. Back in Brynderi, most people worked on the land or in garages and shops. Farmers, mechanics, shop workers. The only suits she saw would be in church on Sundays.

'There you go, luv.' Mrs Brown was back. She plonked down the breakfast and a mug of tea, the colour of mahogany. 'Sugar's on the table over there,' she said, pointing to a trestle table covered in a red plastic tablecloth. 'I'll get the toast.'

Annie's stomach churned when she saw the plate of greasy bacon and eggs placed in front of her. She sipped the tea. *Strong enough to stand a spoon straight up in it*, as her father always said of a cup of tea he approved of. Annie was sure it would taste better in a cup and saucer, but at least the drink was hot. She took a piece of toast from the chrome toast rack when Mrs Brown had brought it over and spread a thin layer of margarine across the surface of the bread before adding some marmalade. Every time she looked up from her food, she felt the gaze of Mr Brylcreem man.

Initially, it was a relief to get outside the boarding house, but soon the smell of car fumes, the drone of the traffic and crowded streets made her realise how much she missed the tranquillity of her secluded Welsh village. Knots in her stomach tightened as she braced herself to make her journey by underground into the centre of London.

It began to rain, and Annie's tears threatened to fall too as she hurried along to the Tube station, weaving in and out of the crowds; people with heads bent downwards, blank expressions on their faces, mouths in taut lines. She looked for the Bakerloo line and then stood to the right on the escalator, letting a stream of commuters flow past her on their way to catch the trains, which she could hear whooshing in and out of the platforms below her. It was the noise that unnerved her. She wanted to place her hands over her ears and shout 'Stop!' Annie promised herself she'd never complain about the village being too quiet ever again.

She didn't have to wait long for her train, and once the doors opened the crowd surged forward, carrying her with them. She stood for the first part of the journey, holding on to the strap above her head until the train reached the stop where she needed to change lines. She managed to get a seat on the next train and scanned the underground map opposite, counting down the stations. Passengers around her made no eye-contact, trapped with their thoughts in private worlds; beige, anonymous people with city pallors, not communicating with their fellow human beings. Another wave of homesickness caused her to blink away the tears.

Emerging from the station and walking out onto the flag-stoned pavement, Annie was struck by a complete contrast. Just a short time before, she'd left a road where the buildings showed clear signs of poverty, but now she'd arrived in an area that exuded wealth. She walked along a wide street of Georgian buildings, lined with neat mimosa trees and wrought iron lantern street lamps that were replicas of the Victorian gas-lamps of a previous era. Each identical building had a blond brick facade and small paned sash windows. Porches supported by white painted ribbed columns protected front doors with gleaming brass knockers and letterboxes. Iron railings in the shape of long arrow heads lined the pavements. Annie searched for house number 246; the place where Clara now called home. Three doorbells for three flats. Diana Knight's name was alongside the bell for Flat 1. She took a deep breath before pressing. As Annie waited, her heart raced and it was all she could do not to run away. How would Clara react? It wasn't long before a tall young woman opened the door.

'Yes?'

'Diana Knight? I've come to see Clara Pryce,' said Annie.

'Yes, I am. Who am I speaking to?' The voice was soft and cultured unlike the brash sounds that had come out of landlady Brown's mouth earlier.

Annie swallowed and gripped the letter in her hand. 'It's Mary-Ann Beynon.'

'Oh.' The young woman's face became serious. 'I-I-I don't know if she'll see you. I'll go and see.'

Annie's heart drummed in her ribcage and her throat tightened. The rain was heavier now and Annie felt her hair clinging to her head, trickles of water finding their way inside her collar.

Before long, the young woman was back. She shook her head. 'I'm sorry. She's adamant she doesn't want to see you. She says she's said all she wants to say to you.'

'Please. I don't want to upset her any further. I understand why she won't see me. She's had a shock. But please give her this.' Annie handed over the letter before Diana Knight could refuse. 'As you can see from the envelope, she returned it unopened. All I want is for her to read the letter inside. Read why I did what I did. That's all I ask. I just want her to know how much she was loved. Please. If needs be, open it and read it to her.' Annie knew tears weren't far away, but she was determined not to break down in front of this young woman. She stood up tall and turned to leave.

Annie didn't wait to see the expression on Diana's face but heard the intake of breath. All she wanted was to get back to the boarding house, collect her things and get on a train that would take her back to the security of home. She never wanted to set foot in London again.

Chapter Thirty-Seven

✦ CLARA ✦

I moved back from the blinds I'd hidden behind to watch what was going on. Was I being cruel to M. leaving her standing there in the rain? I still hadn't been able to forget the look of hurt on her face when I left the village. But what she did was unforgivable, and I was unforgiving. I hated myself but I couldn't wipe away what she'd told me.

'I'm sorry you had to deal with it, old thing. But I couldn't face it,' I said when Diana entered the room.

'Well, you know what I think. You could have at least asked her in and heard what she had to say. She was on the point of tears the whole time, poor woman. I know you said you'd had a row, but it must have been about something pretty serious for her to come all the way from the middle of Wales only for you to refuse to see her.' Diana stormed out and I could hear her stomping around in the kitchen. It wasn't like her to react like that so M. must have really got to her. I followed her and put my arms around her, kissing her cheek.

'I'm sorry, Di. You of all people should know everything. Let's make some tea and I'll tell you the whole sorry tale.'

Back in the sitting room, we sat close on the sofa and I told my friend everything, from being found on a doorstep as a baby, being brought up by parents who never breathed a word to me about the truth, to my uncle's outburst when he revealed I was not a blood relative.

Diana took me by the shoulders and looked straight at me. 'You've kept all this bottled up since you moved in here. I thought you were grieving your mother. But what happened between you and M.? I know you'd had a row ... but refusing to see her today doesn't make sense.'

I clenched my fists and stood up. I began pacing the floor. 'Because she was the one who dumped me on the bloody doorstep! She's my birth mother.'

Diana's mouth gaped open.

'And there's more. The man who I thought was my brother, the beloved Edmund, was really my father. Not even my parents knew that. M. only told me to prove I *was* a blood relative and thought I'd have a better chance to claim Cefn Court. My nanny is my mother, Di! She let me live a lie for all these years. I had no idea.'

Tears streamed down my face. Diana got up from the sofa and hugged me. 'Oh, darling. Let it all out.'

It was the first time I'd cried properly. When I first found out, there were a few angry tears but now, once I'd started, I couldn't stop. Uncontrollable sobs wracked my body and Diana held me tight until they subsided before handing me a handkerchief.

'She also wanted me to give you this,' she said, handing me a cream envelope I recognised.

'I don't want to read it. She can't say anything that will undo what's happened.'

Diana slid her nail under the seal and opened the envelope.

'What are you doing?' I hissed at her.

'M. asked me to read it to you if you refused to open it,' she said.

My heart thumped. I wondered what was so important that M. had ventured all the way to London on her own.

Diana began reading. 'My dearest Clara, I understand what a shock it must have been for you—'

'She can say that again,' I retorted.

'*Sshh*,' said Diana. 'Listen to this. Poor Nanny M. "Your

father and I were very much in love and I have grieved for him from the day the telegram arrived to say his plane had been shot down over France." They were going to get married when the war ended. That's so sad.'

I hadn't given M. the chance to tell me that.

'Listen to this bit. "It broke my heart to give you up, *cariad*"– is that how you say it? "Girls like me were shunned by the village back then, and I'd have ended up having to take you to an orphanage to be adopted by strangers. You deserved better than that." Oh, that's awful, Clara. Can you imagine what she must have gone through?'

Diana was right, and I was starting to feel awful for the way I'd treated M. 'Here,' I said. 'I'll read the rest.'

Diana handed me the letter and I read the rest in silence, my hand shaking. 'Oh God. She gave birth to me all alone! I can't begin to imagine how frightened she would have been, and at that age too!' Overcome with guilt, I just wanted to take M. in my arms and give her a big *cwtch* to say sorry. 'My father gave her a gold locket, apparently. I bet it's the one she never takes off and she's always fiddling with when she's concentrating. Oh, Di. I've been so horrible to her.'

Diana took me in her arms. 'Do you see now why she wanted you to read this? You can make it up to her though, I'm sure of it.'

I broke away from Diana's embrace, holding out my left arm. I pulled up my cuff.

'See this,' I said, pointing to the heart-shaped birthmark on my wrist. 'Apparently, Edmund, my father, had an identical one and she thinks my mother would have recognised it, too. So, perhaps all those years ago, she did know she was leaving the estate to a blood relative after all.'

Diana smiled. 'There you are. Now promise me you'll make it up with M. I shall be haunted by the look on her face as she left for as long as I live.'

There was another shock later that week in the form of an official letter, franked not stamped, lying on the mat in the hallway. My hand shook as I opened it, not knowing who could be writing to me with official business. Edgar Watkins' glowering face came into my head. He was soon to be lord of the manor. Could it be something about the second will? The upcoming probate court case was an open and shut case, according to Winston Gibson.

Dear Miss Pryce,

I'm writing to inform you of something that has recently come to our attention regarding Squadron Leader Edmund Pryce, only son of Sir Charles and Lady Delia Pryce (both now deceased) of Cefn Court, Old Radnor.

A Mademoiselle Françoise Lefèvre has visited me at our offices in Pen-y-rhos to inform me that Squadron Leader Pryce did not perish in action in 1943 as feared and reported by his RAF regiment.

Goosebumps formed on my arms. I couldn't believe what I was reading. My parents had been devastated. My mother told me how she thought her world had ended. Missing in action it says on a memorial stone next to baby Marjorie's in the family plot, where my parents both rest now too. Just who was this Françoise Lefèvre anyway?

It would appear that Squadron Leader Pryce found refuge in a local farm and was taken in by the family.

He had no memory of who he was prior to the crash. Mademoiselle Lefèvre has told us that he and her mother became close and eventually married. She is their daughter.

I steadied myself by placing my hand on the hall table. My father had a secret life in France!

I rushed into the sitting room where Diana was reading. 'Whatever's wrong, darling? You're as white as a sheet!' she cried, jumping up.

I forced the letter into her hand. 'Read this! If you thought M.'s was a shock, wait until you see what this says.'

Diana frowned, but her mouth dropped open as she began to read. 'So, he survived. No word for twenty years. But why are you only finding out now?' She turned over the page. 'Hang on. It says here that both her parents are now dead. Odile is her mother's name but she calls her father Charles *Lefèvre*, not Edmund. There must be some mistake.'

Diana read the rest of the letter aloud. 'Enquiries are now underway to verify the facts. I felt as your solicitor it was only courtesy to inform you of this new information. Of course, if proved to be correct, it means that Mademoiselle Lefèvre is your half-sister ... Oh, Clara. M. will be heartbroken when she finds out after all these years that he'd survived and married a French woman. Poor M.!'

Chapter Thirty-Eight

That night, I took ages to get to sleep as I went over in my mind how my life had changed since Mother died. I had decisions to make about my future. Next year I'd graduate from university but had no idea about what career path I was going to take. Life in London was such a contrast to rural Wales. It was now the capital of the world, full of freedom and hope where anything and everything was possible.

'There'll be no rush, *cariad*,' M. had told me. 'Take your time and follow your dreams.'

There was one thing I was certain about. London was where I was going to make my home … with Di. But that was in the future. M. was right; there was no rush. I had more important things to sort out now.

Dear M. Making it up with her was at the top of the list. How must she be feeling after I rejected her for the second time?

The one decision I had made was to find out as much as I could about my father, and M. had to be part of that discovery. I owed her that at least. I had so many questions. If he'd really survived the war, I needed to know why he'd stayed in France rather than returning home. I wanted to know all about his life with his new family, wanted to visit the place he'd made his home and visit his grave. The person to help me was Françoise Lefèvre, my supposed half-sister.

'I wonder, is it convenient to speak to Mr Winston Gibson, please?' I waited as the receptionist put me through. 'Hello, Mr Gibson. It's Clara Pryce. Thank you for your letter with news about my father. The news was … a shock. I still can't quite take it in.'

The mellow tones of a voice with a cultured Welsh accent on the other end of the telephone took me back to the place I called home. As he spoke, I jotted down the facts of what he was telling me. He explained that enquiries had taken place with the war office, and RAF records verified that my father's body had never been recovered and officially he was listed as missing in action. He gave me the address where Françoise Lefèvre was residing. She was in London on holiday and recognised her father from an obituary in a paper that had a picture of the woman's son who had been killed in France. She went to Gibsons' to stake a claim on the estate. In France, that could happen, he'd explained.

I placed the receiver down after saying goodbye and looked at the address written on my pad. *368a Henrietta Street. SW London.*

'Di, I've just found out that Françoise Lefèvre is still here in London. Fancy paying her a visit with me? I want to meet her,' I called.

There was no answer.

Diana was in the dining room and only looked up as I entered. 'Please Please Me' by the Beatles was blaring from her transistor radio and she was nodding her head in time to the beat. The table in front of her was covered in newspapers. I sat on a chair beside her and saw they were open on the job vacancies pages. She'd circled several and, fascinated, I peered to see what they were. Diana didn't really need to work. The hours spent at the gallery were just to indulge her passion for art, and she received a generous allowance from her father. She turned off the radio.

'Anything take your fancy?'

'Not really. I'm hoping to work with the less fortunate, to do something worthwhile with the time when I'm not working at the gallery. Anyway. What were you shouting? I heard something about a meeting. Who do you want to meet?'

'Françoise Lefèvre ... my supposed half-sister.' The solicitor had said she'd been at my mother's funeral. *Perhaps the woman hiding by the tree was her?* I suddenly felt the same uneasiness I had experienced when I'd noticed her watching us, but I continued anyway. 'Mr Gibson has given me an address here in London. Will you come with me?'

Diana put down her pen and swung round in her seat to face me. Her sage-green eyes looked deep into mine. 'You don't have to ask, darling. This is a rollercoaster for you. One minute you're grieving for your mother and now you have another shock to deal with. I'm here for you. If all is true, it's important that Françoise tells you everything about your father. If he's recently died, there's a gap of twenty years to fill. Exciting but scary too, I imagine.'

I nodded. As always, Diana was the only one who seemed to know exactly how I was feeling.

'I don't think I'll write to her. I'll just turn up. If she's not in, then I can always leave a note.'

'Good idea. There's no time like the present. Why don't we go this afternoon? I'll book a cab.'

Henrietta Street was not the most salubrious of areas. The black cab drew up outside a block of grim brick-built dwellings about half way down the street. Litter scattered in concrete front yards and along the pavement gave the place an unkempt and unloved appearance. Diana paid the fare as I walked to find number 386. Behind rusty railings, a set of stone steps descended to the basement flat.

Through the dingy net curtains behind the small paned window, I could see a light was on, even though it was afternoon. I rang the bell and, not knowing what or who to expect, welcomed the fact that Diana had joined me on the flagstones in front of the front door. It opened a fraction.

'*Oui?*' said a young woman's voice.

'I've come to see Mademoiselle Françoise Lefèvre,' I said.

'*Elle n'est pas là.* Not 'ere.'

The woman opened the door to face us. Dressed in a long patchwork purple skirt and cheesecloth blouse, she wore multiple rows of brightly coloured beads. Her pale complexion and mousy coloured hair seemed at odds with her Bohemian appearance. 'She's out. I tell 'er you call. Your name?'

'Clara. Clara Pryce. When is the best time to come back?' I asked. I took a deep breath. 'I think I might be her ... sister.'

It was the first time I'd said it out loud and it felt strange.

The woman looked puzzled, her brow wrinkling into a frown. 'I do not know she 'as the sister. She will be back at six o'clock.'

Diana looked at her watch. 'We can come back then. It's four o'clock now. Let's go and get a cup of tea.'

The woman started to close the door. 'I tell 'er.'

'Thank you. I don't know your name, sorry?' I said.

'Angélique.'

Angélique shut the door with a slam and left us standing there. We looked at each other and smiled.

'End of conversation, I think. Come on, I spotted a greasy spoon caff on the other side of the street. I'm sure we'll get something there,' suggested Diana.

I fumbled in my pocket with the note I'd written in case

Françoise wasn't there and wondered how she would react when we faced each other for the first time.

Later on, we wandered back along Henrietta Street as the nearby church clock struck six o'clock. Late sunshine was clothing each building in a mellow glow.

'I wonder if she's home yet,' I said.

'We'll soon find out. Come on.' Diana crossed the road and I followed. She stood back for me to descend the steps to the basement flat first.

'Here goes,' I said, pressing the bell. I shifted from one foot to the other.

Nothing. I put my finger on the bell for a second time, holding it there for a longer time. This time, I heard footsteps in the hallway. The door opened, and a very striking looking woman stood facing me. If this was Françoise, she didn't look anything like the image I'd formed of her in my head. She wasn't a blonde-haired replica of me or the father I'd seen in photographs. She had glossy dark hair that fell in tresses over her shoulders and, instead of the pale lavender grey eyes most of the Pryce family had, she had dark chocolate, almost black, eyes. I supposed she must take more after her mother. There was no mistaking this was the mystery woman I'd seen in the churchyard when we buried my mother.

'Are you … Françoise? I called earlier.'

'Yes, Angélique told me.' The woman had hardly a trace of an accent. Her eyes bored into me. 'Yes, I'm Françoise. I don't know why you are here. Angélique said something about being my sister, *ma soeur.* You are mistaken. I am an only child.'

'You came to my mother's funeral in Brynderi. I saw you at a distance but you went before I could speak with you. You told my solicitor that you are Edmund Pryce's daughter.'

She went to close the door.

'Look, I've only just found out that Edmund Pryce was my father too. I was brought up by my grandparents. I have no problem with him having another family in France, but it does make us half-sisters. Please. All I want to know is what was he like. Until you arrived at the solicitors, everyone thought he'd been killed when his plane was shot down in 1943. Twenty years ago ...'

Françoise hesitated. For a moment I thought she was going to ask us in but she shook her head. '*Non*, there is no point now. He has died and lies with my mother in the ground. I did not know Edmund. He forgot who he was. I only know Charles. When I saw his photo in the *journal*, I realised Charles was Edmund.' Just before finally shutting the door on us, she gazed at me intently. 'You are very like my father.'

My heart felt as though it was shrinking. That was that, then. Telling me how like her father I was seemed to make her rejection worse. She'd had twenty years with a father who didn't even know the existence of another daughter. I would still remain the outsider, the illegitimate daughter of a pilot and an employee. *A bastard*. Isn't that what my uncle called me?

Chapter Thirty-Nine

It was a week since I'd visited Françoise, and I didn't know anything more about Edmund than what I'd been already told by my mother and M. Something didn't feel right. I'd expected Françoise to want to tell me all about growing up with Edmund, or Charles as she called him, give me snippets of what he was like as a father, reminisce about what they'd done together … but nothing. It was as if she didn't want to let me into their world. No one knew better than me what it was like to lose a parent, but her attitude was indifferent. Perhaps she was just more mature than me in how she dealt with things. Younger in years but more adult in her attitude, perhaps. M. had always protected me.

Thinking of M. brought a lump to my throat. I owed her a huge apology for my childish behaviour. I needed to see her. Leaving me with the woman who was my grandmother and who could provide for me in a way she couldn't was the greatest gift she could have given me, but it was clearly also her biggest sacrifice. Why couldn't I have seen it when she first told me? It would have saved so much heartache.

'I'm going away for a few days, Di. Going to sort things out with M. I was a real cow, wasn't I? I should have gone after her once you read the letter to me. You can come with me if you want.'

Diana got up from her chair and hugged me. 'I knew you'd come to your senses, darling. No, I think you and M. need some private time. Maybe it's time you stopped calling her "M." and started calling her "Mum"?'

I hugged Diana and nestled my face into her straight

brown hair, expertly cut into the new Mary Quant bob style that was popular now in fashionable London. It smelled of lemons.

'She'll always be M. to me. When I was little, I thought it was short for Emma or Emily. Mother told me that they always called her Nanny Mary-Ann but it got shortened to Nanny M. to be easier for me to say when I began to talk. She brought me up, you know. Mother was often too busy with her meetings and committees. But M. was there for me, always.'

It was a beautiful day when I arrived at Pen-y-rhos station. Walking up from the station into the main town, a few people nodded in recognition but I didn't see anyone I knew well enough to talk to. I didn't have long to wait for the green and cream bus to take me home.

'My, how the mighty have fallen!' I looked across the aisle to see a man smirking at me. 'Born the wrong side of the blanket so I hear.'

I felt my cheeks burn and was glad when the conductor arrived at my seat to take my fare. The man got off the bus at the next stop, and the conductor watched him leave with a look of disapproval on his face. 'Don't take any notice, *bach*. Fred Rhys. Always was a nasty piece of work.'

'Don't worry. I won't. Thank you,' I said.

So, everyone in Brynderi must know about me? I vaguely remembered Fred Rhys from an incident that happened when I was home on holiday from boarding school. He and M. had words when he called at Cefn Court to deliver some horse feed. I could never find out from her what the row was about but I'd never seen her so angry.

The bus came to a halt at the bus stop opposite the village shop. I'd deliberately picked a Thursday when it was half-day closing, hoping M. would be in.

M.'s house gleamed in the sunshine. The windowpanes shone like mirrors, and I could see she'd been out with the scrubbing brush and bleach to get the front step opal-white. *A throwback to how her mam kept house*, she once told me. I bit the inside of my cheek. At Cefn Court it would have been the housemaid's job. Yet again, a sign of a privileged life granted me by M.'s unselfish act. I placed my small suitcase down on the step and knocked on the door.

'Clara!' M.'s eyes filled with tears as she opened the door, and she hugged me so hard that I could hardly breathe. The comforting smell of lavender made me realised how much I'd needed to be *cwtched* by her. I'd been cruel to the one person I loved more than anyone. Wherever I went, wherever I travelled, the smell of Yardley's English Lavender always transported me back to M. It was my mother's treat for her every Christmas. *'If it's good enough for the Queen Mother, it's good enough for Nanny M.,'* Mother used to tell me when I was a little girl.

'I've come to say sorry.' I burst into tears.

'There, there. Let it all come out, *cariad*.' Her voice was soft and soothing as she led me into the warmth of the cottage. We sat together on the settee and she held my hands in hers. 'You've got nothing to be sorry about, Clara. I handled it very badly and I've been beside myself with worry that I'd lost you for good. I couldn't live with myself if I had.'

I looked around the small sitting room and relaxed. The pretty pastel flowered wallpaper and patterned carpet were so typical of M. The decor was in such contrast to both Cefn Court manor, with its heavy antique furniture and dark soft furnishings harking back to a bygone era, and Diana's fashionable London apartment with its luxurious fittings and modern art works. No modern geometric patterns for dear M. Nick-nacks and photos of her parents adorned every surface. My school leaving photograph took pride of place in the centre of the sideboard. Little had I realised that day that I was accompanied by both my mother and my grandmother, both having such different reasons to glow with pride. M. had created a home here. It was much more than a house. It exuded love, and I knew then that the bond between a mother and a daughter could never be severed whatever happened. Di's face came into my mind. I'd made peace with the fact that I might never experience motherhood, but if circumstances had been different, M. would have been my inspiration; showing me a model of true maternal love.

M. let go of my hands. Fumbling with the locket that meant so much to her, she began to talk. 'I'd like to tell you about your father if that's all right. I want you to know everything about him. We knew both families would disapprove, but you can't help who you fall in love with, can you?'

'No, I suppose not.' A certain face came into my head again. *No, you can't.*

M. told me how she'd been friends with Edmund since they were children and spent their summers together when he came home from boarding school. When Edmund got his own horse, a beautiful chestnut mare he named Kenna, her brother, Reggie, became his personal groom.

'In spite of their different backgrounds, Reggie and Edmund became best friends and I tagged along. I grew to long for the school holidays when Edmund would return home. I worshipped him.'

As M. talked, she became more and more animated. Her eyes sparkled as she reminisced about her time with Edmund. She told me about their picnic, and from the way a flush crept along her neck, I guessed that their private time in the boathouse was when I was conceived. It only happened once, she said later, and I believed her. Another innocent girl carried away by love.

She took off her locket.

'Here. Look at the photo. That's your father. The message he left for me inside the locket proves his love. I'd like you to read it. See for yourself. He was so excited at the prospect of us being together forever.' Her voice cracked. 'It was not to be.'

I took the locket and opened it. The photo inside was a smaller version of one that I'd brought with me from Cefn Court. That one showed detail of a smiling young man, his fair hair brushed with a side parting, with light-coloured eyes I suspected to be lavender-grey like my mother's. They'd have creases at the corners. When she'd laughed, her eyes sparkled like amethysts, and I knew his would have done too.

I unfolded the paper and read the message aloud.

'"To my dearest Mary-Ann, All my love until the end of time, Your own, Edmund." That's so romantic, M.'

M.'s voice became scratchy. 'I thought the end of time was when that telegram arrived. But he didn't, did he? Love me till the end of time. He went on to love another and they had a daughter together.'

I stood and handed her the locket, putting my arm around her shoulders. 'Oh, M. He didn't have any memory of his early life. I've been to see my half-sister, you know.'

M.'s mouth dropped. 'You didn't say.'

I explained how I'd tracked Françoise Lefèvre down to an address in London given to me by Winston Gibson.

'She didn't tell me anything more than Mr Gibson had told me. He wrote to let me know about how this new information changed things. She's very grown up, much more than me, but perhaps she hasn't had a wonderful nanny to look out for her like I have. There's something about her I didn't take to, though. I can't put my finger on it. She didn't want to talk about our father for a start. It was as if she didn't want anything to do with me. If it had been me, I would have wanted to know every little detail about her, but it seemed that she couldn't get away from us quick enough. Didn't even ask us in. I think we're going to have to find out about Edmund's life in France ourselves. She doesn't look a bit like him either.'

M. gave me one of her looks. 'As for looking like each other, you don't look anything like me, do you? Poor girl has had a big shock. Just like you did.'

She smiled at me, and for the first time I noticed the dimple on one cheek in the same place as mine when I looked in a mirror. It was true. We looked nothing like each other apart from that. She had wavy auburn hair and hazel eyes that appeared to change from green to nut-brown depending on the colour she was wearing.

'Sorry, M. I was thinking about Mother. She must have guessed who I was, you know. All the comments about the likeness between Marjorie and me. And as you said in your letter … this.' I pointed to the birthmark.

Chapter Forty

It was now a month since I'd travelled to Wales to make it up with M. The four days I spent with her in Brynderi repairing the damage I'd done were some of the best days of my life. We'd talked about my childhood and her pride at how well I'd done in school and was doing at university.

'Can you imagine how proud your grandad would have been if he'd known the truth, *cariad*? As it was, he couldn't help telling people what a good job I'd done helping to bring you up!'

We both laughed, comfortable at last in our new relationship. Mother and daughter, not nanny and someone else's daughter.

We'd already been seen out and about in the village, and what did it matter if people whispered when we approached?

'I don't care at all if I was "born the wrong side of the blanket",' I said, after passing two women who stopped chatting when we got nearer to them.

M.'s mouth gaped open and I laughed. 'Where on earth have you heard that expression?' she asked.

'Oh, this old man on the bus. The conductor told his name was Fred Rhys.'

'*Humph*! He would. Less of the old too, my girl. He's my age.'

Thirty-nine, I worked out. That was her age and still young in many people's eyes. I'd never really thought of M.'s age before. How different her life would have been if my father had returned from the war. Perhaps they could have eloped and got married in secret. She could have been a Pryce herself.

We talked about my Uncle Edgar and Aunt Eliza and the changes they planned to make at Cefn Court once the probate court case went their way.

'I get all the latest gossip from Sara and Elsie when they come into the shop. They say your Aunt Eliza can't bear living in the country. She's never there. Stays back in Credenford most of the time. And as for your uncle, when he's there, he treats them with utter contempt. I feel so sorry for the staff. They need the jobs but are so unhappy. Her ladyship always treated everyone with so much respect. Yes, we were all servants, but she appreciated every one of us for the jobs we did.'

I hugged M. She'd known her place with my mother, but where would we have been without her?

One afternoon, we visited the churchyard at St Mary's church to put fresh flowers on my mother's grave. I swallowed a lump that had filled my throat. The last time I'd walked through the kissing gates was when I attended her funeral service inside the imposing grey stone building. What a lot had happened since then. There was no polished headstone for my mother's grave yet; instead, a nameless mound of earth between ostentatious marble gravestones. Details of the life and death of Sir Charles Pryce were inscribed in gold leaf lettering. In stark contrast, on the other side was a tiny white marble headstone, shaped like a heart and engraved with a cherub where baby Marjorie lay.

I brushed away a tear. *This is where Edmund should be properly buried*, I thought. With his family. Not just a commemorative stone. Not in an unknown grave on foreign soil. I scooped out a space for a jam jar and pressed it in firmly while M. went to the tap by the wall for water. We placed a bunch of flowers inside and filled up the jar.

'There,' said M. 'It looks as if somebody cares. Rest in peace, your ladyship.'

'Rest in peace, Mother.'

A tiny robin flew close. It perched on baby Marjorie's headstone.

'You know what that means, don't you?' whispered M.

I shook my head.

'It means your loved ones are close by. We'll bring a posy for the baby next time.'

M. and her superstitions. I smiled to myself. Over the years I'd heard them all, but that was a new one for me.

The visit to the grave helped me reach a decision. I hadn't yet confided in M. because I still wanted to find out more about where my father's plane had been shot down. I suspected that I wasn't going to get any more information from Françoise Lefèvre, although I *was* going to pay her one more visit …

London seemed so noisy after the peace of Brynderi but did nothing to alter the inner calm I now felt after my visit to M. Leaving her was hard, but we both knew it would not be long before we saw each other again. She promised to contact the solicitor to see if they'd found out anything more about Françoise's claim.

Diana was out working at the gallery all day, so I decided to use the time to research everything about Edmund. It was time to go and see Françoise again.

Later that day, I walked down the steps to the basement flat and waited after ringing the bell. I tried again but, coming to the conclusion no one was in, I turned to go. Then I noticed Angélique walking towards me, laden down with bags of shopping in each hand.

'What are you doing 'ere? I thought Françoise made it clear she 'ad nothing more to say to you.' The young woman's voice was curt and clipped. Françoise had obviously primed her well.

'I need to speak to her about our father,' I said.

Angélique put her bags down and rubbed her hands. 'That will be impossible now.' I waited for her to explain. 'She has gone. Back to France.'

My heart sank. 'Can you let me know her address in France, please?' I said. 'It really is important I speak to her.' I picked up a couple of bags and walked with Angélique towards her flat.

When we got to the top of the steps, she stopped. 'It is no good. She left without saying goodbye. No address. I'm sorry. She became very secretive after your visit. She does not talk to me about it. I go now. *Au revoir.*'

Well, that was that. A weight formed in my chest. I'd been so determined to find out where my father had lived for the last twenty years and where he was buried. Perhaps now I'd never know. There had to be something I could do!

Back at Diana's flat, I went through the possibilities in my head. I had to find out all I could about Edmund's war record with the RAF. I needed to find the name of his training base and if anyone in his squadron remembered him.

When Diana returned, she found me compiling a list of possible places to contact. The thick telephone directory was open and I'd written down all the telephone numbers of possible organisations that might be able to help me.

'You've been busy,' she said. 'Any luck with the uncommunicative Mademoiselle Lefèvre? I thought you were going there today.'

I shook my head. 'No. She's gone. No forwarding address. It's up to me now.'

'I'm sure you could research it, darling,' said Diana.

I got up and kissed her. 'It will be my research for tomorrow. Come on, let's go out for something to eat. I'm starving.'

I grabbed my new red PVC raincoat and we walked down the street, arm in arm, to our favourite bistro. I'd developed a taste for French food when I'd been in the country on exchange as part of my degree. I'd spent six months in a little town called Ville de Roi and had taught English in a *lycée* there. It felt odd to think that my father might have been living in France with a new family, not remembering anything about his life in Wales. Had he ever spoken English again, or had he been totally immersed in French life? What was his French wife like? What was he like as a father to Françoise? Even though I was very young, I remembered Sir Charles as a man with a serious face. It was M. who allowed me to have fun. She arranged for me to play with her friend Gwennie's children in the village. She was the one who invited them back to the Court for tea. We would make Welsh cakes and *bara brith* before they came. It was always dandelion and burdock to drink. Jam sandwiches were my favourite, I remembered, and here I was looking across at Diana studying a menu written only in French and deciding whether to have *chateaubriand* and *pommes dauphinoises* or *lapin à la moutarde*.

The next morning, another official looking letter came for me. I put it on the side for a few minutes, not wanting to open it. But it could only be one thing: a letter from Winston Gibson telling me about Françoise's claim. So many thoughts whizzed around in my head as I picked up the letter and finally opened it.

Dear Miss Pryce

*I'm writing to inform you of the latest development in
the case of Mademoiselle Françoise Lefèvre claiming
to be the daughter of Squadron Leader Edmund Pryce,
deceased. Without explanation, we have been notified
by Mademoiselle Lefèvre that she no longer wishes to
proceed with the claim and that she intends to return
to France.*

Yours faithfully,
W. T. Gibson

I sat back on my chair and folded the letter, returning
it to its envelope. So, Angélique was telling the truth? I
wondered what could have changed my sister's mind.
I couldn't ring M. to tell her about Gibson's letter, but I
could ring the shop in Brynderi and leave a message to ask
her to ring me.

I still had some digging to do, but after that I had an
idea.

Chapter Forty-One

By the time I visited M. and Brynderi next, I'd acquired myself a little car. A duck-egg blue Austin A40 Farina, the latest model. Mother's very generous allowance each month had been put to good use at last. I'd had no need of one before. Whenever I came home from university, Mother had sent the chauffeur to meet me from the train. But with a car, I could visit M. whenever I liked, and that would be essential for the plan I had in mind.

I'd had some success with my enquiries into my father's accident. A cold shiver crept along my arm and goosebumps formed as I'd read the report. A Spitfire fighter plane had been shot down over southern Normandy not far from the border with Brittany in June 1943. Squadron Leader Edmund Charles Pryce was the pilot. Wreckage was found strewn across farmland but my father's body was never found.

I purposely arrived on another Thursday afternoon when I knew M. would not be working. We sat at the kitchen table and I told her all that I'd found out.

'But don't you see? Now we know where Edmund's plane crashed, it would make sense if he'd lived in the area near the crash site.'

'But you don't know that, *cariad*. Wishful thinking on your part maybe?'

M. was as surprised as I was that Françoise Lefèvre had returned to France.

'Didn't I tell you there was something about her I found strange? And why did she duck out of sight at Mother's funeral? If she wanted to find out more about her father's family, you'd think she'd have made herself known to us.

Part of me wouldn't be surprised if she didn't know my father at all,' I said.

'We may never know now, *cariad*. If she's gone back to France and not left a forwarding address.'

'Perhaps I frightened her off,' I said.

'Well, you can be pretty scary.' M. laughed and I made a face at her.

We both sat for a moment in silence, hands around our cups of tea. Perhaps M. was thinking of her beloved Edmund and what might have been. I thought the time was right to tell her about what I'd planned.

'M., I think we should go to France to look for his grave.'

She put down her cup into the saucer with such a force that the bone china rattled and the tea slopped over the edge. 'But why? You said yourself his body wasn't found after the bombing, and we only have a stranger's account that he survived and died last year. Be realistic, Clara. It may be all lies.'

I had all my answers to her protests ready. 'Think of it as a holiday, M. You've had a terrible few months – and you've never been abroad, have you? I've never been back since my placement at the *lycée* in Ville de Roi, and the area of Normandy the War Office gave me is near there and so beautiful. It will be a chance to take a holiday before going back to university to finish my final year.'

M.'s face still looked shocked, but part of me hoped that she'd come round to the idea.

'If we don't find his grave when we're there, I'll never mention looking for it again,' I promised.

M. remained silent, deep in thought, for what seemed an age. 'No promises ... but I'll think about it.'

The next morning there was a tap on my bedroom door.

'Here you are, *cariad*,' she said. 'A cup of tea for you

before I leave for the shop. I know you haven't decided when to go to France yet, but I'll sound Mrs Howells out. See what she says about me having time off. Now the girls are older, perhaps Gwennie would cover for me. The extra money would be a real help. She always does that at Christmas time or when the Howells family go away.' She placed the tea down on the bedside table and sat beside me on the bed.

I was overjoyed that she'd already decided she wanted to come on the trip with me. 'Oh, M. Thank you. You'll love France, I know you will. We'll sort out a passport for you and then we can go,' I said.

'If Mrs Howells says I can go, remember.'

Suddenly, the rocking horse in the corner of the room began to rock back and forth. Neither of us were close enough to have knocked it, and we looked at each other, aghast.

'Think of it as a sign, *cariad*.'

M. left the room before I could ask her what it was a sign of.

While M. worked in the shop, I drove into Pen-y-rhos. I wandered around the town and entered the gardens next to one of the large Victorian hotels the area was famous for. I made my way over to the granite memorial in the shape of a cross that took pride of place on a raised plinth. It had the names of young men inscribed around the base. I spotted a couple of Beynons there; two of M.'s brothers who never returned. Only Reggie had returned in honour. I found my father's name: *Edmund Charles Pryce, aged twenty-three years, missing in action, 1943*. It was always the ages of the servicemen that got to me. So many names, so many men lost at a young age with what should have been their lives ahead of them. If Françoise Lefèvre was to be believed, perhaps Edmund did have a longer life than those poor souls listed there. Despite everything, I found myself hoping he had. I hoped he'd been happy.

I returned to the street that split the town in half and found the solicitors' offices on the corner. I opened the wrought iron gate and walked along the stone flagged path through the rose gardens. Well-tended and pruned, these would be a show of pastel colours in the summer.

When I entered the reception, a middle-aged woman with softly curled white hair looked up from her typing.

'May I help you?' she said. I hadn't seen her before.

'Is it convenient to see Winston Gibson, please? I don't have an appointment, I just thought I'd see if he was free.'

The woman picked up the telephone and dialled. Putting her hand over the mouthpiece, she said, 'Who shall I say wants to speak with him, please?'

'It's Clara. Clara Pryce.'

She spoke briefly into the phone. 'He said he can see you.'

I walked down the corridor, knocked on the heavy oak door and waited for a response. Winston Gibson opened it and offered his hand.

'Please. Sit down. I take it you received my letter, my dear,' he said.

We talked about Françoise Lefèvre. He told me what the investigators had found out about her, and in return I told him about her attitude towards me when I had visited her.

'If I look here in my diary ... Phone call from Mademoiselle Françoise Lefèvre confirmed by letter two days later to say she was withdrawing her claim. She said she was returning to France.'

'I wonder why she didn't pursue it if what she said was true,' I mused.

'The investigators were trying to establish the date and place of her birth.'

I asked the question I'd wanted to ask from the moment I'd entered the offices. 'Do you have an address in France for her, Mr Gibson?'

'Unfortunately not. She only mentioned an address in London.' The solicitor sat back in his chair.

My heart sank. That was where Diana and I had visited her.

'She did mention something about arriving by a passenger ferry. She could have travelled a great distance from her home to the port, of course. You know how vast France is, my dear,' he said.

I thanked Mr Gibson and left. I was no closer to finding out more about Françoise and where she came from, which meant I was no closer to finding my father either.

Driving back from Pen-y-rhos, I was struck by the beauty of the Radnorshire countryside. Lush and verdant, the landscape glowed in the afternoon sunshine. I remembered Normandy; beautiful villages with rustic stone farmhouses and cottages. But it was the stunning coastline that had left an imprint on my memory. On my free days, I'd left the town where I was staying and travelled to the Brittany coast. I'd found picturesque fishing villages with a variety of sea-going vessels, the fishermen delivering their hauls every morning to supply the gourmet restaurants dotted around the quayside; timber-framed auberges down cobbled streets selling cheap rooms and bistros offering excellent food. Françoise Lefèvre or no Françoise Lefèvre, I began to allow myself to get excited about a return trip to France.

Chapter Forty-Two

It was all arranged and the ferry booked. M. and I were going to be spending our holiday travelling around northern France and I couldn't wait.

For the last three months, I'd spent practically every weekend with M. talking about what we were going to do once we got there. If Diana wasn't working at the gallery, she came with me and I had great fun showing her all the places of my childhood. Although I couldn't show her round Cefn Court itself, my uncle couldn't stop me using a public footpath that crossed the land that would soon be legally his. To me, time seemed to be dragging, but Winston Gibson assured me that it was normal when things were not straightforward. One Saturday we climbed the hill that rose behind the manor house. At the top, I bent over with a stitch and took deep breaths.

'I think we need to get fitter,' I said, gasping.

We sat down on the grass and admired the view over the valley in front of us.

'You can really see how amazing the manor house looks from here, can't you?' Diana said. 'It's just a shame it's now going to be owned by that obnoxious uncle of yours.'

I thought back to the scenes after the reading of the will and how cruel he'd been to me, as well as to M. and the rest of the staff.

Diana took my hand and pulled me up. 'Water under the bridge now, darling. Just concentrate on planning your trip with M. I do hope you'll find your father's grave. It would mean so much to both of you.'

As always, my friend was right. Even though I would never meet Edmund, just knowing where his final resting place was would be important. The fact that M. had agreed to accompany me on the trip suggested that she felt the same way, but what if we didn't find it? Was I building her up for disappointment? I brushed off the idea.

'See that building to the left of the house?' I said.

Diana's eyes followed the direction I was pointing. 'The white-washed building with the slate roof?'

'Yes. That's the one. Well, that's where I was born. Up in the hayloft of the stables.'

'No swanky private hospital for dear M. Poor thing!'

'She must have been terrified.' My voice cracked.

We continued with the walk, mostly in silence. As we descended the other side of the hill, Brynderi nestled below us, bathed in pale sunshine.

'Come on,' said Di. 'Last to get to the gate makes the tea.'

We raced to the bottom of the slope, laughing and screaming like silly schoolgirls, our serious thoughts forgotten.

When we arrived at the cottage, M. was already home from work. 'I saw you coming up the road, so I've put the kettle on for a cuppa,' she said. 'Had a good walk?'

We looked at each other and giggled.

'It's Clara who should be making the tea, M.,' said Diana. 'She lost the race. Her mini skirt was too tight. Too slow for her own good in it.' She looked at me and laughed.

'Oh well, she'll need to rest then.' M. winked at me. 'It's so good to have you both here. I really don't mind making the tea.'

Each time we'd visited M., I showed Diana a little more about my family. I'd always shied away from telling anyone about who I really was when M. first revealed her secret, but now I wanted my friends to know. I was proud

238

of who I was and, above all, I was proud of the strong woman M. was.

The next day was Sunday. The shop was closed, and M. and I were left alone to plan the last details of our trip whilst Diana went out for a walk. I spread a large map of France on the kitchen table and found the village nearest to the place where Edmund's plane had crashed. Collinac. It was about ten kilometres from Ville de Roi, which in turn was about fifteen from the ferry port.

'I think we should start there, M. That's where the War Office said Edmund's plane went down. Can you believe it, M.? I was living so close to the actual spot for six months. I've booked a cabin for a ferry sailing in two weeks' time, and we'll arrive in France at eight o'clock in the morning ... Oh, have you got a pen and something to write on?'

M. stopped studying the map and got up, retrieving a writing pad and pencil.

'We'll get on the road straight away and stop for breakfast en-route. Write down the name of the road we need to take out of the port, will you?' I watched M. scribble them down. 'N176 in the direction of Ville de Roi. I know the area well from my time in the *lycée* so I've booked us into a little *pension* not far from where Edmund's plane came down. How does that sound to you?'

'I'm in your hands, *cariad*. I'd never been further than Aberystwyth on my own ... before I came to London to see you, of course. I thought I was being brave doing that.' M. laughed.

I leaned across and squeezed her hand. 'I know how hard that was for you, M. And I was ghastly to you, wasn't I? I promise all you'll have to do on this trip is be the navigator.'

'What?' Her mouth gaped open.

'Don't worry. You can read the map and look out for the road numbers as I drive. We'll mark it all out for you before we go.'

M. went into the sitting room and returned with a number of books. 'I've been to the library in Pen-y-rhos and got these out.'

The books were all about Normandy. The villages, the seaside towns, French food. M. had used picture postcards as bookmarks. When she opened one of the books, she placed the postcard on the table, and I noticed it was a photo of a beautiful park I recognised. 'Is that in Ville de Roi?' I asked.

She turned it over. 'Yes, it's one of the ones you sent me when you spent your exchange there. I've kept them all, *cariad.*' She handed me the book, open on the page she'd marked. 'This chapter is all about the area around there as far as the coast and Mont St. Michel. I remember you writing to say how when the tide is out there's a part of the day when you can walk across the causeway. I'd love a visit to see it, if we have time.'

'Of course,' I said. 'We're going on holiday, M. If we find Edmund's grave, that would be wonderful, but I don't want us to spend so much time on a search that may be fruitless. Let's think of it as a bonus. I want you find out what a wonderful place France is and understand why I love visiting.'

M. showed me each of the books in turn. 'I'm not sure about some of this food, though,' she said, grimacing. She turned to a photo of a plate of *escargots*. 'If these are what I think they are, you won't see me eating them!'

'Don't worry. By the end of the holiday, you'll love them.' I winked at Diana, who had by that time returned from her walk and was standing in the doorway.

By the time we left for our return to London, the journey to France was finally all worked out. M. seemed to be even more excited about it than I was. It was going to be a long drive back and we wouldn't be arriving until very late, but it had been worth staying to get everything sorted.

M. walked us to the car and *cwtched* each of us in turn.

'Bye, *cariad*. Safe journey. Make sure you write,' she said. 'Goodbye, Diana.'

'Bye, M.,' I said. 'Thanks for another lovely weekend. The next time I see you will be in London, ready for our big French adventure.'

M's eyes sparkled, and I knew I was doing the right thing.

Chapter Forty-Three

✦ MARY-ANN ✦

Northern France

Annie took her first glimpse of French soil. The crossing had been uneventful, and Clara had commented on how smooth it was. Standing up on deck, it was good to see the port from the sea and watch as the buildings along the quayside become more defined the nearer they got. The tannoy announced that drivers and their passengers on deck three could descend to reclaim their vehicles. As they queued in an orderly fashion by the stairwells, Clara turned to her and grinned.

'Remind me to drive on the right-hand side of the road when we leave the ferry, won't you?' she said. 'They say more accidents happen on the roads nearest to the ferry terminals than anywhere else.'

Annie felt the butterflies in her stomach flutter. This was really happening. After all the planning, they were on their way. Would they find Edmund's resting place? If they did, she knew it would close one part of her life. The not knowing was worse.

Leaving the ferry in an orderly convoy and following the line of cars in front of her, Clara was soon driving on the right-hand side of the road away from the ferry terminal. Annie had the map on her lap, open on the page for the first part of their journey. The red line that Clara had marked for her made the route they'd chosen stand out, and paper clipped to the top listed road numbers they needed to take.

'Well, here we are, M. Welcome to France. *Bienvenue*, as

the locals would say. About fifteen kilometres from here, look out for the road to Ville de Roi for me, okay?'

The steel-grey sky overhead threatened rain, but ahead it looked brighter. Annie relaxed in the passenger seat and looked around at the open countryside. It was flatter than Radnorshire; larger fields dotted with rolled hay bales appeared to stretch for ever, but with its hedgerows and farmland it was similar to the countryside she knew.

'There's a crossroads up ahead, M. Can you check the map and road for me?'

Annie looked for the N176 on the map as Clara approached the junction. 'It's signposted left,' she said.

Clara signalled and turned as Annie had instructed. After a while the road became narrower and narrower. It was clear that they had taken the wrong direction. Clara turned the car around and went back to the crossroads. Although the signpost clearly appeared to be facing to the left, the road they needed was straight on. This was to happen a number of times, and Annie started to think something was very wrong with her map reading skills.

'Don't worry,' said Clara. 'I should have warned you. It happens to everybody the first time they drive in France. I was too busy concentrating on the road.'

'Now you tell me.' Annie smiled. 'At least the countryside off the lanes is pretty.'

'We'll stop at the next village. *Petit déjeuner,* I think, and strong coffee.'

Annie's stomach rumbled. She hoped they served tea. She'd never get over how strong the coffee was that Clara made. When she'd moved into Annie's, she'd brought a steel percolator to make fresh coffee. The smell in the kitchen had been wonderful, but Annie had only ever tasted it once and preferred her usual Camp coffee in a cup of hot milk.

'That sounds good. What do you call those pastries you were telling me about?'

Clara smiled. 'Croissants. You're going to love them.'

Clara was true to her word, and the first village they came to had both a bakery and a café in the main street. She parked the car and the two of them walked the short distance to the small café. There were several wrought iron tables and chairs outside on the pavement.

When they entered, the smell of home baking and freshly ground coffee made Annie realise how hungry she was.

'What do you fancy, M.? Croissants?' she said. 'Or something more fancy?'

Standing beside Clara at the counter, Annie's eyes widened when she saw the vast range of delicious looking pastries and cakes on display behind the glass screen. 'Oh, croissants for breakfast, I think.'

Clara led her to a table by the window where a young girl soon approached to take their order. Clara spoke to her in French. '*Deux croissants, s'il vous plaît. Et du café et du thé, aussi. Merci.*'

The girl soon returned with their pastries and drinks. The croissants were huge, golden and shiny. Annie poured her tea from a stainless steel pot. 'My tea looks as weak as your coffee looks strong,' she commented. She took a first sip and grimaced, confirming what she thought. The croissant made up for it, though. It was buttery and flaky and seemed to melt in her mouth.

She looked around the rest of the café. There were a few other people sitting at the tables, leaving very little space for the waitress to move around. Paper tablecloths were placed at an angle to reveal corners of dark wood. Bentwood chairs with woven raffia seats were tucked underneath the tables when not needed. Some people were dipping large chunks of what looked like bread into their drinks.

Clara noticed Annie's confused expression. 'It's *brioche*, A soft crumbly bread, and I wouldn't mind betting it's hot chocolate in the mugs. If you're not keen on the tea, you should have a hot chocolate next time,' she said. 'It's the milk, I expect.'

After paying at the counter, Clara and Annie left and walked on to the bakery they'd spotted a few shops down. The bell tinkled as they entered. The queue of people in front of them, mainly women, soon disappeared as loaf after loaf was sold from the shelves.

'*Bonjour.*' The woman serving was dressed in black and wore a green apron displaying the same logo as the sign on the glass door. *La Boulangerie Rustique.*

'*Bonjour, madame,*' said Clara. She turned to Annie. 'We'll take something for our lunch to save stopping again. Maybe a baguette? We can tear it in half. We'll call in the butchers to get some cooked ham to go in it.'

On shelves behind where the woman stood were loaves of bread in every shape imaginable. Round white loaves with tops scored in diagonal patterns, nutty brown loaves, plaited bread and a stack of long, thin baguettes standing upright behind a wooden rail.

'I've never seen such a choice. A bit bigger than the rolls I normally buy.' Annie laughed. 'Yes please. We won't need to eat anything else after that.'

'*Une baguette, s'il vous plaît.*'

The woman slid the baguette into a long paper bag. '*Voilà.*'

Clara counted out the exact change in francs, bid *au revoir* to the woman and then, after calling in at the butchers for some ham, they returned to the car. Back on the road again, Annie relaxed. The route Clara had marked on the map showed almost a straight line to the small village where they were going to centre their search for Edmund's grave. She wondered what his life with his French wife and Françoise had been like. What a different way of life from his privileged upbringing at Cefn Court. Annie had been disappointed that Françoise had not been more welcoming towards Clara when she called on her in London. If she'd been telling the truth, they were only half-sisters – but sisters all the same. They shared Edmund's blood. And now he was dead. She'd only had brothers, but she'd known how good it was to share things with Alf, Jimmy and especially with Reggie. Edmund's daughters could have become friends ...

The road in front of them was perfectly straight and flanked by evenly spaced poplar trees. Clara came up behind a pale blue-and-white caravan with a British number plate.

'Someone else off the ferry like us, I expect,' said Clara. 'I'm going to need your help now, M. Can you let me know when it's safe to pull out to overtake?'

Annie leant her cheek against the window to have a clear view of the road. Just as Clara went to pull out, there was a loud blast on the horn from a speeding car overtaking them.

'*Merde. Imbécile.* Sorry for the language M., but he was nowhere to be seen when I looked in my rear mirror.'

Annie watched as the driver of the car overtook the caravan at the same time and only just managed to get back in before an approaching car. The road was now undulating its way through the French countryside and there wasn't another opportunity for Clara to overtake. They came to a small town and found parking alongside the central square.

'I think we'll stop here for lunch and stretch our legs,' said Clara.

Benches were dotted around with plenty of space in between each one. There was a stone building with a door each end and a long stainless-steel sink for washing in the middle. *Femmes* and *Hommes*. Annie guessed what these were before noticing the corresponding pictures.

'Just a word of warning when you use the toilet, it will most likely be the traditional French type. A hole in the ground. You may get wet feet when you flush it.' Clara laughed at Annie's horrified expression. 'I'm not joking, M.'

People came and went; families spilling out from hot cars, others carrying picnic baskets to the spare benches. On the nearest bench to them, Annie watched as a woman spread out a brightly coloured tablecloth and laid out what appeared to be a feast for the family along the slatted seat. She cut a long baton of bread into thick slices and placed them in a basket. The children and the man Annie presumed to be their father stood or sat on the pavement and tucked in. It was all so different from the narrow lay-bys back in Britain where people unwrapped squares of sandwiches and ate them on their laps, often inside their cars when the weather was inclement.

They were soon on their way and left the roads edged with poplar trees behind. The scenic coastal route they now took was much prettier with magnificent views out over the Atlantic. The sea sparkled like a mirror in the afternoon sun, and coves and inlets surprised her around each bend as she continued to follow the map to the village they were staying in.

'Not long now, M. Watch out as we go around the next bend for the view of Ville de Roi above us. When we get close, look out for a large expanse of green in the middle. The *Parc des Orchides*. The gardens are beautiful; there's a glass house with a wonderful display of orchids. I'll take you there.'

They were approaching a town where buildings with smooth charcoal slate tiles glistened in the sunshine. The park and gardens Clara had pointed out were focal points in a very built-up area. Away to the left was the sea.

'It looks a lovely place, Clara. Bigger than I imagined from your letters, *cariad*.'

Clara nodded. 'We need to turn off now. Look for the sign to Collinac.'

Annie concentrated back on the map.

It wasn't far until she saw the sign they wanted. *Collinac. Dix kilometres*. She inhaled deeply. The real adventure was about to begin …

Chapter Forty-Four

The road up to the *pension* was a narrow lane, and at the end of it stood two stone cottages. Clara had chosen this place because it was in the village closest to where Edmund's plane had been shot down. The car crunched to a halt on the chippings that formed a wide parking space to the side. A hand painted sign with the *pension*'s name, *Les Deux Chaumières*, was fixed to the wall by the left-hand door.

'The Two Cottages,' said Clara, pointing to the sign. 'The brochure said they've kept it as two separate houses to give privacy to the guests, but apparently there's an adjoining door on the ground floor inside for the madame to serve us our breakfast in our own kitchen.'

They took their luggage from the boot of the car and pulled the bell. It was one of those rustic cast iron ones where the clapper was attached to a thick rope. An elderly woman dressed in a sombre black dress answered. Her grey hair was dragged back into a large chignon, and Annie had visions of her brushing it loose each night and it reaching her waist at least. Her dour appearance was completely at odds with the warmth of her smile and the way she welcomed the two of them.

'Ah, *bonjour. Bienvenue, bienvenue. Entrez!*'

Inside, the cottage was full of polished wooden furniture with floral soft furnishings. Hand-crocheted antimacassars covered the backs of the chairs, and white lace curtains like the ones often seen in cafés hung from brass rods a short way above the window sills.

'Madame, I'm Clara Pryce, and this is my ... mother, Mary-Ann.'

'*Enchantée*. Sylvie Chevalier.'

Annie's chest tightened, and for a split second she thought she would start to cry. That was the first time that Clara had referred to her as her mother. She continued speaking with Madame Chevalier, and Annie marvelled at the way her daughter was able to slip into speaking French so easily.

Madame Chevalier led them through to the second cottage and up narrow wooden staircases to the second floor. A simply furnished bedroom was tucked up in the eaves, and Annie bent her head to look out of the window at the view. The room overlooked the back garden with its extensive orchard and across a patchwork of fields.

Two single beds with wrought iron bedheads were pushed up against opposite walls, each with a small bedside table alongside. A painted wooden wardrobe and chest of drawers almost filled the rest of the space, but the room looked clean and fresh. A heady aroma of dried lavender came from a ceramic bowl placed in the centre of the chest.

'Swing and cat spring to mind,' Clara said, raising her eyebrows once madame had left them to unpack. 'But we'll only be using it as a base, won't we? As long as the breakfast is good in the morning. I think we also have our own sitting room, and we can use the small kitchen for making coffee too. It seems we're the only guests at the moment, so at least we have the place to ourselves.'

Annie thought of Edmund. He'd never told her much about his time at university and she only realised he'd studied French, when she'd overheard his mother mention it. Would he have been fluent in the language when he met his French wife? She wished that Françoise Lefèvre had knocked on her door to tell her that he had survived the war and not gone straight to the solicitor in a formal way. She would have invited her in and asked her all about Edmund's life in France. How he met her mother, how he made his living, what was he like as a husband and father. There was so much Annie wanted to know. From what Clara had told her, the young woman hadn't said much. Perhaps she was still grieving for her father. *Yes, that would be it*. She pushed more uncharitable thoughts away.

'Penny for them, M.?'

Annie realised Clara was talking as she unpacked her suitcase. 'Sorry, *cariad*. I was thinking about your father. There's so much we don't know ... and we might never know.'

Clara came over to her and put her arm around her shoulders, pulling her close.

After unpacking and asking Madame for directions, Annie and Clara walked into the village of Collinac. There was a main street with shops selling groceries, interspersed between private houses and café bars. As far as Annie could see, the village boasted a small convenience store that resembled the one she worked in at home. Pretty window boxes adorned the upstairs windows and scarlet summer geraniums and tumbling blue lobelia gave a blaze of colour. They hadn't walked far when they reached a large paved area in front of an ornate building. Red brick formed a pattern around the gable and rendered façade, and the word *MAIRIE* was spelled out using the same brick.

'Even the smallest village has a square and a town hall, it seems.' Clara nodded to the imposing building. Well-trimmed linden trees surrounded the perimeter and several cafés overspilled onto the paved area with tables and chairs.

Annie couldn't get over how many cafés and bars there

were in a such a small place. As the two of them ambled along the wide pavement, Annie caught the smell of strong cigarette smoke wafting from groups of older men. They sat at tables with small cups of coffee and tumblers of water in front of them. To Annie it seemed they spoke so fast that they hardly stopped for breath.

In the centre of the square, a pale grey stone obelisk stood in the middle of a well-tended raised flower bed. The base of the obelisk was surrounded by white chippings that sparkled in the strong sunlight. Annie and Clara walked over to read what was written on it in black lettering.

GUERRE 1939–1945
À LA MÉMOIRE DES
MORTS DE COLLINAC

Annie thought back to the war memorial in Pen-y-rhos and how she'd accompanied Lady Delia every Armistice Day to honour the young men and women who had given their lives. It seemed Clara was remembering too.

'Do you remember, M., how, every November, Mother always gave me a little wooden cross with a poppy on to remember Edmund? Little did I know then I was honouring my own father,' she said.

Annie squeezed Clara's arm. *You didn't know … but I did, cariad.*

They read the list of names in silence. Annie was shocked to read how young many of the men were and remembered how Alf had forged his age so he could fight for king and country.

Clara had moved on to the opposite site of the obelisk. 'M. look at this. Roger Lefèvre, Michel Lefèvre. You don't think it could be the same family, do you? Our first day here. Surely we can't be that lucky!'

Annie rushed round to read the names of the young men for herself. Eighteen and nineteen. *So young*. The spelling of the surname was exactly as Winston Graham had written down for her.

'I don't think we should read anything into that, *cariad*. Don't get your hopes up. Perhaps Lefèvre is common in this part of France,' she said.

Clara agreed and led them to a small café directly in front of the town hall. They sat facing the square, letting the sun warm their faces. Although the purpose of their visit was to pay respects to Edmund by finding his grave, anyone looking at mother and daughter would just assume they were holiday makers relaxing and enjoying the good weather. A waitress approached the table and Clara ordered a coffee for herself and a tea for Annie. Annie understood those few words, at least. Already she'd found that the tea did not taste like tea back home so she'd started drinking hers black.

'I thought we could go into Ville de Roi tomorrow, M. I could show you the *lycée* where I spent my placement, and I'll catch up with the English teacher there. He may be able to help us in our search.'

Chapter Forty-Five

When they left Collinac the next day, the sun was high in a sky the colour of cornflowers. Annie caught the spectacle of Mont St Michel glistening in the distance across a narrow band of sea. She thought again about the guidebook that had told her that there was a causeway you could walk across when the tide was out. The book had shown the narrow street winding up to the Gothic abbey of St Michel perched on the top.

As they drove along, the roads got wider and Clara pointed out the places she'd visited to Annie when she'd stayed there just a couple of years ago. They entered the town of Ville de Roi and Clara turned the car into a space in front of an imposing building, which was three storeys high and shaped like a horseshoe. The name *Lycée et Collège Charles De Gaulle* stood out in large black letters. Row upon row of small cars, many the same make but in a variety of colours, were lined up in the car park.

'The popular mode of transport for staff and students alike! Citroën 2CVs.' Clara turned off the ignition and they got out of the car. 'This is where I called home for six months in my second year, M. See that window up there? That was my room.' Annie let her eyes follow the direction Clara was pointing. She remembered looking forward to receiving translucent blue envelopes full of exciting news from Clara when she'd stayed as an *assistante* here.

They walked to the main entrance, and almost as soon as they got inside the young woman on reception came round from behind her desk and flung her arms round Clara.

'Ah, *chérie*!'

Clara beamed and the two of them proceeded to talk in French so quickly that they hardly took a breath. Realising that Annie couldn't understand a word, Clara turned to her. 'Sorry, M. That was rude of me. This is Delphine. She was so kind to me when I first arrived here. If it wasn't for her, I'd have turned around and gone back home. Delphine, this is *maman*.'

Annie swallowed hard. She was going to have to get used to Clara introducing her as her mother after all these years. Delphine smiled. '*Bonjour*.'

The young woman led them through the double doors along the corridor to the study where Monsieur Loiret, the Head of English, was waiting. He was not teaching until the afternoon and seemed pleased to see them.

'*Ma chérie*,' he said, kissing Clara on both cheeks and shaking Annie's hand. 'You said in your letter that this visit is part holiday and part trying to find your papa's resting place. Firstly, you must take time to enjoy your time in Normandy again and show your companion all the wonderful places we have to offer.' Bernard Loiret smiled at Annie.

'This is M., my mother … Mary-Ann,' said Clara.

'Ah, I see. M. for *mére* and *maman* as well as Mary-Ann.'

Annie and Clara looked at each other and smiled. Neither of them explained further and Monsieur Loiret didn't ask. Annie noticed his face had suddenly become quite serious. 'The reason that I suggest you enjoy the holiday side of your visit is that I do think you will find it difficult to find your father's grave. In your letter you explain where his plane was shot down. I've made some enquiries with the history society based here in Ville de Roi, and they confirmed that a British Spitfire did crash just outside Collinac but no body was recovered.'

Clara stretched across to Annie and squeezed her hand.

'I'm very sorry, my dear, and to you too, Mary-Ann. I may call you that?'

Annie nodded. All she could think of was Edmund's lifeless body, rotting and undiscovered. *But Françoise said he'd survived and changed his name to Charles Lefèvre ...* 'A young French woman came to Wales claiming to be his daughter. She said a British pilot who had survived a crash married a local woman and her name was Odile. Odile Lefèvre. He took a French name, she said. Charles Lefèvre,' she found herself explaining.

Monsieur Loiret sat back in his chair and spread out his fingers on the desk. 'Now if the surname had been mine, Loiret, it would be easy to narrow it down, but I'm afraid Lefèvre is a very common surname in north-west France. However, Odile is more unusual. Leave it with me. Odile seems to ring a bell ... but I may be just thinking about the Black Swan in Tchaikovsky's ballet.' He smiled at both women.

'We did find a number of Lefèvres on the war memorial where we're staying.' Clara smiled and nodded at Annie. 'You were right, M., about it being a common surname.'

After saying goodbye to Monsieur Loiret and Delphine, they left the *lycée*. The teacher had promised to make more enquiries now he had the name of both Odile and Charles. Annie knew it was pointless to build up her hopes of finding Edmund's grave, but having the help of someone who had lived all his life in the area gave her hope. He was right, though; this visit should be a holiday for both Clara and her.

They went into the centre of Ville de Roi and found Clara's favourite creperie for lunch. The house *galettes* were all she could talk about, and Annie couldn't wait to try one.

La Belle Époque was situated down a narrow cobbled street branching off from the main square. Outside, tables covered with red-and-white tablecloths and bentwood chairs were placed along each of the two large windows. Ornamental fruit trees in brightly glazed pots separated each table.

'Is it warm enough for us to sit outside, do you think?' Clara asked as she walked towards one of the tables.

This was a real treat for Annie. None of the cafés in Pen-y-rhos had outdoor seating. 'Oh yes. It's a beautiful day.'

They sat down and studied the menu. Annie had never seen such a choice and couldn't decide from the images between a savoury *galette* filled with ham and cheese, topped with a fried egg, or, to satisfy her sweet tooth, a crêpe, oozing with cooked local apples and whipped cream. Pancakes were only ever eaten on Shrove Tuesday at home and then always with sugar and lemon juice.

Clara laughed at her indecision and Annie wondered if her eyes were as wide as she felt them to be.

'I tell you what. Why don't you choose one now and then we can come back again for you to try another one? That's what I used to do. And you have to wash it down with some Normandy cider. Don't tell Mother how many francs I spent here ...' Her face drained of colour when she realised what she'd said. Her eyes misted with tears. 'You know, M., after all this time I still can't believe she's gone. I often think "I must ring and tell Mother that".'

Annie patted her hand. 'It's going to be like that for a long time I'm afraid, *cariad*.'

Clara sighed. 'Here's the waitress,' she said, quickly rubbing her eyes.

A young girl came to take their order, and then the two women chatted about their plans for the next few days.

Annie reminded Clara about a visit to Mont St Michel. Clara got out a map and showed Annie some of the places that she thought were worth visiting. By the time the galettes arrived, Annie was pleased to see that Clara's mood had lightened and she allowed herself to get excited about the holiday. She placed her hand on her gold locket and reassured herself that Edmund would have been happy that she'd tried to find him.

'*Voilà!*' said the young waitress, placing each plate down in front of them. '*Bon appetit!*'

Annie looked at the steaming *galette* overflowing with the savoury ingredients and could see why Clara had wanted to return.

'What did I tell you? My idea of heaven would be to go through each item on the menu,' she said.

'And then you wouldn't be able to fit behind the steering wheel and we'd be stuck here.'

They both laughed, but then didn't talk for the rest of meal; it was so delicious. After paying the bill, they walked to the gardens that Ville de Roi was famous for. At this time in the summer, the flowers were in full bloom and the strong sunlight transformed the lake into a sparkling ellipse at the far end of the grounds. As they looked across the bay to Mont St Michel, Annie reflected on the last few months. When Clara had been a baby, all she'd thought about was making sure she was looked after in the best way she knew how by surrounding her with love, just as her mam had done for her and her brothers. Being Clara's nanny was the next best thing to raising her herself, and she was so proud of the confident young woman sitting on the bench next to her. A blonde tendril had escaped from her ponytail, and Annie admired the sculpted high cheekbones and fair colouring Clara had inherited from Edmund. If only he could see his beautiful daughter. But that was not to be, and she wasn't even sure they'd find his final resting place either.

'I think we'll go to Mont St Michel tomorrow, M. I can remember the last time I went there. It was a horrible misty day, not sunny like today. The mist was so thick on the approach over the causeway. I was driving a little 2CV like the ones we saw at the *lycée* and the other *assistante* was with me. I could hardly see my hand in front of us.'

Annie and Clara strolled back up into the town, stopping to look in shop windows on the way until they reached the central square. A group of elderly men were playing a game Annie hadn't seen before.

'*Pétanque*,' said Clara. 'It's very popular in this part of France.'

They found a bench and watched the game in progress. One man threw a small white ball onto the dusty gravel; a "jack", Clara explained. In turn, each player threw a larger silver-coloured ball, a *boule*, as close to the jack as they could. The men became more animated as the game went on, especially when someone's *boule* knocked another's further away from the jack.

'Apparently every village has a square for *pétanque*. Can you see how seriously they take the game?' Clara laughed. 'You must never disturb a player when they are about to throw.'

Before leaving Ville de Roi, Annie and Clara called for a coffee and a cup of tea at one of the quaint café bars edging the square. They sat outside amongst pots of trailing geraniums in full bloom. The scalloped canvas awning, stretching along the whole length of the front of the café, shielded their eyes from the strong sun. They'd been tempted by the mouth-watering array of pastries and *gateaux* inside, and Annie took her time to savour each delicious mouthful of her fresh strawberry tartlet with *crème pâtissière.* Clara laughed at Annie's reaction. 'You're like the cat that got the cream, M.'

Annie wiped her mouth on the napkin and sat back in her chair. *This is the life*, she thought.

Chapter Forty-Six

The next morning they awoke to misty grey skies, and immediately Annie thought back to Clara's account of arriving on Mont St Michel in thick fog. How could two days be so different?

She stood at the bedroom window and looked out over the fields at the back of the cottage. The vibrant clear colours from the previous day had been transformed to hues of grey; with the scene came the greyest of moods. Even though the search had only just started, she realised that going home without finding Edmund was a real possibility. But hadn't Monsieur Loiret said to enjoy this as a holiday? He was right of course, but where could they go in the mist and the fog?

'We'll have to change our plans, Clara. There's no point going anywhere in this.'

Clara joined her by the window.

'You'd be surprised. The mist will clear to be a fine afternoon. You watch. Come on, let's get dressed and enjoy Madame's breakfast. That wonderful smell of freshly ground coffee is beckoning. You really should try it, M.'

Clara was right. By two o'clock the sky had changed to patches of blue interspersed with white cotton-wool clouds. The famous landmark Annie wanted to visit stood proudly on the horizon. The roads wound through farmland, and Annie noticed a signpost to a war cemetery on the way. If Edmund's body had been found, he could have been buried in a well-tended graveyard like that one. If Françoise was telling the truth and he had only recently died, he could be buried anywhere. The sea on the right-hand side of the road was like a millpond with only an occasional ripple. The sunlight transformed it into a mirror, reflecting rocks and foliage along the water's edge.

The road into the car park was straight with water either side. This was where the causeway was covered by the sea when the tide was in. To one side, a raised walkway edged in rough shrubbery flanked the wide road. The car park attendant directed Clara to a free spot. Annie got out of the car and stood admiring the abbey perched on top of the small island. The buff-coloured stone edifice with its pointed steeple glowed in the sunlight. She fumbled in her shoulder bag and took out her Kodak camera that had been a gift from Clara in preparation for their trip. After taking a number of snaps of Mont St Michel itself, she and Clara took photos of each other.

'Come on, M. You're going to love it.'

Annie and Clara walked along to the main entrance through an archway and entered the narrow street. Both sides were lined with shops displaying souvenirs to attract visitors. Annie and Clara walked up the steep stone steps to the abbey at the top of the island. They wound their way up, taking regular stops to catch their breath. The view from the very top was spectacular and worth the effort. They wandered around the arched cloisters that edged formal gardens and then found a bench for Annie to read the guidebook she'd bought about the abbey.

On the descent, they both agreed it was a lot easier going back down.

'Well, M. What did you think? Was it worth the climb and dodging the crowds?'

Annie smiled at Clara. 'Yes, definitely. I'm so glad I've been. Thank you for bringing me here, cariad.'

It was still so strange to think that she was there in

France sampling delicious food and visiting French tourist attractions when she'd barely left Wales before.

When Clara parked the car at the side of the pension, Annie noticed that Madame Chevalier was waiting for them by the front door. She spoke to Clara in French, but she picked up the words *téléphone*, Bernard Loiret and Odile Lefèvre. Annie's pulse raced.

'What is it? Has he found out something?'

'Yes. He wants us to call at his house tomorrow after college. He has news about Odile.' Clara beamed at Annie. 'Perhaps we're in luck after all.'

That night Annie couldn't settle. She went over and over things in her mind, imagining every possibility. Could Monsieur Loiret know where her grave was? Would Odile and Edmund be buried together? Why hadn't Françoise told them more? She lay awake listening to the gentle breathing of Clara in the opposite bed. Outside in the clear air an owl hooted.

It was a Saturday the next day. Bernard Loiret would be home after taking his morning classes, and Clara had arranged for them to arrive at his isolated château at three o'clock. The word *château* conjured up a vision of grandeur in Annie's mind, but the further they travelled into the French countryside the more she began to wonder why someone would want to live in the middle of nowhere, completely away from civilisation. On one side of the narrow lane was an expanse of open fields, and on the other orchards of apple trees.

Clara parked the car when they came to a passing space in the road. 'Want to have a look?' she said. 'When I was here before, I remember the apple blossom was spectacular in May.'

They crossed the road and walked over to the trees. 'The apples have a lot of growing to do in this summer sun yet, but they're on their way, aren't they? These will end up in a bottle of Normandy cider or *calvados*, you can bet. The area is famous for it. Monsieur Loiret makes his own. He'll probably offer you some and show you around his orchard.'

The rest of the journey was spent in silence, and soon a huge old building came into view. In its day, it would have been quite grand with its three circular turrets and floor-to-ceiling windows. Duck-egg blue painted shutters were peeling in the strong sunlight and covered the windows at an angle to keep the rooms inside cool. Monsieur Loiret was standing in the large arched wooden doorway as they drove through imposing iron gates. He walked out and signalled for Clara to park the car at the shady side of the house.

'Clara, *ma chérie*.' He waited with open arms for them to get out of the car. He kissed Clara and beamed at Annie, his ice-blue eyes twinkling. 'Good to see you again, madame. Welcome to my home.'

'*Merci*,' said Annie.

Monsieur Loiret led them into the house. The heavy wooden doors led into a vast square entrance hall. Portrait paintings in heavy gilded frames adorned each of the four walls, and a sweeping staircase led up from the centre of the room. Together, they hinted at a life of luxury long gone; the rest of the space was shabby and in dire need of renovating. Plaster flaked on the spaces between the paintings and a large patterned rug was threadbare on the stone flagged floor.

'As you can see, Clara, nothing has been done since you were last here. We've concentrated on decorating the sitting room and updating the kitchen before running out of francs.'

He pointed up at yellow stained patches on the high ceiling. 'False economy, I think. We should have started with a new roof first.'

They both laughed, and Annie wondered who the "we" was he referred to. Surely this ramshackle building was too big for one person? She thought back to how empty Cefn Court had felt when Clara was away, but at least there was a staff of kitchen and chamber maids to fill the many rooms. The Court was a fraction of the size of this building.

Monsieur Loiret walked in front of them along a corridor leading off the hall and entered a room bathed in pale afternoon sunshine. A young woman, possibly a little older than Clara, stood when they entered, and Monsieur Loiret moved to her side. 'Clara, you remember Monsieur Maçon who taught history at the *lycée* when you were there? Well, this is his daughter, Béatrice. She speaks fluent English and has been studying the period in history when your father would have been shot down, and especially the local history around Ville de Roi. I think you will be interested in what she has to say.'

Béatrice Maçon was tall and slim, dressed in elegant well-cut slacks and a grey silk blouse. Her glossy black hair fell in tresses over her shoulders, and her smile was warm and welcoming. Annie felt immediately at ease with this stunning young woman.

'It's nice to meet you both. I understand that Edmund was shot down near here, but you have reason to believe he survived and that he has only recently died?'

Clara explained how his daughter had come to Wales after reading the obituary of Lady Delia and that the only clue they had was that her mother's name was Odile Lefèvre. Béatrice agreed with what Bernard Loiret had said about her surname being commonplace. 'But Odile is less so. And one such Odile Lefèvre was famous for a role she played during the war. I think you may be in luck.'

Béatrice took some papers out of her bag and unfolded them. She stood and walked to a highly polished table at the side of the room. She spread the papers over the table and called everyone over to see. The heading on one large sheet was written in bold black capitals. *LA RÉSISTANCE ET FORCES FRANÇAISES DE L'INTÉRIEUR, VILLE DE ROI.*

'If your father was shot down in 1943 and survived, it is probable that he was here when this organisation was formed in the later stages of the war. Let's look,' she said.

Underneath the heading was a list of names in alphabetical order starting with the surnames. Row after row showed the name Lefèvre, but there was one that jumped out at Annie. *Odile Lefèvre, aged twenty-three years. Home village: Sainte Marie-Hélène, Normandy.* Annie's pulse raced and she saw Clara's mouth drop open. She placed a finger on the name. 'Look, M. Odile Lefèvre. Do you think it could be her?'

Annie crossed her fingers. If Béatrice's information could take them to Odile's grave then perhaps they would be able to find her husband's as well?

'I understand, the word resistance, but what do these words mean?' she asked.

'Forces Françaises de l'Intérieur – The French Forces of the Interior is the name of the French *résistance* fighters in the later stages of the war. Charles de Gaulle used it as a formal name for the *résistance* fighters who carried out intelligence missions and the repatriations of Allied airmen. So you see, if this Odile is the one you are looking for, she may be the one who can lead you to your father, Clara.' Béatrice smiled. 'I love this sort of puzzle. All we need to do now is find out when and where she is buried. Up for some detective work?'

Annie and Clara looked at each other. 'You bet,' said Clara. 'This is the best news we've had since we arrived, eh, M.?'

Béatrice spread out another sheet of paper on the table. It was a map of the locality around Ville de Roi, detailed enough to pick out all the roads and lanes leading through tiny villages and hamlets. Sainte Marie-Hélène was situated a few kilometres away from Collinac where Annie and Clara were staying.

'You take this with you. I'll spend some time in the town hall looking at the archives about the *résistance* activity in Ville de Roi. Here's my telephone number. Ring me and let me know how you get on and we can meet in a few days' time.'

Bernard Loiret got up from the seat where he'd been silently observing the three women absorbed in the search for Clara's father and Odile.

'Now I think it's time for some tea. I've bought in some English tea in your honour, Mary-Ann. I understand you don't like *café* ...'

Chapter Forty-Seven

Sainte Marie-Hélène was tucked away from the main roads that criss-crossed that part of Normandy. As they entered the tiny village, a yellow road sign with three flower symbols proudly welcomed the visitor to a *Village Fleuri*. Clara explained that the accolade was part of a national initiative established just a few years previously. France was still in a period of reconstruction after the devastation caused by the war, and it was felt that the planting of flowers helped renew and repair communities.

'What a lovely idea,' said Annie. 'It certainly is a village of flowers, *cariad*.'

The sign was set in a bed planted with scarlet begonias in full bloom alongside white alyssum and blue lobelia.

'The colours of the French flag. No doubt where we are, eh, M.?'

Clara drove into the square and parked the car. Everywhere they looked were tubs of flowers in vibrant colours, edging the cobbled pavements, in front of each shop window, formal beds set in neatly clipped lawn areas. An elderly man in faded navy overalls was weeding a flower bed around the village memorial that took pride of place in the centre of the square like some of the other villages they had visited.

'Stay here, M. He's bound to be a local.'

Annie sat on a bench and watched as Clara wandered over to him and spoke in French. He put down his hoe and became animated as he spoke, gesturing with his hands. Annie understood '*Mais, oui! Mais, oui!*' and could tell by the expression on Clara's face that she had some good news from him.

floor, full-length windows led on to balconies protected by twisted iron spindles that supported window boxes of trailing petunias. Two French flags flew either side of the columns of a porchway. They walked up the steps and into a large reception hall. A young man in a dark blue uniform behind a huge wooden desk welcomed them and spoke in perfect English before they'd said a word.

'I wonder if you can help us, please,' said Clara. 'We are trying to trace a woman called Odile Lefèvre and wonder if she is buried near here as we've been told this is her home village. We've also been told there is a booklet written by an English woman about the *résistance* fighters who used to live locally.'

'Yes, of course. Odile Lefèvre is very famous. It was a very big funeral.'

He pointed to the local map under glass on the counter of the desk.

'*Ici*. Here. You will find her grave in this churchyard. Église de Saint Augustin. It is about half an hour away in the car. I give you the map.'

The young man handed Clara a folded pocket map. 'Thank you so much, monsieur. And the English lady, do you know how we could find her?'

He came around from behind the desk and walked to a display of books and pamphlets in the section marked *Anglais*/English. He picked out a buff-coloured booklet about the size of a foolscap notepad.

Local Heroes of the Résistance
Margaret Barnard

He handed the booklet to Annie. 'I think this is what you are looking for. Inside the writer has left a card with her contact details. She now lives in Ville de Roi. She wrote the booklet in French but we have had it translated into English, Italian, Spanish and German.'

After paying for the booklet and thanking the young man for his help, Annie and Clara walked back to the car. Not able to wait any longer, they decided there was enough time to visit the graveyard at St Augustin's church. Their hope was to find Odile's grave and that it would lead them to Edmund's.

The journey was only a short distance on the map, but as each kilometre passed Annie felt her heart beat a little faster. For twenty years, she'd believed the man she loved to be dead – now to know he might have had a life in this region of Normandy was strange. Perhaps he'd travelled along the very road Clara was driving along now. Had he visited the church where Odile was buried? *Would he be buried there too?*

As they approached a small hamlet, the striking stone church towered with importance above several cottages. Clara parked the car on the grass verge next to the wall surrounding the graveyard, and they entered through the wooden gate. The blond-coloured stone glowed in the late afternoon sun. The graves came in all shapes and sizes, from simple crosses to marble head stones to huge stone family vaults. Many had ornate sculpted angels and inscriptions.

'Where do we start?' cried Annie. 'There are so many!'

She was immediately taken back to the tiny churchyard in Brynderi where her mam and dad lay resting, side by side. Their graves were marked by simple wooden crosses in such contrast to the finery of the Pryce family graves where they had so recently buried Lady Delia.

'I think we should split the area in half. You do the half from the yew tree up to the porch door of the church, and I'll do the part up to the boundary wall,' suggested Clara.

The two women separated and methodically made their way down each row of graves searching for the name Lefèvre. Annie found a number of graves with the surname, but they were not close together which suggested they were from different families. Three rows across from the last Lefèvre grave, she spotted an unusual headstone. It was a simple square of polished black marble with an enamelled French flag and an unusual cross in the centre; instead of one horizontal piece, it had two, the top one slightly narrower than the other. When Annie got close, goosebumps prickled along her neck and her arms as she read the inscription.

ICI REPOSE
ODILE MONIQUE LEFÈVRE
À l'Age de 39 Ans
le 5 MARS 1960

'Clara, come quick! I've found her.'

Clara was by Annie's side in seconds, and she hugged her when she saw the inscription. 'The *résistance* flag! The French Forces of the Interior Béatrice was telling us about. It's definitely the right Odile. That's so sad. She was only thirty-nine. Well, we've found part of our puzzle. Now, let's look for the graves near this one and find Edmund's.'

Annie and Clara read every stone, and nearby they found another cluster of Lefèvre gravestones lying near the boundary wall. One in grey unpolished stone signified the grave of Monique and Henri Lefèvre. The inscription was simple; their ages, the date of their deaths and the words *En Mémoire*.

'Maybe we should go now. We haven't found Edmund's grave, but at least part of the jigsaw has been completed. All in all, it's been productive! We'll read her book tonight and then see what Madame Barnard has to say.'

Chapter Forty-Eight

Annie and Clara had telephoned and arranged to meet with Margaret Barnard the next morning at her apartment in Rue de Maqueville on the edge of Ville de Roi. Hers was one of the luxury apartments overlooking the bay with Mont St Michel in the distance. Large balconies, most with ornamental garden tubs overflowing with trailing flowers, provided an outside space for the residents. On pressing the bell, a voice with an English accent sounded on the intercom telling them to enter and take the lift to the second floor. A smell of lavender and wax polish greeted them when they entered the hallway, and immediately Annie was transported back to the days at Cefn Court when she'd rubbed the silky wax polish into the mahogany antique furniture until she could see her face in the gleam. The door to the lift was a metal concertina affair, and once Annie and Clara were both inside the ancient contraption clinked and clunked noisily as it climbed to the second floor. They arrived on the level with a shudder.

'Blimey,' said Clara. 'I didn't think it was going to make it. Imagine being stuck in there.'

'This place oozes money but still has an ancient lift.' Annie laughed. 'I think we'll take the stairs on the way down.'

Margaret Barnard's apartment was number three; she had already opened her door and was waiting for them in the wide corridor. 'Welcome and please come in. I'm Margaret.'

Annie was trying to place her accent, and soon after inviting them to sit on the sofa in the sitting room, Margaret explained that she had come to Ville de Roi from her home in Bristol to undertake research for her history degree and had never left. She had not only fallen in love with the area but found the love of her life too. 'I transferred and finished my degree in Nantes University and married my beloved Didier.' Her expression changed and she continued. 'He died last year. Taken before his time. I've decided I'll never leave here, though. I've made it my home ... but that's enough about me. I understand from what you said on the phone that you have a connection with Odile Lefèvre?'

Annie explained about Edmund and how it had been a shock to know he might not have died in a plane crash after all. She patted Clara's hand. 'This beautiful young lady is his daughter. And mine. We've been told that he died recently, and although we now know where Odile is buried, we know nothing of where his final resting place is.'

Clara reached in her bag and pulled out Margaret's booklet. 'From your research, we can tell how important Odile was as a *résistance* fighter but did you find anything about a British airman? Their supposed daughter said he had no recollection of before the air crash, so it could be that he couldn't remember his name either. She said he was known as Charles Lefèvre. Did you find out anything about anyone of that name married to Odile?'

Margaret shook her head. 'Nothing.' She stood and crossed the room to the bureau to retrieve what looked like an exercise book. 'Let's see who was active about the same time as Odile. You say his plane was shot down in 1943?'

Annie nodded, and Margaret flicked through the pages. When she reached a certain page, she stopped and let her finger trace the names. 'Here we are. Lefèvre – there are so many. Lefèvre, O. Female. That must be Odile. All the women are listed first and then the men. There are three C. Lefèvres.'

Annie and Clara went to sit either side of her so they could see the book.

'Let's check the addresses. O. Lefèvre, Le Vieux Moulin, Sainte Maire- Hélène. C. Lefèvre, no … but look! This one has the same address. "Le Vieux Moulin". Voilà.' She slammed the book shut. 'You see, I was following up the fighters who were famous for what they did, like Odile. I didn't go through each one individually. Many were supporters and quietly went about their *résistance* in anonymity. Charles must have been one of those. I'll make a pot of good English tea. Fresh milk, of course. None of that awful tinned stuff.' Margaret laughed and left Annie and Clara to let the information sink in.

Annie's heart thumped in her ribcage. Could this Charles Lefèvre be Edmund Pryce? She looked at Clara and suddenly noticed that she was crying. 'Aw, *cariad*. Don't cry. It will be good to know where his final resting place is. If it's anything like that beautiful churchyard we visited yesterday, he'll be at peace.'

Margaret returned with a wooden tray set for tea. 'I'll just get the cakes,' she said. 'I had to bring the teapot with me when I moved here. Many French people don't own one! Will one of you be mother?'

'I think that's me, don't you?' Annie winked at her daughter who had now composed herself. She poured the tea into the cups and handed one to Clara. 'You don't take milk now do you, *cariad*?'

'No, that's lovely. Thank you,' she said, placing her cup down on the small table at the side of the sofa. 'If Charles *is* Edmund, it's so sad to think he'll never know about me – and yet I could have visited him when I was here. I was so close!' She blew her nose. 'It's too late now.'

Margaret brought in a plate of delicious looking individual gateaux and fresh fruit tarts. 'Here we are. The French may not appreciate a good cup of tea like we do, but you can't fault their delicious cakes. Tuck in.' She handed individual plates to Annie and Clara and offered the cakes around. 'I do know someone who knew Odile very well in the *résistance* movement, and if anyone knew anything about Charles Lefèvre and his connection to her it would be Lucien Aubert. They worked on many sorties together and he still lives in Ville de Roi. I'll try to arrange a visit for you. In the meantime, you now have the address where they both lived in Sainte Marie-Hélène. That may be worth a visit.'

Before leaving Margaret Barnard's lovely apartment, they sat on the balcony in the sunshine and chatted about how it felt to be a British woman living abroad. She talked about all the landmarks in the Normandy town and pointed out where she had met Didier for the first time. Annie wondered if Edmund had felt like the same as Margaret when he'd spent almost twenty years living in a foreign country. Perhaps they'd never know. He was dead; she'd already accepted that – so why did she feel so unsettled now? Perhaps Lucien Aubert would be able to provide answers. Perhaps he could also tell them about Françoise Lefèvre, Charles and Odile's daughter.

The next day, Clara and Annie drove to Sainte Marie-Hélène again and tracked down the farmhouse where Odile and Charles had lived – Le Vieux Moulin. Planned visits to the nearby coast and the beautiful seaside towns Clara remembered seemed to have been abandoned, as Annie was more interested in finding out about the life Edmund had potentially lived in France.

'We can always return for another holiday now you've

got a passport and liking for France,' Clara said, as if reading her thoughts.

'I'd love that, *cariad*. This has been a real experience for me.' Annie looked across at her once secret daughter. Spending time together in France had brought the two of them closer together.

'I'm quite excited, aren't you, M.? I feel we're getting close to finding out what happened to Edmund.' She paused for a moment. 'It's strange. I can refer to you as my mother now, but because I've never met him I don't feel I can talk about him being my father. I still think of him as the big brother who died when I was a toddler.'

Le Vieux Moulin was situated down a narrow lane with fields either side where brown and white cattle grazed. The main farm building was situated close to a stream, and the old mill from which the farm's name must have derived was at one end with a now silent water-wheel testament to its past history. Clara parked the car, and she and Annie walked towards the gate. Two large black dogs with tan patches of fur bounded towards them, barking furiously.

'*Arrêtez*! Silence,' shouted a young man who'd emerged from one of the outhouses. He approached and began stroking the dogs who nestled into his legs.

Clara began speaking in French but switched to English once the man said, 'English?'

'Welsh, actually,' said Clara. 'This is my mother. We want to find out some information about the family who lived here before you. I'm Clara Pryce, by the way.'

The man smiled and offered a hand first to Clara and then to Annie. 'I'm Peter. Peter Hinton. As you'll have gathered, I'm English but I live here with my French wife, Danielle, and our son. Please come through. It will be good to speak English for a change.' He laughed. 'The dogs are harmless, but I'll put them in the barn if you're not sure.

They are Beaucerons and are good for letting us know when we have visitors.'

As Peter led Annie and Clara towards the farmhouse, the dogs lost interest in the newcomers and lay down in a shady corner of the yard. The stone farmhouse with its painted shutters was cool inside. The kitchen was a hive of activity when they entered. Peter introduced Danielle, who was up to her elbows in flour, kneading dough. The smell of freshly baked bread from an earlier batch cooling on a wire rack filled their nostrils. An overhead pulley once used as a clothes airer now held copper pots and pans of every size and shape, and shelves on the back wall were lined with jars of preserves. The large dresser there wouldn't have looked out of place in a Welsh farmhouse kitchen, thought Annie.

'*Bienvenue.*' The pretty, dark-haired woman spoke rapidly to her husband in French. Clara smiled and nodded.

'Danielle apologises for not being able to shake your hands,' said Peter. 'She is almost done. She'll just finish here, then she will join us. Please. Sit down.'

He directed them to the large wooden table in the centre of the room. Then he moved to the corner where a playpen was set up around a young boy with a mop of dark curls who was playing with a set of wooden farm animals.

'And this is Louis. He's fifteen months. *Dis bonjour*, Louis.'

'Pa- pa,' said the little boy, then resumed baby talk before lining up his tractor and farm animals.

'Can I get you to drink?' asked Peter.

'Coffee for me, please,' said Clara.

'Tea, please,' said Annie.

'Good. I can have an excuse to share a cup of good English tea with someone who'll appreciate it.'

Peter continued to chat as he made the drinks. He and Danielle had lived at the farm for three years. He explained that they'd bought it from a young woman who had inherited it after her grandparents had died. It had taken a while to be settled as there were others living in the farm who refused to leave. Clara looked at Annie and raised her one eyebrow.

'I don't suppose this woman's name was Françoise Lefèvre, was it?' she asked.

'I don't think so. That doesn't ring a bell. We only dealt with the estate agents. They said she lived just outside Paris.'

Peter walked to the dresser and took out an official looking folder from the right-hand drawer. 'Let's see,' he said, unfolding a cream-coloured letter. 'No, the owner's name is Dupont. Françoise Dupont. So she was Françoise, but not the person you mentioned.'

Clara pulled her mouth into a taut line and reached for Annie's hand. 'I knew it. She's *not* Odile and Edmund's daughter. You don't know who the previous tenants were, do you, Peter?'

Peter turned to his wife and spoke in French. When Danielle answered, Annie recognised the words "Odile" and *résistance*.

'Danielle says that Odile Lefèvre, the *résistance* fighter, lived here with her parents. They died without leaving a will and the farm was split between her and Françoise Dupont, who was the daughter of the eldest son who was killed fighting for the *résistance*. The other brothers died in concentration camps after the war, she believes. They were not married. Danielle thinks Dupont is the granddaughter's married name. Odile Lefèvre tried to stay but could not afford to buy the niece's share. Even though she had nursed her parents to the end and built up the farm, she had to move out. Very sad. The villagers were very angry with

Madame Dupont as she had never visited her grandparents before. It seems all she wanted was the money.'

'Ah, that would explain why she gave up on her claim in Britain then. Inheritance rules are very different there,' said Clara, looking thoughtful.

'Was Odile Lefèvre married, Peter?' asked Annie.

'No, I understand she never married.'

Annie's heartbeat raced. 'So, who was Charles Lefèvre?'

By now, Danielle had joined them at the table. Having heard the name of Odile's friend, she began speaking in French again very quickly. The name Charles came up, as well as *résistance* again.

'Listen to this, M.,' Clara said.

Peter translated what his wife had said for Annie. 'Danielle remembers the talk in the village that Odile had a lover, *un amant*, who lived here at the farm with her and the Lefèvres. Rumour had it that he was an Allied airman who survived his plane being shot down during the war. He spoke perfect French and helped Odile in the *résistance* efforts. He took on the family name to save being exposed and reported to the Germans when this part of France was occupied. Odile and Charles moved out, but it seems that Odile was already very ill when they left the farm and died not long after moving away.'

'We should tell you that Françoise Dupont, or Lefèvre as she told us, claims to be the daughter of Odile and Charles, but what you've told us has cast even more doubt on that. She also said that Charles had died too, and she came to lay claim to his family home in Wales.' Clara's expression told its own story.

'It doesn't sound like Danielle has heard of his death,' said Peter, looking confused. Annie gasped and placed her hand over her open mouth.

'No wonder she wouldn't tell me anything about her

so-called parents. *Arrgh*! We think Charles is really my father, Edmund Pryce, and the two of us have come to France to try to find his grave. Are you really saying he might not be dead? Do you have a forwarding address for him?' asked Clara breathlessly.

Peter rushed to get a pen and notepad from the top of the dresser. 'We'll help in any way we can. Why don't I get in touch with our estate agent and see if they have one? Do you have somewhere I can contact you?'

Clara took the pen and notepad. She wrote down the telephone number. 'You can ring this number if you have any information. It's the telephone number of the *pension* where we are staying at in Collinac. It would be so good to find Odile's Charles. We have to prepare ourselves that he may not be Edmund at all, but the fact that Françoise came looking for his family in Wales, and now with what you have told us, it makes it worth a try.'

Annie had one more idea. 'What's the word for "horses", *cariad*?'

Clara looked puzzled. '*Chevaux*. Why?'

Annie turned to Danielle who had picked up baby Louis and was balancing him on her hip. 'Madame. Charles Lefèvre. *Chevaux*?'

The French woman's face lit up. '*Mais oui.*'

She spoke to her husband and Clara translated for Annie. 'Apparently he was a friend of all the horse owners around here. He set up a business as a farrier and kept all the horses' feet in tip-top condition, well shod.'

Danielle pointed to a row of horseshoes fashioned into coat hooks behind the door leading outside. '*Bonne chance.*'

Would those horseshoes bring them good luck too? Good luck in finding out what happened to the man who was her one and only love and Clara's father?

'Madame Chevalier will pass a message on to us. We'll let you know if we find Charles Lefèvre. We can't thank you enough, can we, M.? *Au revoir*, Louis,' she said, tickling the little boy's tummy. He snuggled into his mother's neck and chuckled.

'Yes, we can't thank you enough, Peter. Goodbye. *Au revoir*, Danielle.'

Annie's heart pulsed with emotion. Perhaps her Edmund had made a life for himself in rural France? All she wanted now was to find out if Charles Lefèvre and Edmund Pryce were the same person.

As they walked away from the farmhouse, Annie put her arm around Clara. 'I can't believe it, *cariad*. He might still be alive!'

Chapter Forty-Nine

'What a day, M.! Not long now until we leave, but I have a good feeling we're going to find him.'

Annie looked at her daughter as she drove along the narrow roads back to the *pension*. Her eyes sparkled, and the determination she'd displayed when she'd first been shocked by Annie's revelation was now being put to good use. If they did find Charles Lefèvre, whether he was Edmund or not, it would be down to Clara's resilience.

'Are you going to say something? I can feel you staring at me.'

'I'm just thinking that if you hadn't forgiven me and invited me on this trip, I would never have known all this. So yes, *cariad*, I have a very good feeling, too. Two leads as well. Margaret Barnard's contact who knew Odile, and Peter's follow-up hopefully finding out where Odile and Charles moved to. But even if they both lead to a dead end, at least we have tried. And I've been abroad!'

When they arrived back, Madame Chevalier was waiting for them and spoke to Clara.

'M., listen to this. There was a message for us. Madame said it was from the English lady, as she calls her. She says it is good news and that we must ring her.'

Annie's stomach somersaulted. *What could the news be?*

Clara thanked Madame Chevalier and they went into the hallway to ring Margaret Barnard. Annie noticed that Clara's hand shook as she dialled the number.

'Margaret, it's Clara Pryce. Madame Chevalier said we were to ring you. Do you have news?' Her words tumbled out, and it seemed to Annie that she didn't give the woman at the other end any time to answer. She smiled and gave Annie a thumbs up. 'Oh, that's amazing news. Thank you so much. You don't know what this means to my mother and me.'

Annie's eyes widened. 'Clara, come on. What did she say?'

'She's contacted Lucien Aubert, the man she told us about. And guess what? He knows Charles Lefèvre well *and* the best news – he knows where he's been living since he was forced to leave the farm with Odile. He's not dead!' Clara flung her arms around Annie and squeezed her tight. When Annie freed herself, there were tears streaming down her daughter's face.

'Aww, *cariad*. Come here. This has affected you far more than you've let on, hasn't it?' It was her turn to do the *cwtch*ing now. They stood in the hallway for a few minutes just holding each other. 'But there's one thing we have to remember. We don't know yet if Charles is Edmund. Lucien Aubert only knows a Charles Lefèvre.'

Clara nodded. 'I know, but I think we should see him first. I said we'd meet him at Margaret's apartment in the morning. Is that all right?'

Annie couldn't get to sleep that night. Outside the clear sapphire sky was jewelled with a myriad stars and moonlight bathed the room in an ethereal silver glow. A fleeting image of a young Edmund, handsome and resplendent in his RAF uniform, stood at the bottom of her bed. It filled her with sadness for the years they'd lost. She looked across at the sleeping form of their beautiful daughter in the bed opposite, hoping that she and the father she'd never known might still have a chance to meet.

The next morning both Annie and Clara were deep in thought as they travelled into Ville de Roi. What would

Lucien Aubert be able to tell them? If it *was* Edmund, what would he look like now?

Clara parked the car in the street near the entrance to the apartments. They walked up the stone steps to the front door and rang the bell. When they arrived by lift on the second floor, Margaret was waiting for them on the carpeted corridor outside the open door to her apartment.

'Come in, my dears. Lucien is waiting to meet you both. He's outside on the balcony and speaks very good English. He worked in London after the war.'

A distinguished looking man with steel-grey hair stood as they went through the double door onto the balcony. He stubbed out a cigarette on a glass ashtray on the coffee table before offering his hand to Annie first and then to Clara.

'*Bonjour*, ladies. I'm very pleased to meet you. Lucien Aubert.'

'Mary-Ann and Clara.' Margaret invited them to sit down after introducing them. The view across to Mont St Michel was clear, and the water in the distance gleamed like a band of silver.

'Please call me Annie. Thank you for seeing us, Monsieur Aubert.'

'Lucien, please. I understand from Margaret that you are trying to trace Charles Lefèvre. During the early part of the war, I was the leader of the *résistance* movement based here in Ville de Roi. We were very active, women as well as men. It was all very secretive, and when the Germans were occupying the area we trusted very few people for fear of being found out. One of my confidantes was a woman called Odile Lefèvre. We were paired up to undertake missions together. She was very brave, and we managed to foil many a German raid. In 1943, she told me about finding an injured British airman in the hayloft at her parents' farm.'

Goosebumps formed on Annie's arms, and she watched the expression on her daughter's face change.

'How does this fit in with your friend, Charles Lefèvre?' Clara asked.

'Because Odile said the airman had no recollection of who he was. Only that he had escaped from the wreckage and sought refuge in a farm. The Lefèvres' farm.'

Lucien Aubert went on to tell them how Odile had hidden the airman even from her own parents to start with and nursed him back to health.

The three women waited for him to elaborate. He took out another cigarette from a slim gilt cigarette case, lit it and inhaled deeply.

'Odile said she'd been terrified he'd be caught. She and her parents would have been shot for harbouring a prisoner. Together they came up with a plan. He spoke fluent formal French but his accent would have given him away, so they would work together on that and he took on a French name. He chose Charles. Had to learn to say it the French way. *Sh*arles – no "s" on the end. From then on, he was Charles Lefèvre. At night, he accompanied her on the leaflet drops, travelling by horseback to the surrounding villages, riding down the narrow lanes and often crossing fields to avoid the wider roads that the German trucks used—'

Clara interrupted. 'His father was called Charles. Perhaps he did remember something about his old life after all?' She looked at Annie, wide-eyed.

'Odile said that, at first, she did all the talking for them both, but very quickly he learned local sayings, and he started to sound like a local. There's a slight trace of an accent if you know what to look for, but after twenty years no one would know. Even back then, no one questioned it. To everyone apart from the group members who knew the truth, he was her cousin from Brittany. He helped Odile with so many missions and was very respected for his bravery.'

'So, they never married and they didn't have a daughter?' asked Annie.

'Odile never said, but I'm sure they were lovers. To my knowledge, there was no marriage. At the farm it was just her parents, Odile and Charles. After the war, he helped Odile run the farm and grow the grain for the mill. Their flour was sold all over Normandy and Brittany. Charles also learned to be a farrier. He loved horses and wanted to work with them. They were just normal farmers trying to make a living until old Monique and Henri Lefèvre died within six months of each other.'

Annie knew what was coming. The mysterious young woman who appeared at Lady Delia's funeral came into her mind. 'Françoise,' she said, glowering.

'You know her?' asked Lucien. 'I will never forgive her for what she did to poor Odile ... and Charles too. No one had ever heard of her. She said she was Pierre's daughter but had not seen her grandparents or her aunt for years. In France, there is a rule about the estate being shared amongst the spouse and the children. Pierre had gone underground and had been killed actively fighting for the *résistance*. Odile did not know it but she was already ill with cancer when this row all blew up, and I'm convinced the unpleasantness and the worry over money just accelerated her death. Poor Charles was heartbroken. They had built that farm up and it was just starting to be a successful business; the Dupont woman insisted on selling it straight away to get her share of the money. *Bitch*!' He thumped his hand into his open palm. 'Sorry.'

The atmosphere was tense, and Annie was relieved when Margaret Barnard suggested a break. She disappeared into the kitchen and brought back a tray with glasses and a jug of homemade lemonade. Slices of lemon floated in the cloudy liquid, and ice cubes clinked as she poured the drinks into crystal tumblers.

'I think we need this,' she said, smiling.

Conversation turned to the weather, their visit to Mont St Michel and the places Clara had visited when she'd stayed in the area previously. The only time Charles Lefèvre was mentioned again was when Annie and Clara got up to leave.

'Here is where Charles lives now. It's not far; a smallholding on the road out of Ville de Roi. He has a few chickens, lots of apple trees and several of his beloved ponies. You'll recognise it by its wrought iron sign, just like the one he made for Le Vieux Moulin. This place is called Les Petites Écuries. The Little Stables.' He handed a sheet of paper to Clara.

Annie's throat tightened. She willed herself not to break down in front of everybody. She was more convinced than ever that they had traced Edmund. He was alive and there was no grave. Her hand instinctively went to the gold locket resting under her blouse.

Chapter Fifty

Another sleepless night for Annie; she tossed and turned for hours. Whereas the previous night had been plagued with questions and uncertainties, tonight's insomnia was caused by excitement at the prospect of seeing the man she loved after a long time of believing he was dead. Lucien Aubert had convinced her that the man they would be visiting in the morning was Edmund Pryce, the father of the baby she'd abandoned on the steps of his family home. Her heart raced and her throat tightened. What would he say when he found out what she'd done? Would he ever forgive her? Through the gap in the curtains, Annie lay watching dawn break. Streaks of pastel pinks, lavenders and lemons brushed across the palest blue sky. A cockerel crowed in the yard below. Again, she closed her eyes and tried to sleep, but the next thing she knew Clara was gently tapping her on the shoulder.

'Come on, M. We're going to find Edmund today! I'm going to ask madame if I could use the telephone. I want to warn Winston Gibson that we are ninety-nine per cent certain Edmund is alive, and he is a beneficiary of Mother's will as well as me. After, I'll go straight to the dining room for breakfast and wait for you there.'

Annie felt bleary-eyed after so little sleep, but once she was washed and dressed she was ready for one of Madame Chevalier's continental breakfasts she'd come to enjoy. Sometimes they had sweet *brioche* buns that Clara had encouraged her to dip into a *bol* of steaming hot chocolate. The first time she felt quite decadent when she remembered her mam had forbidden her and her brothers from dunking even a biscuit, proclaiming it was the height of bad manners. She had smiled and said "Sorry, Mam!" to herself before tucking in.

That morning breakfast consisted of a selection of croissants, *pains au chocolat* and a large bowl of fruit. There was also a jug of freshly squeezed orange juice.

'Sliced white toast isn't going to be the same after this, is it, *cariad*? Did you get through to Mr Gibson?' Annie sat down at the table opposite Clara.

'I did.' Clara's eyes sparkled. 'He said we didn't need proof that the man was really Edmund. M., he had the most wonderful news. Uncle Edgar's lost his court case! It turned out that the will he talked about was, in fact, a fraud. He did get Mother to sign it, but he was the only other witness at the time and the bogus solicitor didn't sign in the presence of Mother. It was declared invalid! It must have been that day she got so upset, M. Do you remember me saying? As well as my statement, Elsie and Sara both testified as to how agitated my mother was after his visits. Can't stand the countryside, he told Winston Gibson. Can't stand the Welsh.'

Annie gripped Clara's hand. 'You know what that means, don't you, cariad? Cefn Court is going back to where it belongs, where your mother wanted it to be. In her children's hands!'

Clara sipped her black coffee with a smile on her face. 'The Court is all locked up and the staff dismissed. As soon as we get home, we must give all of them their jobs back. I'll have to let Di know. She's going to be so pleased too.'

Annie thought of her friends; Elsie still working at the Court after all this time, young Sara, and Frank Baker still working in the stables. When she thought of Frank, she wondered what would have happened if she'd taken his offer of becoming more than friends. Lucien had said Odile and Charles were lovers. Was it possible to fall in love more than once? She knew she couldn't. It wouldn't have been fair to Frank if she couldn't have loved him in the same way she'd loved Edmund. Today, she might find out. Would he remember who she was? Would he remember the special time they spent together before he left to fight for his country?

'We've just got to hope he has proof,' Annie mused. 'If only he'd had something to identify him. Even if he couldn't remember anything before the crash himself, he surely would have some kind of documentation to prove who he was so he could return to Wales once he recovered.'

'But, M., he fell in love and wanted to make his life here. It sounds like he had no memory of you. No memory of his parents. Odile loved him and he loved her. He made his life in France with her. We have to accept that.'

A feeling of sadness dawned on Annie and her chest tightened. She no longer held a part of Edmund's heart. He'd asked her to wait. And she had. But he wouldn't have any recollection of what he'd asked of her.

The journey to Les Petites Écuries did not take long. Annie acted as navigator with the map spread over her knees. Her map-reading skills had improved since they'd first arrived in France. How the holiday had flown! The route took them along the coastal road where the fields were flat, and a view of the sea and Mont St Michel in the distance glistened in the sunshine. A sign to the smallholding took them left down a narrow lane. Clara braked to allow a youth to herd a flock of sheep from one field to another on the opposite side of the lane. It took so long that Clara turned off the engine.

'Almost as bad as being back in Wales,' said Clara, laughing. 'What do they say? There are more sheep than people in Radnorshire.'

Annie chuckled and watched the large flock huddle together to get through each of the gates on either side. Closing the second gate, the young lad rose his hand and mouthed '*Merci*'.

Clara drove for a few more kilometres, and with each passing minute Annie's stomach churned and somersaulted. She'd told herself not to build her hopes up, not to expect too much. Soon the lane led to a pretty stone cottage. Pale blue shutters graced every window. To the side of the house was a small field where several horses and ponies were grazing. Annie gasped. One of the horses looked so much like Kenna, and memories of her time as a groom in 1941 came flooding back.

'M. Whatever is it?'

'The chestnut horse,' said Annie, pointing. 'She's identical to Edmund's horse, Kenna. He must remember!'

'Don't get your hopes up, M. Remember what I said.'

Clara left the car by the gate behind a parked blue-and-white Citroën 2CV, and the two of them walked the long path to the door of the cottage. There were several outhouses across a yard from the house, and Annie recognised that they were kitted out as stables. There was another building alongside the main house that was obviously used as a workshop, judging by the iron implements and machinery visible through the open door.

'We'll try the house first. Do you want me to do the talking? Prepare yourself. Here it goes, M.'

Annie's heart raced as Clara shook the rope tassel to ring the brass bell suspended from a black wrought iron bracket. The door opened.

'*Oui*?' said the man.

Annie willed herself not to break down in tears. She clenched her fists so tightly that her knuckles became white. *He was alive! Standing in front of her, living, breathing but unaware of who she was*. Edmund looked almost exactly as he had when she'd last seen him. His blond hair now had a few silver streaks at the temples, and the fine white line of a scar traced his cheekbone from the corner of his eye to his jaw. He had the tanned appearance of someone who worked outdoors; so different to the fair skin she remembered.

'Monsieur Lefèvre?' said Clara. For the next few seconds, they spoke in French then Annie heard her ask in English, 'Do you mind speaking so that my mother can understand too?'

Edmund Pryce properly focused on Annie for the first time, his lavender-grey eyes intense and puzzled. 'Of course, madame.'

'We've come here after talking to your friend Lucien Aubert, and the couple who bought Le Vieux Moulin. They bought the farm from a young woman called Françoise, but I think you used to live there with Odile Lefèvre?' For a second, Edmund's face became serious, his eyes misting over at the mention of Odile.

'You'd better both come in.' At first, he spoke slowly and deliberately with a heavy accent, as if working out each English word in his head, but as he continued to tell them about the unpleasant way they'd been ousted from Odile's family home, his English became more fluent and his cultured accent returned.

Annie looked first at her daughter then Edmund and wondered if they saw what she saw; they were almost a mirror image of each other. Not just the shade of the hair and unusual colour of their eyes, but the way they angled their heads when listening to each other, the way they splayed their fingers as they spread out their hands. She noticed the small birth mark on the inside of his wrist that had been passed onto Clara.

Annie plucked up courage to speak. To begin with, her voice sounded scratchy. 'Monsieur Aubert said you were shot down during the war but have no memory of your life before that.'

Edmund paused and looked at Annie again. 'That's right, but every now and then certain things come back. For example, did you see the chestnut pony in the field when you arrived? Well, something in my mind told me there was a connection and then it went. I knew I had to buy her from the farmer when he brought her here to be shod.'

'Kenna,' said Annie.

'I don't understand. What's Kenna?'

'The name of your horse.' Annie rummaged in her bag and brought out a faded black and white snap of Edmund on Kenna that she carried everywhere with her. 'Do you recognise the rider?'

Edmund's mouth gaped open. 'Is that me? I don't understand.'

'Before your air crash, we think you were Edmund Pryce, a British airman, but it would appear that your injury meant that you have no memory of your life before then,' Clara explained slowly.

He nodded and placed his hand on his forehead, pulling back his thick hair to reveal another scar where the skin puckered. 'This. Odile found me in her barn and patched me up. It was too dangerous for me to go to hospital. This one on my cheek healed quickly, but this one did all the damage. A trusted family doctor came out to the farm in the dead of night and did what he could.' He stared at Annie. 'Did I know you then? Your face looks familiar. Your red hair. Such a beautiful shade.'

Annie felt her skin burning. 'I was your groom. I looked after Kenna for you.' *That's enough for now.*

Clara explained how when his mother, Lady Delia, had died her brother felt he should inherit the estate. She and Annie had come to France to find his grave. 'A young woman calling herself Françoise Lefèvre turned up claiming she was yours and Odile's daughter and that she had a right to inherit the estate. Things are different here in France, I understand.'

Edmund stood and began pacing the floor. 'That woman. Dupont. I have no daughter. Odile had no daughter. Odile was heartbroken. She was forced out of the farmhouse in order for her obnoxious niece to get her share. She lived only a short time after we moved here.'

Clara continued. 'It was a shock to find you hadn't died in 1943 and more of a shock to find you are still alive and living here. Do you know, I spent six months here in Ville de Roi, teaching at the *lycée* and you were just a few kilometres away?' Annie squeezed her hand.

Edmund fidgeted. 'I have a confession to make to you. I *did* know that I was a British airman from what Odile told me, but because I couldn't remember my name or who I was, I decided I would make my life here in France helping the family who took me in. I owed my life to Odile and her parents. We decided on a new identity for me. I chose Charles – God knows why Charles – and I took on the family name.'

'Charles was your father's name,' said Clara. She hesitated before broaching the subject of what finding him alive could mean. She looked across at Annie who nodded her approval, reading her daughter's thoughts. 'Once you've got over the shock, perhaps we can tell Winston Gibson, our solicitor, that you are alive and able to inherit Cefn Court and its estate, as your mother wanted. I've already explained some of the situation to him.'

It seemed to take a while for Edmund to understand

what that meant. He sat in silence with his head in his hands. 'A simple man who works with horses can't suddenly become lord of the manor, can he?'

Annie smiled at him and knew at that moment that, whatever happened, she still loved him and she was right to wait for him. Her hand went to the chain of her locket and she unfastened the clasp.

'There is something else you should know. You won't remember but you gave me this locket when you left for RAF training.' She handed her precious necklace to him. 'Go on. Open it and read what's inside.'

Edmund flicked open the oval locket. He unfolded the note tucked inside. 'Well, that's my handwriting all right. This is a photo of the same man as the one on the horse you showed me ... you had long auburn ringlets then, didn't you? And we went to the boathouse. A picnic to say thank you.'

Annie's heart thumped. It was as if a secret box of memories was being unlocked in Edmund's brain. She looked at Clara and beamed. 'Yes, we did.'

'You weren't Annie then, were you? Mary-Ann. Yes, that was it. My groom was called Mary-Ann.' He leaned back on the sofa. 'I remember lavender, I think.'

Annie smiled, remembering how her mam had shown her how to make muslin pouches filled with lavender seeds and tied with a ribbon. They were placed in drawers and wardrobes to ward off moths. All her clothes smelled of it.

'She's wearing lavender *eau de cologne* now. We got some on the boat coming over. Show him, M.,' said Clara.

Annie lifted her wrist to let Edmund inhale the fragrance. He closed his eyes. When he opened them, he looked at Annie shyly. 'Mary-Ann, I remember you now.' He placed his hand on her arm and tingles fizzled across twenty years, and she was back with the man she fell in love with when she was a young girl.

He reddened and stood. 'Come. Let me make you something to drink. We can sit outside in the sun and you can tell me all about Wales.'

The paved area in front of the cottage windows was sheltered from the sun by a cream canvas awning and home to a round iron table and four matching chairs with cream linen cushions. Annie recognised a female touch and wondered about the woman who had stolen Edmund's heart. She'd have to be satisfied that at least he had some memory of her, but that would be all. One thing was bothering her. He didn't yet know who Clara was and how she came to be brought up by his mother. Edmund returned with a tray of hot drinks and a plate of iced biscuits.

'Coffee for you, Clara. And tea for Mary-Ann. Do you know I've always drunk tea? We have to boil the water in a saucepan, no pot, but it still tastes good. I was the only one to drink it at the farm. Odile and her parents always made black coffee so strong you could stand your spoon up in.'

They laughed and he pressed the plunger down into the cafetière, pouring the coffee for Clara into a pottery mug. As she reached across to pick up the mug, Edmund sat bolt upright and pointed at her wrist.

'You have the same birthmark as me,' he said. 'Look!' He turned his arm over and the two of them compared the heart shapes on their wrists.

'There's something else you should know,' said Clara. She hesitated and looked at Annie again for reassurance. 'This will come as a shock for you, as if you haven't already had enough already, but … you're my father. I'm Clara Pryce.'

Edmund's face paled. 'I don't understand. How can I be?'

Annie wanted nothing more than to take him in her arms and tell him everything would be all right. He looked at Clara as tears formed along his reddened eyelids. He took her hand.

'I would have loved a daughter, and I've missed the first twenty years of your life. If only I'd followed up who I was when I recovered from my injuries. I'm so sorry, *chérie*. There is no doubt you are my daughter. Now I know who you are, it's like looking in a mirror.'

Clara smiled. 'I've only just found out myself. Your parents brought me up as their own and gave me a wonderful home.'

As things began to dawn on him, he turned to Annie. 'The boathouse. It was then?'

Annie lowered her eyes. 'Yes. I didn't know I was expecting when you left for the RAF. I never received your letters or heard from you again. I couldn't tell anyone.'

'But if my parents brought Clara up, I presume my mother knew she was mine?'

Chapter Fifty-One

Annie had dreaded this moment ever since she suspected Edmund was still alive. How was she going to tell him the truth about what happened and how would he react? Her heart pounded and she felt heat spreading to her neck and cheeks. The silence was deafening and felt like it went on for a lifetime. Clara came to her rescue. She grabbed Annie's hand and stroked it gently.

'M. did what she knew was best for me, Edmund,' she explained. 'She had no means of supporting the two of us. I would have ended up in a children's home or adopted by strangers. But she was very brave and gave me to your parents so that I would not know poverty like that.'

Annie's vision blurred with tears. She squeezed her daughter's hand, wondering what Edmund would say next.

'I don't remember my parents, but did they really just take in a baby? Didn't they guess you were mine?'

Again, it was Clara who took charge. 'Your mother told me I looked the image of your baby sister who died.' She turned over her wrist. 'I'm sure she would have guessed when she saw this too. Your mother appointed M. as my nanny. So, you see I had the best of both worlds. Two mothers who showered me with love.'

Edmund didn't ask any more questions and neither Clara nor Annie elaborated. Talk moved on to what to do next. The only life he'd remembered in detail began here in northern France in 1943, but he was now being given a glimpse of a very different life he'd had before his accident. He looked at Annie and reached for her hand.

'I do remember that you were very special to me,

Mary-Ann, but that's all. It's so frustrating. If we have a daughter, just knowing you *were* special is not enough.'

'You asked me to marry you,' Annie said. 'And I told you I'd wait for you until after the war. And I did.' Her voice dropped to a whisper. 'I *have*.'

Clara quickly stood up and walked in the direction of the horses. 'I'll give you two some time together. You need to talk. I'm going to explore the orchard and look at your ponies, if that's all right, Edmund?'

'Of course. Make yourself at home.' He turned back to Annie. 'You said *have*. Surely you must have married since then. After news came through that I was missing in action?' Edmund held her hands in his, and old familiar feelings soared ... but she was still a stranger to him. *He's just being kind*, she told herself.

'There was someone. Frank. I liked him and I knew he loved me, but I couldn't marry him. It wouldn't have been fair. I didn't love him, you see,' she said.

'I'm so sorry, Mary-Ann. You've wasted your life because of me. I didn't deliberately fail to keep my promise. You must know that.'

Annie knew that whatever Edmund decided to do – return to Wales and run Cefn Court as a gentleman farmer or stay in Normandy living a simple life with his horses – there would be no romantic reunion between them. But she was still better off than when she'd arrived in France with the intention of finding Edmund's grave and final resting place. Here he was, alive and well, and because they shared a beautiful daughter, they would remain close. She had to be content with that.

'I'm just happy to know that you're alive, and that at last you have met our beautiful daughter. Once you get to know her, you will be very proud of her. Not only is she very clever but she is kind and a lovely person. It's because of her determination that we found you. We leave on the ferry very soon, but I know she will be back to get to know you better. You two have so much catching up to do. Perhaps she will bring her friend Diana to meet you.'

Clara was walking towards them. 'Did I hear Diana's name?'

'I was saying that although we leave soon, I thought it wouldn't be long before you'd be back. You two need to spend time together and get to know each other. As Di is part of your life now, I thought she'd be coming with you, that's all.'

Edmund put his arm around his daughter and pulled her close. 'There's nothing I'd like more than get to know everything about you, and if Diana is a special friend, then I would love to welcome her here too. Next time you must stay here. You, too, Mary-Ann.'

They stood to go. It seemed that no sooner had they found Edmund that it was time to leave. But Annie noticed he appeared deep in thought.

'Ebony!' said Edmund suddenly. 'A handsome black stallion belonging to my father. More is coming back to me.' He held Annie's hand. 'You are the trigger, Mary-Ann. The more time you're here with me, the more is coming back. Oh, this is so frustrating. If only—'

'Take your time, Edmund. Goodbye for now. *Au revoir.*'

As her hand slipped away from his, the look in Edmund's eyes as he gazed so intently into hers caused her pulse to race. Could there be a flicker of the old feelings he had for her coming back?

'*À bientôt*, please. Not *au revoir*. Write and send photos. Anything to unlock these memories.' He pressed his hand on the side of his head. He turned to Clara. 'I understand that you have to leave, but it's too soon, *n'est-ce pas?* Ah well. From the ferry port along the coast from here? I'd like to meet you there before you drive on to the ferry, to wave you off.'

Annie could see that it was hard for them both. Father and daughter. More than twenty years of catching up to do, only to be separated again.

'That would be lovely. Hey, before we go, let's get some photos of you two together.' She took out the camera Clara had bought for her and began snapping away to finish the roll of film. Clara and Edmund standing in front of the house with the horses in the background. Clara posing like a model. Clara and Edmund making silly faces. A photo of them holding up their arms showing the matching birthmarks on the insides of their wrists. She then handed the camera to Clara to take a photo of her and Edmund.

'Say cheese!' said Clara.

'Camembert!' said Edmund.

The three of them burst out laughing. They spent the next few minutes still putting off the inevitable.

Annie took a deep breath. 'Come on. We really do have to go now. We'll write and send you the photos, Edmund. This has been the *best* day. One we could never have imagined when we arrived in France.'

Clara and Edmund kissed each other on both cheeks, the French way. Then her eyes became teary and she walked away without looking back.

'She'll be fine, Edmund. Knowing you are her real father is still quite new for her. Clara will be back here before you know it. I'll look after her until then.'

'I know you will, Mary-Ann. I'm starting to understand how easy it would have been to love you. I can tell you are a good person. One day you will tell me how you persuaded my parents to take our daughter. I'm so glad you did. I want to know everything about my life in Wales before I left for France.' He kissed her on both cheeks, his lips soft on her skin.

Am I being stupid to dream? Annie's insides somersaulted.

It was the day they were leaving to return home, and Annie and Clara were up bright and early. After saying goodbye to Madame Chevalier and settling the bill, and with the car packed, they were ready for the journey to the ferry port.

'*Arrêtez*! Stop. *Un petit cadeau*.' Madame rushed back into the house and came back with a present for them, gift-wrapped in flowery paper.

'*Merci, madame*,' said Clara. 'Open it, M.'

Annie pulled off the paper, revealing a wheel of camembert cheese and a small bottle of local Calvados. 'That is so kind. Thank you. *Merci*.'

A wide grin spread across Madame's face. By this time, she had been joined by her husband. 'Calvados. *Mmm*,' he said, making a circle with his thumb and forefinger and bringing it up to his lips.

Everyone laughed. Clara put the gifts in the boot of the car and they left their hosts standing in the lane, waving them off as they drove away.

'That was nice of them, wasn't it?' said Annie. 'What a time we've had, eh, *cariad*?'

'You can say that again. When I rang Winston Gibson last night, he said he's started putting into motion the shared inheritance of Cefn Court and its estate on Edmund's behalf, but of course he will need proof. If Edmund comes to visit us, he'll need a passport, and I'll send him a copy of his birth certificate for him to know details of his full name, his parents' and their occupations.'

Annie had dreamed of this moment since Lady Delia had passed on. That was why she'd risked everything by divulging the true circumstances of Clara's birth. But what she could never have imagined was that Cefn Court would also transfer to another of its rightful heirs. *Edmund Charles Pryce*.

By the time they joined the main N roads, the sun was at its highest in a cloudless periwinkle-blue sky. In the distance, the sea glistened like silver. *Magical*. But as they got onto the A40, something wasn't right. 'What's that smell?' asked Annie. 'It's really horrible!'

They wound the windows down and, although it was better, they could still smell it.

'I thought it was coming from outside when I first noticed it, but it's getting worse. I think it's inside the car,' said Clara. When it was safe, she stopped the car and got out. She looked everywhere before opening the boot. She stood back. 'Phew! It stinks.'

'What is it?' asked Annie, getting out to join her.

'It's madame's camembert! The heat is obviously making it even more ripe. I'm going to have to throw it. Sorry, madame!'

She walked to the lay-by bin, already overflowing with rubbish, and managed to place the melting cheese in what seemed the last available space.

Driving with the windows down and the outside air clearing the smell, the rest of the journey continued without incident. The port loomed into view and they could see the ferry in the distance. Edmund had said he'd wait for them near the entrance to the terminal and, true to his word, they spotted his small blue-and-white Citroën parked in a space on the left-hand side of the car park. He was leaning on the bonnet in an open-necked shirt and navy slacks. He waved when he saw their car approaching. Annie thought of the Daimler that had been his usual chauffeur-driven mode of transport when he'd left Cefn Court for the RAF. How on earth would he adapt to a new life back in Wales? If indeed he was going to.

'Thank you for coming to wave us off ... Papa,' said Clara.

Edmund's mouth broke into a smile. 'Come here, *ma chérie*. That's the first time you've called me that.' He pulled his daughter into a bear hug.

She pulled herself free. 'Isn't "Papa" what French children call their fathers? Maybe that's what I should call you, as you've spent almost as much of your life in France as you have in Wales.'

'By the look on his face, I think he loves it, *cariad*.'

More goodbyes, and then it was time for them to join the queue for the ferry. Neither Clara or Annie knew how the story would end. It was up to Edmund Charles Pryce; they would both be there to help him every step of the way, whatever decision he made. As Clara kept her eyes on the ramp as she drove up into the ferry, she wouldn't see how Annie's fingers were tightly crossed. *I've got a good feeling about this.*

Epilogue

A year later

This was the day we'd been waiting for. I looked in my rear mirror and checked my father was still behind me. He was driving the Austin Gypsy and horsebox I'd taken out to his home in Normandy to bring his belongings and his chestnut mare, Phénix, home to Cefn Court. The manor and its estate were, at last, legally ours. It was strange driving Papa's left-hand drive 2CV on Welsh roads. He'd found it hard leaving the home he'd lived in with Odile, and we'd made a final visit to St Augustin's churchyard to lay flowers one last time.

'Happy?' said Diana, smiling.

'Very,' I said. 'After all the visits back and forth over the last few months, it's been worth it. It was a genius idea to suggest *Les Écuries* is kept to use as a holiday home. That's what clinched it, I think. Papa isn't giving everything up in France. Between all of us, the cottage will be well used. I'm looking forward to holidays there, just the two of us.' I squeezed Di's hand.

'They won't be as broad-minded as in London, mind,' she said, winking. 'Does this thing go any faster? I can't wait to see your father's face when he sees Cefn Court again.'

'No, it doesn't – and I don't want to lose sight of him. Because the Gypsy is new, he has to make sure it doesn't go over forty. Mr Evans at Auto Palace was insistent that it would damage the engine if we drove it too fast.'

The Radnorshire countryside appeared to glow that

day. Emeralds and limes, jades and olives, interspersed with citrus and chartreuse, all mingled in bright sunshine to form a verdant landscape welcoming home one of its own. We turned off the main road. The side roads became narrow and edged with thick hedgerows and grass verges full of wild flowers as we dipped down into the valley where Cefn Court stood.

'Do you think he'll settle? It's a huge wrench for him,' said Di.

'We'll see. He wants to try, and that's the main thing. We've managed to re-employ a few of the older members of staff who are still alive in the hope that he'll remember. I think the fact that he came to visit a few times has helped him. More memories came back each time. In fact, in the last year, he says he can remember some of the chaps he went to school with and certainly some of the airmen he flew with in the RAF.'

The journey continued in silence as we sat, deep in thought. As so often happened, I knew we were thinking about the same thing.

'What about M.?'

'Well, remember she's already moved in to help him run the house. She says she's happy with that, but I know she still has feelings for him. They've never gone away,' I said. 'I really don't know what's going to happen. Her philosophy is to take one day at a time. All I know is that Papa has asked her to build up the stables and horses with him and maybe help with showing and eventing that was cut short so abruptly during the war when she worked as his groom. I think she's looking forward to that.'

I turned off into the long gravel lane that led to Cefn Court. A lump formed in my throat as the significance of what was about to happen hit me. The manor and its surrounding land had been in the Pryce family for generations, and today one of its sons was returning home. I looked in the rear mirror and slowed to wait for Papa to manoeuvre the Gypsy and the horsebox into the lane behind me. We'd stopped a number of times to check on Phénix, but soon she would be able to enjoy the freedom of the paddock in fresh air. At the stable block, Papa stopped and, just as I thought he would, led the chestnut mare out of the horse box and into the field adjoining the stable yard. He left the vehicles there and walked the rest of the way down to the main house where I'd parked the little car.

In front of the main doors of Cefn Court, M. and the staff had assembled to welcome Edmund home. Watching my father join us, I saw his face break into a wide grin. It seemed he only had eyes for one person and increased his walking pace to embrace M, nestling his head into her auburn hair. A cheer went up from the staff, and when they pulled apart there were tears in M.'s eyes and her cheeks were flushed.

Di discreetly held my hand and whispered, 'Love is in the air, darling.'

Thank You!

Dear Reader

Thank you for reading my third novel, *Her Nanny's Secret*. I do hope you enjoyed Annie and Clara's stories and finding out about the special relationship they shared as well as the secret Annie kept from her daughter for over twenty years. I hope you will understand why Annie made the decision she did and not judge her too harshly. I've tried to give you a glimpse of what it was like in the early years of World War Two in both rural Wales and occupied northern France. When Annie accompanies Clara to Normandy in 1963, I was able to indulge myself by reminiscing about the many family holidays we spent in a country we love. Through Annie's eyes, I hope I've captured what it was like to visit there for the first time and experience some of its beauty, culture and foods.

Just as with my first two novels, it's both exciting and nerve-wracking to introduce you to characters I now know very well. I'd love to hear how you enjoyed *Her Nanny's Secret* and would really appreciate you taking time to leave a review in order for the book to reach more readers. Thank you.

My contact details appear at the end of my author profile and I'd love to hear from you. I'm fascinated by family secrets and how past events can have a bearing on future generations. Look out for more novels in future.

Love

Jan x

About the Author

After retiring from a career in teaching and advisory education, Jan joined a small writing group in a local library where she wrote her first piece of fiction. From then on, she was hooked! She soon went on to take a writing class at the local university and began to submit short stories for publication to a wider audience. Her stories and flash fiction pieces have been longlisted and  shortlisted in competitions and several appear in anthologies both online and in print. In October 2019, her first collection of stories was published. Her stories started getting longer and longer so that, following a novel writing course, she began to write her first full-length novel. She loves being able to explore her characters in further depth and delve into their stories.

Originally from mid-Wales, Jan lives in Cardiff with her husband. Having joined the Romantic Novelists Association in 2016, she values the friendship and support from other members and regularly attends conferences, workshops, talks and get togethers. She is co-organiser of her local Chapter, *Cariad*.

You may find out more about Jan here:
Twitter: @JanBaynham
Facebook: Jan Baynham Writer
Blog: www.janbaynham.blogspot.com

More Ruby Fiction

From Jan Baynham

Her Mother's Secret

The Summer of '69

It's 1969 and free-spirited artist Elin Morgan has left Wales for a sun-drenched Greek island. As she makes new friends and enjoys the laidback lifestyle, she writes all about it in her diary. But Elin's carefree summer of love doesn't last long, and her island experience ultimately leaves her with a shocking secret …

Twenty-two years later, Elin's daughter Alexandra has inherited the diary and is reeling from its revelations. The discovery compels Alexandra to make her own journey to the same island, following in her mother's footsteps. Once there, she sets about uncovering what really happened to Elin in that summer of '69.

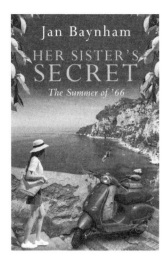

Her Sister's Secret

The Summer of '66
How far would you travel to find the truth?

It's the 1960s and Jennifer Howells is a young woman with the world at her feet, just on the cusp of leaving her Welsh village for an exciting life in the city.

Then the contents of an inconspicuous brown envelope turn Jennifer's world upside down. The discovery leaves her spiralling, unsure who she is. Overnight, Miss Goody Two Shoes is replaced by a mini-skirted wild child who lives for parties and rock'n'roll.

But Jennifer's experience with the excesses of sixties' culture leaves her no closer to her true identity. She soon realises she'll have to travel further – first to Cardiff, then across the ocean to Sicily – if she wants to find out who she really is …

Visit www.rubyfiction.com for details.

Introducing Ruby Fiction

Ruby Fiction is an imprint of Choc Lit Publishing.
We're an award-winning independent publisher,
creating a delicious selection of fiction.

See our selection here:
www.rubyfiction.com

Ruby Fiction brings you stories that inspire emotions.

We'd love to hear how you enjoyed
Her Nanny's Secret. Please visit
www.rubyfiction.com and give your feedback or
leave a review where you purchased this novel.

Ruby novels are selected by genuine readers like yourself.
We only publish stories our Tasting Panel want to see in
print. Our reviews and awards speak for themselves.

Could you be a Star Selector and join our Tasting Panel?
Would you like to play a role in choosing which novels
we decide to publish? Do you enjoy reading women's
fiction? Then you could be perfect for our Tasting Panel.

Visit here for more details ...
www.choc-lit.com/join-the-choc-lit-tasting-panel

Keep in touch:
Sign up for our monthly newsletter Spread for all the latest
news and offers: www.spread.choc-lit.com. Follow us on
Twitter: @RubyFiction and Facebook: RubyFiction.

Stories that inspire emotions!